D0029955

ELLEN ELIZABETH HUNTER

is the author of twelve mystery and suspense novels.
Her Magnolia Mystery series consists of ten cozy mysteries set in
Wilmington, North Carolina, featuring Ashley Wilkes, a historic
preservationist who restores old houses. If you like crumbling
antebellum mansions, moss-draped live oak trees, sultry Southern
nights and unsolved mysteries from the past, then you'll love
Magnolia Mysteries. Ellen's suspense novels are *Lady Justice* and
Dead Ringer, both published by Harlequin's Worldwide Library.

As a student at New York University, Ellen studied American
literature and creative writing. She is a member of the National
Society Daughters of the American Revolution and is confirmed
in the Episcopal Church. Dedicated to helping others, Ellen
frequently uses book sales to raise funds for worthy causes. To
learn more, visit her website at ellenhunter.com.

ELLEN ELIZABETH HUNTER

DEAD RINGER

WORLDWIDE®

TORONTO • NEW YORK • LONDON
AMSTERDAM • PARIS • SYDNEY • HAMBURG
STOCKHOLM • ATHENS • TOKYO • MILAN
MADRID • WARSAW • BUDAPEST • AUCKLAND

Recycling programs
for this product may
not exist in your area.

ISBN-13: 978-0-373-18974-8

Dead Ringer

Copyright © 2012 by Ellen Elizabeth Hunter

A Worldwide Library Suspense/July 2015

First published by Magnolia Mysteries

www.Harlequin.com

Printed in U.S.A.

DEAD RINGER

Acknowledgments

A bouquet of orchids to my sister-in-law Lorrie Taylor. Thanks to Lorrie, I was able to realistically and convincingly describe Kate Callahan's career as a television journalist. Lorrie shared the inner workings of a TV newsroom, the insiders' lingo and the excitement of venturing out to a crime scene to interview witnesses and law enforcement.

Lorrie is a nationally recognized investigative reporter for WJW Fox 8 News in Cleveland, Ohio. Her investigations have saved lives, changed Ohio law and put criminals behind bars. She is the recipient of the coveted National Edward R. Murrow Award, five regional Edward R. Murrow Awards and numerous other professional awards. I'm proud to call her "sister."

ONE

Kate was in the newsroom when the call came in. A woman's body had been found in a Dumpster behind a bar on Second Avenue. "I've got it," she yelled to Mike Cramer, her producer.

Kate and a news team jumped into the remote van and headed across town to Second Avenue at breakneck speed. Even though Kate was the host of a popular magazine-format news show called *New York at Seven*, she was first and foremost a newshound. She couldn't resist covering the big news stories that broke at all hours, and the strangler story was the biggest serial killer case New York City had seen since "Son of Sam." The remote van would feed her broadcast live to the station, and Mike would cut into the afternoon soaps with Kate's breaking news bulletin.

Second Avenue between Forty-ninth and Fiftieth streets was closed to traffic with police cruisers parked crosswise in the avenue. Seeing a clearing on the sidewalk, her driver nosed the remote van between a fire hydrant and a fruit stand, then veered out into the avenue mid-block.

"No!" Kate warned, too late. "You should have dropped me at the corner, Gino. Now you're in for it."

A uniformed cop stationed at the intersection to prevent just such disregard for public safety and police work hurried to the driver's window to give her driver a chewing out and a ticket. Gino tossed the ticket into the glove compartment where it had lots of company. Legal took care of his traffic violations. The thing was to get ahead of the competition.

Kate was already out of the van, a cameraman trotting at her heels. Law enforcement vehicles had converged in a snarl at the curb in front of Devon's Irish Pub. An overcast sky pressed down on tall buildings. Emergency lights whirled, red and blue strobes that raked over dusty brown brick facades. Crime scene technicians and plainclothes detectives scrambled, their comings and goings seemingly without direction. Suddenly, a knot of uniforms parted, making way for two paramedics who emerged from the narrow, dark alley. The gurney rolling between them bore a black body bag.

"You got that?" Kate yelled to her cameraman.

"Got it, Kate!" he called back over the roar of voices.

Spotting Detective Rick Smith, Kate pushed her way through a crowd of reporters and shoved the mike in his face. Rick frowned, but did not push the microphone away. Kate spoke for the benefit of the camera. "I'm with Detective Rick Smith of the Violent Crimes Division. Detective Smith, you're the lead investigator on the strangler case…"

Rick interrupted. "Me and my partner, and a lot of other detectives," he corrected.

Kate didn't miss a beat. "Is this another one of the strangler's victims?"

Smith seemed angered by the question. "We don't know that yet. We won't know until the coroner does his job."

"But was she strangled?" she persisted.

"Yes. Now I've got to go." Rick turned to leave. Kate knew that he'd accompany the body to the coroner's office. She couldn't imagine how he'd get through the autopsy.

He treats me like he doesn't know me, she thought. He won't make eye contact with me, he resents my questions. He refuses to acknowledge that we know each other. Well,

I can be just as cold. "Thank you for your time, Detective Smith," she said coolly.

Back at the TV station, the secretaries would be swooning. They all joked that Rick Smith was the cutest cop to ever walk in a gumshoe's shoes.

Kate looked squarely into the camera. "If this morning's victim is the work of the strangler, the body you are seeing being conveyed to the coroner's wagon will be the strangler's fourth victim. On December 21st, nineteen-year-old Ashley Fuller from Scarsdale was found in a Dumpster on Eighth Avenue; she'd been strangled to death. Celeste Parker, an aspiring actress from Madison, Wisconsin, was the strangler's second victim, discovered on April 1. The third young woman to meet her death at the strangler's hands was Courtney Dixon from Mobile, Alabama, who had come to New York to study art. Each of these young women possessed talent and promise in abundance, each had a rich life to look forward to. All three had their lives cut short by the strangler. Although the Police Commissioner has assigned a special task force to investigate these horrible crimes, to date the police have no suspects they're telling us about. For TNYC-TV, I'm Kate Callahan, broadcasting live from Second Avenue."

SPOTLIGHTS, AS BRILLIANT and hot as miniature suns, blazed down on the set of *New York at Seven*, illuminating Kate's shiny auburn hair, her milky white skin, her slow, infectious smile.

Across the Metropolitan viewing area, audiences tuned in to the young yet highly respected anchorwoman. Kate had been on the New York news scene at TNYC for ten years now, first as an intern while juggling her senior year classes. Fresh out of NYU, with a B.S. in Broadcast and Theatre, TNYC offered her an associate producer's title, which sounded glamorous to her at the time but turned out to be little more than a gofer's job. She did the scut work for the talents—broadcast lingo for the anchors and reporters—edited their copy, charted their tapes, all the while maintaining a sharp lookout for her own big break.

That break came one freezing, sleeting night when all the talents were covering the First Lady's bid for the New York Senate seat at a five thousand dollar a plate dinner in the Plaza Hotel Ballroom. A motorist spotted a jumper on the Queensboro Bridge, tipped the cops from his cell phone, then, to Kate's eternal gratitude, phoned the story in to TNYC. Grabbing a sleepy cameraman and a microphone, Kate jumped into one of the station's trucks. Bad weather had cleared the streets of motorists, and they sped to First Avenue and Fifty-ninth Street in a matter of minutes.

Slipping and sliding on the icy pedestrian walkway, sleet biting her cheeks, Kate raced to the middle of the bridge, the cameraman struggling to keep up. When the cops arrived moments later, they found Kate talking calmly to the desperate woman, her hand clutched tightly in Kate's own. The camera and Kate's microphone had recorded the woman's heart-wrenching confession: Her baby had drowned in the bathtub when she wasn't looking. Now she wanted to end her own life.

With barely thirty minutes till the eleven o'clock news, the cameraman drove like a maniac back to the station where the producer decided to run Kate's brilliant rescue right after the First Lady spot. Kate's career as a news reporter was launched.

Over the years, she'd connected with city viewers because they trusted her; they'd seen her get down and dirty in the trenches. And she was one of them, not some import from L.A. A born and bred New Yorker, Kate Callahan had made hers a household name in the Metropolitan viewing area.

Leading into the program's first news item, Kate's expression grew somber, her tone grave. "Police are now attributing the murder of a woman found in a Second Avenue Dumpster this morning to the strangler."

The tally light on camera two flashed red. Kate turned in its direction as the camera captured her and investigative reporter Evan Wallace who had joined her at the anchor desk. "Evan, has there been any progress today in identifying the dead woman?"

Wallace, sandy-haired and possessing a boyish face, said, "None, Kate. The woman was approximately twenty years old and apparently had never been fingerprinted in New York. But detectives at NYPD's Violent Crimes Division are accessing the FBI's fingerprint system, in hopes of identifying the woman as quickly as possible so that next-of-kin can be notified."

"I assume the police are reviewing missing persons' reports," Kate speculated.

"You bet, Kate. And the media coverage today has been comprehensive and ongoing. Although relatives of missing young women have contacted the police, no positive identification has been made as of this evening. The three previous victims have been positively identified, however."

The screen flipped to head shots of three women and Evan recapped their names and the dates their bodies had been found in Dumpsters in various locations around the city.

How dreadful, Kate couldn't help thinking, to have to go to the morgue, hoping against hope that the murder victim is not your loved one. Kate had spent her whole life wondering what had become of her mother. She hoped she'd never have to accompany her grandfather Jerry to the city morgue to make a possible I.D.

"Evan?" Kate hesitated out of a sense of propriety. "Were there any signs of sexual assault?"

"None, Kate. And none of the previous three victims had been sexually molested either."

In the Control Room, producer Mike Cramer, longing for the old days when he could smoke any place he damn well pleased, sat on the edge of his seat. The director next to him scrutinized the monitors and snapped, "Take camera two."

"Thanks, Evan." Kate tracked the tally light to camera two which zoomed in on her as Evan stepped off the set.

"Rumors of scandal rocked the New York art community today—a marketplace where a single painting can bring millions of dollars, where investors speculate fortunes on whom among today's artists will become the Vincent Van Gogh of tomorrow. The Gotham Group, an association of art dealers, filed a lawsuit in New York District Court, charging Lorneby's International Auction House with collusion to fix prices and defraud buyers. The Group is asking for one billion dollars in compensatory damages. Their suit accuses Lorneby's of bilking buyers out of millions of dollars on important sales. The Gotham Group is demanding that New York's Consumer Affairs Department launch a full-scale investigation, and they are hoping the FBI and Interpol will join the probe. Chairman Neil Lorneby, grandson of founder Laurens Lorneby, could not be reached for comment."

As Kate read from the teleprompter, the monitor flashed to footage of the prestigious auction house's marble exterior. Austere and imposing, the seven-story structure presided over half a block on New York's Upper East Side. Colorful flags, representing the world's great industrial powers, fluttered over the entrance. Lorneby's legal counsel was filmed being mobbed by reporters. Susan Waxman, TNYC's very pregnant arts and entertainment reporter, extended a microphone to the lawyer as he exited the auction house. "No comment," he growled.

Kate said, her voice pitched low, "For over a century, Lorneby's reputation has been unimpeachable. Now, that reputation is tarnished."

Kate leaned confidently toward camera one. "And on a brighter note, members of the art world, and ordinary citizens like you and me, are calling Thomas Shipley a hero. In a press conference which I attended late this afternoon, Shipley, owner and director of the prestigious Shipley Galleries on Madison Avenue, announced his gallery's acquisition of *The Embrace*, a celebrated Art Nouveau painting that has been missing for over seventy years. This is what Shipley had to say."

The screen switched to footage that had been filmed earlier. Kate took advantage of her off-camera break to sip water from a glass and to study the interview on her monitor. She saw an elegantly dressed man of about forty step onto a podium and speak into a clutch of microphones.

Shipley read from a prepared statement: "I'm pleased to announce the recovery of a long-lost work of art, *The Embrace*, painted by Gustav Klimt in Vienna in 1910. Art historians and curators agree *The Embrace* is one of Klimt's most important works. The painting disappeared from the art scene in 1939 when it was confiscated by Hitler's Nazi regime. From the Reichstag, *The Embrace* was transferred to a wealthy private collector in France. Since then, it has changed hands many times, each exchange doubling or tripling its value. Independent experts have confirmed that the painting is authentic and have appraised its worth at five million dollars."

As reporters shuffled impatiently, eager to fire off their questions, Shipley calmly removed tortoiseshell reading glasses and looked over the assembled press corps. "I'll take a few questions now."

Kate had been the first to ask, "Mr. Shipley, now that you have the painting, what do you intend to do with it?"

Shipley darted sharp eyes in Kate's direction and replied in a tone that implied there could be but one answer, "Why, I intend to return the painting to its rightful owner, of course."

Cries rose from the press corps, each member vying for Shipley's attention. One voice carried above the din. "Who *is* the rightful owner, Mr. Shipley?"

Nonchalantly—or nervously, Kate couldn't decide which as she studied the video—the art expert extracted an immaculate white handkerchief from his breast pocket and began to slowly polish his spectacles. Whatever his motive, Kate acknowledged that the ploy was effective. The homely act made Shipley seem accessible and human, thus all the more credible. "The painting was originally owned by Herman Greenbaum, a prominent Berlin art collector and dealer during the thirties. Sadly, Greenbaum did not survive the holocaust; he died in Auschwitz. But his only son managed to cling to life in that death camp until the liberation forces rescued him. Later he moved to America and married. His widow lives right here in New York. Her name is Irma Greenbaum. I telephoned her earlier today with the news."

Shipley paused for dramatic effect, allowing himself a small smile as he tucked the handkerchief back into the pocket of his finely tailored jacket. "Naturally, Mrs. Greenbaum is quite pleased."

As Shipley turned to leave the podium, Kate fired

a parting shot, "But don't you stand to lose millions, Mr. Shipley?"

Shipley ran a hand over thinning hair, then swung back to face the microphones. "True enough, Kate. But someone's got to make amends for the crimes committed against the European Jews. I've done very well in this business of buying and selling paintings. I can afford to do the right thing." Tossing a self-satisfied smile over his shoulder, Shipley stepped off the podium and disappeared into a crowd of backslappers.

After reviewing the footage, Kate's estimation of Shipley soared. The man's a remarkable showman, she thought. I'm glad I've got him lined up for an interview tomorrow, but I'll have to stay on my toes to keep up with him.

She wound up her report. "Few tales of stolen paintings end happily. I think I speak for all of us when I say the art world could use more dealers like Thomas Shipley. Throughout the week, *New York at Seven* will devote a segment of each broadcast to the topic of looted art treasures. Together, we'll learn how paintings were stolen, how they were sold and resold, and how they were concealed from the public for decades. Tomorrow night's guest will be the man of the hour, Thomas Shipley himself."

For the remaining thirty minutes, Kate and *New York at Seven*'s feature reporters covered the important stories of the day. "And that's our report for *New York at Seven*. Thank you for tuning in. Good evening, New York, and good evening to you, Granddad." She blew a kiss to the camera.

Opinion polls showed that Kate's fans loved her signature sign-off. It reminded the oldsters of Jimmy Durante's "Goodnight, Mrs. Calabash, wherever you are." They liked this cozy glimpse into Kate's private life, feeling that in the final moment of the broadcast they got a peek at the real Kate Callahan. Jerry Callahan—self-described as 'just a regular Joe'—was a celebrity now too, a fact that did not set well with the eighty-five year old. But the public ate up stories about the devoted twosome. TNYC's public relations people couldn't be happier and played up the relationship for all it was worth. *People Magazine* had featured Kate and her grandfather in a recent edition. And *Architectural Digest* had just run a photo spread of Kate and Jerry in their Fifth Avenue apartment.

TWO

IN HIS HIGH-TECH OFFICE, with its bank of television monitors on the opposite wall, TNYC's CEO Vaughn Thompson leaned back in his leather executive chair to appraise Kate's delivery. She's a knock-out, he told himself, but there's a powerhouse brain behind that pretty face. When she first joined his station, she was just a kid and he barely noticed her. Still, there had always been something plucky about Kate Callahan that earned her the respect of her colleagues and that her superiors brought to his attention.

Thompson had kept tabs on Kate by regularly watching the *Eleven O'Clock News* where she'd been a contributor. He'd been alerted at home the night TNYC covered a fire at a Soho nightclub. Kate was on the scene, broadcasting a Special News Alert via the remote van. Her face was smeared with soot, she was miserable from the heat and smoke, yet she brought in her story. Eight young lives had ended that night when an arsonist with a grudge torched the old warehouse turned disco.

Kate's coverage of the tragedy on nine-eleven that crushed the once invincible New York City earned her an EMMY. While other newscasters broadcasted from cool, secure newsrooms, Kate was as near to the World Trade Center site as law enforcement would permit her. She interviewed firemen and their families. She interviewed relatives searching for their loved ones. She worked from dawn till dark, rarely taking a break. She made many friends and loyal supporters on that tragic day.

But the scoop she landed for the station that made Thompson sit up and take notice had been another tragedy of smaller but no less mournful proportions. Kate handled the bizarre turn of events with grace and humility. An Iowan on a class trip to the Big Apple had somehow defied the security system and ventured out onto the prow of the Staten Island ferry. Later, his pals told police that the boy had boasted he would re-enact the famous "flying" scene from the movie *Titanic*. The sixteen-year-old fell into the cold, choppy waters of Lower New York Bay.

In all the excitement, Kate managed to stow away on board an NYPD Marine Search and Rescue vessel. She must have had a friend on the team, although she refused to say. An eight millimeter camera concealed under her oilskin slicker, Kate filmed the rescue effort, and hung on for hours while the mission was downgraded from rescue to recovery, until the body was fished out of the black waters. Overhead, the competition's helicopters circled at a distance—and at a disadvantage.

Thompson had glued himself to the monitors when that newscast was broadcast. The next thing Kate knew she was being summoned to the big boss's office. Only now Kate was all grown up, an elegant woman of thirty-three who could hold her own with any supermodel when her hair wasn't plastered down with ocean spray or her face wasn't blackened with soot.

After exchanging pleasantries, it suddenly dawned on Thompson, who'd always gotten every woman he ever wanted, that this might be one relationship that put him on the groveling end. It wasn't at all necessary, but he found himself trying to convince Kate to accept the anchor spot on a new show he was experimenting with: a combination straight-news, magazine-style format that he was calling *New York at Seven*.

Research showed that more and more people were getting their news from the Internet, clicking to those news stories that interested them the most. Thompson instructed the news director to put together a research team to track which stories were getting the most Internet traffic. Those were the stories they'd feature in depth on *New York at Seven*.

Ironically, research also showed that New York viewers were loyal to their favorite newscasters. Kate had a loyal following. And why not? She was gutsy. She was articulate and aggressive, yet humble. Rarely did she fluster. And that smile. It could light up a runway at JFK.

But Kate didn't want to be harnessed to an anchor desk. "As long as I can continue to work the stories of my choice, I'd love to do it," she said, standing and stretching out her hand to Thompson.

The unattainable Vaughn Thompson had met his match. He invested big bucks in promoting the show. Now the public was rewarding him for his innovation. His investment was paying off and advertising revenues were soaring. He had plans for Kate—important plans.

THREE

KATE UNCLIPPED HER lapel microphone and remained seated as a technician unthreaded the wire that ran down her back under her jacket. Producer Mike Cramer barreled out of the Control Room to join her on the set. It was Cramer's policy to conduct a postmortem of the show with the staff while his observations were fresh in his mind. Kate was relieved to see the hint of a smile on Cramer's normally impassive face.

In his mid-fifties, Cramer was the picture of an old-fashioned newsman with his broken nose, bald pate, shirtsleeves rolled up over thick muscular forearms. He had started the day wearing a tie, Kate knew, but as the pressure mounted, with telephones chirping and crisis brewing, he'd yanked it off. Right now it could be lying on a chair or desk in any one of a dozen different offices in the TNYC-TV news center.

In the privacy of their own home, her outspoken grandfather referred to Cramer as the Lou Grant of TNYC. "Who does that make me?" Kate always grinned and asked, "Mary Tyler Moore?"

THE SPOTLIGHTS DIMMED, and Kate felt her eyes and facial muscles relax. Always tense and on an adrenaline high during a show, she seemed to experience meltdown after the sign off.

"Powerful show, Kate," Cramer complimented. "Well done."

"Thanks, Mike. I have to admit I prefer reporting good

news about paintings being restored to their rightful owners over telling viewers we've got a serial killer stalking the city's streets. Makes me feel creepy." She rubbed her upper arms. "And the news about the Nazi's theft of paintings from the Jews during the war *is* powerful stuff. It's a red hot topic these days, as newsworthy as the secret Swiss bank accounts were several years ago. There's still a lot of sympathy out there for the holocaust survivors."

"Yeah," Cramer agreed. "Imagine going through what they did only to find out years later that neutral Swiss bankers and supposedly reputable art dealers were part of the conspiracy to swindle them."

Kate started across the studio, stepping gingerly over cables and wires that crisscrossed the floor. Cramer walked with her down the corridor to his conference room. There, the staff would rehash the show, figure out what they'd done right, what they'd done wrong, and how not to make the same mistake twice. "I'm glad Shipley's agreed to give us an exclusive interview," Cramer remarked.

"He sure is a cut above the average dealer," Kate said. "I can't wait to get to know him better."

"We're sure to win the ratings war this week." Then Cramer scowled, his forehead furrowing. "Now if only we could get Irma Greenbaum to talk to us. But she won't take Susan's calls," he said, referring to the show's arts and entertainment reporter, "and I've tried myself." He shook his head. "Well, at least, she's not talking to any of the competition either. I know that for a fact."

Kate gave him a thoughtful look. "I'm working on it, Mike. I think she'll talk to me."

Cramer clapped a hand on her shoulder. "I've seen you pull rabbits out of a hat before, Callahan, but what makes you think she'll talk to you when she's not talking to anyone else?"

Kate ducked her head before saying, "Because Grand-dad was one of the soldiers who liberated Auschwitz in 1945. And Irma Greenbaum's husband was one of the survivors he rescued."

JERRY CALLAHAN CLICKED the remote and the television screen in his comfortable den went black. Although he thought Kate's piece on the stolen Klimt painting was outstanding, the story brought back memories he'd rather not be reminded of. Yet, could he ever forget his first sight of Auschwitz? The inmates they'd rescued looked like scarecrows, with their skin-and-bones bodies and too-large heads. They'd looked threatening even, and he knew his buddies shared his initial revulsion.

But then Jerry's common sense prevailed. The good Lord sent you here for a reason, he told himself, so get a grip on yourself and help these poor souls find a better life. One inmate in particular, a boy of eighteen, attached himself to Jerry. Jerry understood only a few German phrases, yet the pair were able to communicate in a universal language. The young man's name was Herman Greenbaum, II. The G.I.'s nicknamed him Harry.

Jerry wrote to a Jewish family he knew in his neighborhood back home, persuading them to sponsor Harry. Then he and his buddies chipped in and paid for Harry's passage to New York. Over the years, Jerry kept in touch with Harry and his wife Irma. As fate would have it, Harry turned out to be a brilliant medical student, then went on to become an emergency room doctor at Beth Israel Hospital. Harry had a genius for diagnosis, his colleagues said of him at his funeral.

Harry passed away peacefully in his sleep five years ago. Jerry attended his *Shiva*. Irma was delighted to see him. Again, she expressed her gratitude for the start Jerry had given Harry.

"So now Irma's getting a picture worth five million bucks," Jerry said out loud to the empty room. Then he thought, There is some justice in this world, after all. That Shipley must be a stand-up kind of guy. I'd like to shake his hand. And with Kate interviewing him, I might just get the chance.

Jerry lifted himself slowly out of his favorite recliner. He was in good health for a man his age, but his joints creaked and ached when he moved suddenly. Not as tall as he used to be, still he was an attractive man with a nice head of wavy white hair and snapping blue eyes. Kate told him he looked like the late Tip O'Neill, except he had a much nicer nose. He'd appraised her with a jaundiced eye when she'd said that. But Kate loved him, of that he was certain. What would he do without her? And, more important, what was she going to do without him when his time came? The two of them were all that was left of their little family.

He walked into the cheerful kitchen, took a bottle of red wine off the rack, uncorked it, and poured himself a liberal glassful. For the old ticker, he told himself. At the kitchen table, he raised the glass and said out loud, "Here's to you, Harry."

Sniffing the air, he announced, "Beef stew's ready." About his habit of carrying on a conversation when he was alone, Jerry argued: "I'm eighty-five. Guess I've earned the right to talk to myself if I want to."

The stew was simmering in a Dutch oven on a back burner of the gas range. Jerry looked around appreciatively. The kitchen was spacious with high ceilings, as were all the rooms in the apartment, and painted a sunny yellow. Kate had redecorated when she'd bought the apart-

ment three years ago. But nothing fancy-schmancy, Jerry
thought. The kid's got good taste. She made this place
cozy, a real home.

She'll be here in a few hours, he thought. I told her to
come straight home. I don't want her out alone at night,
not with that psycho on the loose. Then, we'll have supper
like we do every night. But she needs some nice guy in her
life. Someone to take her out and show her a good time.
Yet, it's like she wears a sign around her neck when a man
gets interested. "Keep your distance," the sign warns. It's
all *his* fault, Jerry thought for the umpteenth time. That
spineless heel who broke her heart. Six years, it's been,
and my baby still has not got over that jerk. "Damn you,
Rick Smith!" he said with disgust.

IT WAS KATE's habit to work in her office until ten each
night. Jerry tried to have a hot meal ready for her when
she got home. He'd have a bite or two with her at the
big, pine, country table, and they'd talk about their day.
Then she'd read in her room—boning up for the next day's
show—until well past midnight, while Jerry watched the
talk shows. Sure, they stayed up late, but the tradeoff was
they got to sleep late. Jerry liked taking care of Kate. He'd
taken care of her all her life.

When they got married, Jerry and Babs planned to raise
a slew of kids. But it just didn't work out that way. There
was only the one girl. "Annie, you broke your mother's
heart and sent her to an early grave," Jerry said aloud.
What's the matter with me tonight? he asked himself. All
the old, sad memories are pressing down on me like rain
clouds at a funeral. He tried to shake them off, but it was
nothing doing.

Annie had been a good girl until high school when she
fell in with a bad crowd. Those were the days of pot, LSD,

and free love. Jerry and Babs tried everything. Grounding her didn't work. She'd just sneak out. "And I draw the line at locking her up," Jerry told Babs.

Talking to the parish priest didn't help either. That gentle, elderly man couldn't cope with Annie's wild behavior any better than Jerry and Babs could. And the therapist they consulted seemed to be on Annie's side. "Give her room," he'd counseled. "Let her grow."

Jerry returned to the den and pulled a thick album from a lower bookshelf. He thumbed through to the last photo he'd taken of Annie. Long hair flowing around her shoulders, she was dressed in the style of the day, midriff-baring tee shirt, hip-hugger jeans. Her feet were bare even though she was standing on a dirty city sidewalk.

Tears filled Jerry's eyes. "You coulda had a good life, sweetheart. Why'd you have to go and throw it away?"

At seventeen, Annie ran away with her boyfriend to San Francisco. "To be a flower child," she'd explained when she called home. At least she'd had the decency to call. Some of their neighbors never found out what happened to their kids.

A year later, Annie showed up unexpectedly on their doorstep. She looked like something the cat dragged in. Her hair was lank and stringy. She was thin to the point of gauntness. Black smudges underscored her red eyes. But her smile was the one she used to give them when she was a little girl, caught before dinner with her hand in the cookie jar.

Jerry grabbed her and pulled her close. "Don't!" she cried, backing away, and fresh pain stabbed Jerry's heart. Then she explained, "You'll crush the baby."

In his excitement, Jerry hadn't even noticed the bundle Annie carried in her arms. A gurgle escaped from inside the blanket, and Babs reached out her arms to receive their first and only grandchild. "Look, Jerry. See how beautiful." She turned to Annie and asked in an awed whisper, "Is the little darlin' a boy or a girl?"

"A girl. Her name's Kate. Kate Callahan," Annie replied, and for a moment she sounded as defiant as she used to in high school.

Jerry and Babs exchanged knowing looks. She's not married, their eyes told each other. Jerry shrugged his shoulders. So what? he thought. At least we've got our little girl back, and we always wanted more kids.

"Come on in, sweetheart," he said. "Your old room's just like you left it. We'll go shopping right after lunch and get a crib and whatever else you need."

Taking the baby from Babs, he crooned, "Kate," and held her up so he could get a good look at her tiny pink face and fists. Already her fine reddish-gold hair was beginning to curl. "She looks like my mother. Welcome home, Kate. Your old grandpa has fallen for you already." And he kissed her cheek.

Jerry slammed the album shut. A week later they'd awakened to Kate's cries. Annie's bed was empty. Her suitcase was gone. She'd sneaked out in the middle of the night. A few weeks later she'd called. "Don't try to find me. You've got to let me live my own life." That was the last they heard from her.

"Are you alive, or are you dead?" he asked the room. "Are you up there in heaven with your mother? I know the good Lord's forgiven you for your weakness, just like me and Babs forgave you long ago. Thanks for giving us Kate, kiddo, at least you done one thing right. She brought us more joy than you'll ever know." And he wiped a tear from his wrinkled cheek.

FOUR

PROFESSOR LEON HABER's female students described him as dark, brooding, and mysterious. They attributed his perpetual glower not to displeasure but to intense concentration. "He's thinking about his book," they told one another.

Each fall Haber told his incoming students at New York University's Institute of Fine Arts that he was writing the definitive history of the Art Nouveau period. He had been telling that story to his classes for the past ten years. The book just never materialized.

There were drafts—there were fits and starts—but no finished product. Haber had many excuses. It's because my work for the World Jewish Congress's Commission for Art Recovery is so demanding, he told himself. He also served on the President's Commission on the Holocaust. Both organizations helped families recover the treasures that had been looted before and during the war. The Nazis were not the only guilty party, Haber frequently pointed out to the uninformed. The Russians and the French had participated in dividing the spoils. In interviews, he described the looting as packs of greedy wolves eviscerating a doe.

Haber got up out of his burgundy leather chair and snapped off *New York at Seven*. He didn't own a remote control. His television set was almost twenty years old. He was above such things as television entertainment. Now and then he turned the thing on to catch a news item of particular interest. Most of the time he looked up items

of interest on the Internet. He was rarely without his lap-
top computer.

He'd been alerted by a colleague at the World Jewish
Congress that Thomas Shipley was going to return a Gustav Klimt painting to its rightful owner, Irma Greenbaum.
He wanted to see Shipley's face for himself. Everyone
thought Shipley was acting out of some sort of *noblesse
oblige*. But Haber, a born skeptic, was suspicious. What's
in it for Ship? he asked himself.

Pacing the length of his main floor library, Haber
stopped at the long front windows and peered out. The
evenings were warm now, attracting riffraff to Washington Square Park. They played boom boxes at deafening
decibels and sold rocks of crack cocaine and their disease-
ridden bodies to one another.

He shook his head in disgust and turned away, his intense brown eyes smoldering like banked fires. Two hundred years ago when this fine old Georgian-style house
had been built, Waverly Place had embodied all that was
genteel about New York City. The park had been a shady
place where tots played under the watchful eyes of strict
nannies. Horses drawing carriages had clip-clopped rhyth-
mically around the Square. Now, only a wrought iron fence
separated him from Sodom and Gomorrah.

Although only forty-six, much had changed since he
was a boy. He'd inherited the house from his great-uncle.
He couldn't move if he wanted to. Besides, where would
he go? The great unwashed surrounded him on all sides
in New York City.

Haber clipped a cigar, lit up, inhaled pleasurably, and
dreamed of an ideal society where his brilliance would
be recognized and rewarded. Suddenly, he experienced a
flash of inspiration. Kate Callahan, he thought. She seems
so clean and wholesome. And intelligent. When was the

last time he'd engaged in intelligent conversation with a woman? His female students? They couldn't articulate a simple thought. But a few were talented, far more talented than he. That right-side of the brain thing was something he'd always resented. An artist didn't need to be able to speak eloquently, only to paint, and either you were born with it or you were not. An old adage chewed at his confidence: Those who can, do; those who can't, teach.

He shrugged off his morose mood and brightened. He was scheduled to be interviewed by Kate Callahan on her TV show on Wednesday evening. The show ended at eight. He'd invite her out to dinner. They could talk about art, music, and literature. Yes, it had been far too long since he'd had an intelligent conversation with an attractive woman.

FIVE

NEIL LORNEBY SLIPPED off his jacket and refilled his glass with single malt Scotch. He'd punched off *New York at Seven* after the piece with Thomas Shipley. Shipley's was the last face Lorneby wished to see tonight but he had to know precisely what Shipley was saying.

He strolled out onto his terrace. This had been one of the worst days of his life. Things had gotten way out of control. He wanted—he needed—to regain control of his life.

Lorneby lived in a penthouse on the top floor of the auction house. When his father had opened the New York branch of Lorneby's International back in the late fifties, he'd converted the seventh floor into spacious living quarters. Neil was just a small chap then but he remembered well the wrenching move from London, knowing he'd never see his playmates again, clinging to his nanny and begging not to be taken. But taken he had been, and ignored by his parents in his new life just as he had been ignored by them in London. His parents were dead now, and last year his third wife had left him, then initiated a punishing divorce settlement.

Absently, he noticed that his potted azaleas were beginning to bloom. His mother had missed her London garden and to compensate had lavished the penthouse terrace with a myriad of plants and greenery. His most frequent memory of her as he was growing up was watching her water the hundreds of potted plants with a garden hose sprayer.

If only she'd tended to him as she had the flowers. After her death, the rooftop garden seemed to fade.

Sipping his drink, he gazed down onto broad Park Avenue. Thanks to a special fund set up by Brooke Astor, the median was always colorfully planted with seasonal flowers. Bright red azaleas bloomed between the north- and south-bound lanes of heavy traffic—mostly yellow cabs.

Anyone watching from a tower window would see a distinguished man in his early forties with prematurely silver hair, wearing a glower on his chiseled face. His chin was cleft, his mouth small, his brows furrowed. Tanned the year round, agile and lean, he favored clothing in dark monotones. A white-gold link bracelet adorned his right wrist, a diamond studded Rolex his left. His fingers were ringless although he owned three wedding bands and was too sentimental to get rid of them.

It seemed like all his life someone had been after his money. But Wife Number One, an art student, hadn't been interested in money, only art, and he'd managed to extricate himself from that marriage with his wealth intact.

Wifey Number Two, Edith, whom he privately called Edie the Greedy, had hired one of the dirtiest divorce lawyers in New York State. Together they'd really put the squeeze on Neil. He vowed then never to marry again. But Neil, an incurable romantic, had taken one look at Serena—the goddess, the Grace Kelly look-alike—and lost his heart, and a large portion of his bank account. For like Grace Kelly, Serena was drawn to Monaco, and she thought that Neil should buy it for her. He'd settled her gambling debts there in a rancorous divorce settlement that had bit into his capital.

Now Thomas Shipley and his pals at the Gotham Group had dreamed up this trumped-up charge just to get their filthy fingers into Lorneby's deep pockets. For years they'd bitterly resented the premium Lorneby's charged them on every buy. The case would be thrown out of court, his legal counsel had assured him in a meeting late that afternoon. The problem was that Lorneby's was going to be tried in the media. Some of the mud would stick, he knew, there was no way to avoid it. And that would be bad for business. The public who bought at the day-to-day auctions were his bread and butter. The acclaimed auctions that brought out the big-time dealers, the museums, and the socialites— the sale of Jackie Onassis's and the Duchess of Windsor's jewels and personal memorabilia came to mind—brought in the big bucks, sure, but they were few and far between. Yes, the ordinary client would grow uneasy and take his business to Sotheby's or Christie's.

That led him to recall that Kate Callahan had furnished her apartment with finds from Lorneby's three years ago. At the time, the receptionist had tipped him that TV journalist Kate Callahan was in the building, previewing goods in advance of the auction. Lorneby made a point of going out onto the floor to meet and greet her. Now that he thought about it, he remembered that he'd invited her up here for lunch. His cook had prepared a light salad for them both and served it out here on the terrace.

Neil had been very taken with Kate Callahan. She was astute and sophisticated, and she played fair and did not manipulate the guests who appeared on her show. If anyone in the media would be willing to give him a fair shake, he thought, it's Kate Callahan. I'm going to nip this lawsuit disaster in the bud. I'm going on the defensive. Didn't Kate say she was doing a series this week on stolen artworks? Well I, as one of the world's leading authorities on paintings, can certainly contribute something to that topic.

And in the process, I'm going to expose the Gotham Group for what they really are: an association of bitter, resentful money-grubbers who are motivated by malice and revenge!

SIX

"THAT'S GOOD, KEVIN. Now you're one of us." Dolly Devereaux sat back on her heels and admired her handiwork.

Seven-year-old Kevin Brown reached for a hand mirror. "Let me see, Posey." He admired his head from various angles. A wide grin stretched his painted red lips almost to his ears. "Now I look just like you."

It's so easy to make these kids happy, Dolly thought. Posey was Dolly's clown name. An amateur clown, Dolly entertained the kids at New York Hospital's Comprehensive Cancer Center. The gaudy makeup concealed Kevin's pallor; the bright orange wig covered his bald head.

They're such little tykes, Dolly thought. They deserve a chance. This is so damned unfair. I wish I could do more for them than paint their faces and perform funny tricks. Well, at least for the hours I'm here they aren't thinking about how bad they feel.

Some of her kids—for that was how she thought of them—went home to experience years of remission and almost normal lives. Others went home to die, or to hospices. Those were the ones she kept in touch with. She was there, to entertain them for as long as they could bravely smile.

Dolly hadn't watched Kate Callahan's show or her earlier news bulletins, although Kate *was* her oldest and dearest friend. Dolly had been here at the hospital since before five, helping the nurses' aides serve the dinner trays, then painting hands and faces, clowning around, but most often just offering a friendly ear. She'd see Kate on Friday night.

That was their routine. Every Friday night for as long as she could remember, she and Kate got together. Sometimes Jerry joined them. Jerry was the grandfather Dolly never had and she adored him. This Friday night the three were going to meet at the Cafe Carlyle so that Jerry could see his favorite entertainer, Bobby Short. Saturday morning, they'd sleep late.

Even if she had not caught the show, Dolly knew that Kate was doing a feature on stolen artworks. They talked on the telephone every day, sharing each other's lives and secrets. On Friday night, Dolly would hear all about how the feature series had been received by Kate's audience.

Dolly wasn't following the strangler story closely, although she taped all of Kate's shows and watched them when she could. While her heart went out to the victims and their families, just coping with the tragic lives she encountered day in and day out here at the hospital used up all of her emotional resources. And Dolly wasn't particularly concerned for herself that a serial killer was out there preying on women. There was always a string of cabs in the hospital's driveway off York Avenue. Some of the cabbies knew her by now, for even though this was New York City where anything goes, how many women in clown suits hailed a cab? At about eight o'clock most evenings, Dolly would hop in one and ride to her secure, twenty-four-hour-doorman building on the corner of Fifth Avenue and Sixty-second Street.

SEVEN

CEO VAUGHN THOMPSON got up from his desk, stretched, and strolled to the huge expanse of glass that comprised one wall of his office. His secretary Mrs. Russo had left hours ago. Even though TNYC was a twenty-four-hour station, the building took on a tranquil atmosphere at night.

Until recently, he'd spent his evenings in the company of actresses and show girls. Now he often worked late, content in the knowledge that Kate Callahan was also working in the building.

Through brainpower, nerves of steel, and plain old-fashioned hard work, Vaughn Thompson had propelled himself to the pinnacle of New York television. He had it all: money, power, prestige, and the women who ran after powerful men. Once exciting, now the women bored him. Everything seemed boring these days; he'd experienced a loss of appetite for the life he'd created. His meeting with Kate a few months ago had given him a glimpse of the kind of life he longed for—and the woman who could make it all possible—a satisfying domestic life that everyone, right down to the janitor who was at this very moment vacuuming Mrs. Russo's office, seemed to possess. Everyone except Vaughn Thompson.

He liked to gaze down at the city at night. His city. The reflection of lights from Manhattan and the New Jersey cliffs sparkled on the Hudson River like those tiny white lights that were strung in the trees outside the Tavern on the Green. Almost beneath his feet, a passenger ship was docking at pier 88. He'd like to take another cruise. Cruises were so romantic, but only with the woman who had captured his imagination.

He checked the time. Above the TV monitors that covered one wall, a row of clocks displayed the time in each time zone around the globe. It was ten here in New York, time for him to put his plan into action.

He removed his unwrinkled suit jacket from his closet. Some men hung their jackets on the backs of their chairs and leaned against them all day as they worked in shirt-sleeves at their desks. Thompson wouldn't dream of doing that; it was a sloppy habit. His suits were custom made. Why would he treat them like upholstery?

The janitor was working his way toward his office so he left the door open, then boarded the elevator to the news floor where Kate had her office.

"Knock, knock," Thompson called as he tapped lightly on her open office door.

Kate stood at her desk, stuffing printouts into a brief-case. "Boning up for the series?" he inquired approvingly. She looked particularly pretty tonight. The tailoring of her suit did not conceal her lush curves. Her hair, the color of ginger, was ruffled, as if she'd been running her fingers through it. The professional makeup she'd worn while on the air had faded, and a smattering of freckles shone through. He was beguiled.

Kate looked up, her wide amber eyes registering pleasure. "Hi, Vaughn."

She's glad to see me, Thompson thought, pleased. He'd taken to dropping in on her after hours recently, so his visit tonight did not appear out of the ordinary.

Yes, it's time I got married again, he thought, as he watched Kate move around the office, grabbing books and files and stuffing them into the already bulging briefcase.

This time I'll marry a woman worthy of my love. And she'll be someone who loves and wants kids. I'm forty-five, not too old to start a family. A man can have kids at any age, and Kate's just thirty-three. Women today are having babies well into their forties.

He studied her covertly. She was as sexy as hell, and the best part was she didn't even know it, and that made her all the more appealing. And that perfume. What was it? He'd buy it for her by the gallon. If only she'd have him.

"I meant to get down here earlier. I'm glad I caught you before you left. Kate, congratulations on an outstanding show. The entire week promises to be a ratings buster. So what's with all the printouts?"

Kate smiled, glad for his company. "Oh, this is my crash course on Gustav Klimt. The Research Department did a computer search, printed out everything they could find on him, plus stolen artworks in general, and how provenance is established." Kate eyed the daunting stack, then continued stuffing. "I'm interviewing the expert tomorrow. Remember?"

"How could I forget? You snagged Thomas Shipley."

Thompson was glad he'd taken time to wash his hands and face and comb his hair before leaving his office suite. He'd even shaved a second time. His aftershave was specially made for Bijan's and it lingered after others lost their fragrance. Thompson worked out and played a mean game of racquetball regularly, taking pride in his physical fitness and his sexual prowess. Those show girls hadn't chased him solely for his money. He knew he looked younger than forty-five. His light brown hair was stylishly cut, and his Savile Row suit was impeccably tailored in the soft, youthful, continental style.

Kate reached for her raincoat from the coatrack. "Allow me," Thompson said, taking the coat from her and holding it so she could slip her arms through the sleeves. Standing close behind her, he inhaled the scent of her hair as its warmth touched his chin.

"Thanks, Vaughn."

"I'll walk you out," he said, snapping off her office lights. "You know, I know Shipley well," he volunteered as they waited for the elevator.

Kate tipped her chin so that her eyes met his. "Oh? I'm looking forward to meeting him. He's quite the hero."

Hero? He beat down jealousy. "Yes," he replied coolly, "he knows the business. I've bought some paintings from him over the years. He's good at spotting the Picassos of tomorrow, and he's never steered me wrong."

The elevator doors opened and Kate preceded him inside. Thompson pushed the lobby button. "My driver's waiting out front. Give you a lift home?"

"Thanks, but I use a car service," Kate said. "They pick me up every night at ten fifteen. The driver's a regular."

"Well, then, I'll see you to your car." Thompson stepped out of the elevator ahead of her and started across the lobby. The guard sprang to his feet. "Evening, Mr. Thompson."

Thompson glanced quickly at the man's identification badge. "How are you tonight, Jesse?"

The guard hurried to the double glass doors, unlocked them and held one open for the chief and the anchorwoman. "Couldn't be better, sir. You folks have a nice night."

Vaughn took Kate's elbow and steered her out onto the cool sidewalk. He paused momentarily, still holding her arm. "There's a little piano bar on Sixth Avenue that I'm fond of. The atmosphere's cozy and sometimes I unwind there after a long day. What do you say? Care for a nightcap?"

Kate hesitated, weighing the invitation. "May I have

a rain check? Granddad's waiting supper for me and I've got all these printouts to read."

"Ah, yes," Thompson said thoughtfully, "your grandfather."

The sidewalk and curb were deserted except for Thompson's shiny limousine. His driver, Tony, jumped out from behind the wheel to sweep open the rear door. Kate looked up and down Eleventh Avenue for her car service. Cars sped by, but none stopped at the curb for her. "I don't understand. They're always so reliable."

Thompson shot his cuff and checked his watch. "It's ten twenty. I don't want you waiting around here at this hour. Obviously your driver's late. I'll take you home." He guided her toward his car.

Kate switched her briefcase to her left hand. The papers were heavy. "Oh, he'll be along soon. I'll wait inside the lobby. The guard's there. I'll be fine." She turned and started to retrace her steps toward the building's entrance. Suddenly, from around the corner, a drunk stumbled directly into her path. "Watch it, bitch!" he snarled as he slammed into her. The collision sent her reeling. Her briefcase flew out of her hand and hit the pavement with a thud. Kate was falling when Thompson lunged for her. He grabbed her and pulled her upright. Then, unable to control his anxiety, he drew her close.

"Are you all right? Kate, are you hurt?" One arm caught her roughly around the waist, the other supported her back. He held her close for a long minute, until her voice in his ear reassured him that she was okay. Desire seized him and shook him to his core. His physical response to her nearness embarrassed him, and he took a step backward.

Tony darted after the drunk who was weaving his way down Eleventh Avenue in a stupor. Grabbing his shoulder, the driver spun the man around and shouted in his face,

"Whatsa matter with you, man? You blind or sumpin? You almost knocked that lady down. Why, I'd like to give you a black eye, you lousy wino."

Still holding onto the slobbering drunk, Tony called to Thompson, "Hey, Boss, you want I should call the cops? Get them to take this wino in?"

"No, Vaughn," Kate protested. "I'm fine, really I am." She stepped out of Thompson's arms and looked into his concerned face. "If we involve the police, it'll get into the tabloids. I don't want that kind of publicity."

Thompson regarded her keenly. *She's as smart as I am. My equal,* he thought again. "Okay, if you're sure," he said gently. To his driver, he called, "Let him go."

"All right, you heard the man. Geddouddaheh! And don't ever let me see you around this building again. You hear me, Mac!"

Swatting at imaginary demons and muttering to himself, the drunk tottered off, and Tony returned to the car. He picked up Kate's briefcase. "Come on, Miss Callahan, you get inside here where it's safe. We'll take you home, won't we, Boss?"

"Help her in, Tony, I'll be right back," Thompson said. He sprinted back across the sidewalk to the plate glass window and tapped. The guard, Jesse, was already hurrying toward the doors, keys in hand. Leaning a head out, he inquired solicitously, "Something wrong, Mr. Thompson? I thought I heard a ruckus out here."

"Miss Callahan's car has not arrived. When, and if it comes, tell the driver she's gone home. Oh, and further," Thompson added irritably, "tell the man he's fired!"

Kate slid across the backseat of the comfortably heated limousine. Thompson slid in beside her.

"Better?" he asked solicitously.

"Look, it was nothing, Vaughn. A little run-in with a

harmless drunk. I'm perfectly okay. Can't say the same for my poor briefcase," she joked, regarding her scratched and battered leather case. She drew her raincoat around her shoulders. Why was she shivering?

Thompson was furious. The neighborhood was remote, and at night, the streets were like empty canyons. What if she'd been alone and attacked by a mugger? Few motorists would stop to assist her. New Yorkers did not like to get involved.

Turning to her, he said, "I don't ever want a repeat of that episode. Starting tomorrow morning, you'll have your own limousine and a driver who's a trained bodyguard."

Kate blinked and looked Thompson full in the face. "You're making too much of an isolated incident, Vaughn. I don't want a fuss. I get along fine with my car service. I don't want a driver sitting around with nothing to do, waiting for me all day."

Thompson chuckled. How could she be so sharp and yet so naive? "They get paid for waiting around, Kate. I don't want an argument. The limo's yours, starting tomorrow. You've earned it."

"I'll agree to give it a try," Kate acquiesced.

"In a month you'll wonder how you ever did without it," Thompson said. It was time to make his move. I don't want to scare her off, he thought, but I've got my chance and I'm taking it. "Kate, you work too hard. I know you can't take time off tonight, but you don't have a show on Saturday. Let's take the afternoon and drive out into the country. We can have lunch at my house in Greenwich, tour the grounds, and be back in New York in time for the gala we've got to cover at the Metropolitan Museum of Art."

Kate opened her mouth to accept, but before she could, Thompson said, "I won't take no for an answer. I'll pick you up at ten."

Kate laughed and placed a hand on his arm. "Vaughn, I was going to say yes."

Thompson smiled to himself. She does like me.

EIGHT

KATE LET HERSELF into her apartment. A drive in the country? When was the last time I did that? "I'm home, Granddad," she called.

"Back here in the kitchen," came his reply.

"I'll go change first." Her clothes were disheveled and her stockings torn from her scrape with the drunk. She was glad Jerry had not met her at the door because she had no intention of telling him about the incident. He'd just worry.

In her bedroom—the apartment's master suite that Jerry had insisted must be hers when they moved in—she removed her business suit, folded it, and placed it on a chair. Tomorrow she'd drop it off at the dry cleaners.

The room was feminine, painted a warm butter yellow. Yards and yards of rose patterned chintz draped the windows and covered deeply cushioned furniture. She'd pulled out all the stops when she'd decorated this room, turning it into her dream bedroom. English antiques she'd bought at auction at Lorneby's shone with the mellow glow of beeswax. Under a bank of windows that looked out across the Central Park reservoir all the way to the San Remo twin towers on Central Park West, a club chair and a chaise lounge were separated by a round tea table. The room had a working fireplace and on cold winter nights Kate lit a cozy fire and curled up in front of it.

She slipped on soft cotton pajamas, pulled a robe over them, and thrust her cold feet into fuzzy slippers. Now I'm prepared to face the dragon, she thought wryly.

Jerry gave her an appraising look as he ladled stew into large bowls. "You're late. I was worried." He broke crusty Italian bread into chunks and arranged them on a tray with a small dish of warm olive oil and balsamic vinegar for dipping.

"Well, you don't have to worry anymore. Vaughn says I'm to have my own limo and a driver who's a trained bodyguard starting tomorrow," she told Jerry.

He looked up, his eyes shrewd. Sometimes he can read my mind, Kate thought, please don't let it be tonight. "Did something happen to you?" he asked. "You look a little washed out."

"Well, thanks for nothing," Kate replied cheerfully. "No, nothing happened to me. Stop your frettin', man," she said, the way her grandmother used to scold him.

"It's about time you had your own limo. There's a psycho out there, you of all people should know, abducting women, killin' 'em. I remember that Son of Sam thing, went on for a whole summer before the cops finally nailed him. So what took Thompson so long to put your safety and comfort above his profits? Ya think Diane Sawyer and Barbara Walters drive around in beat-up car service junkers? No way. Glad Thompson's finally doing right by you."

Kate sipped red wine. "This is nice." Then, "Granddad, did you reach Mrs. Greenbaum?"

Jerry grinned. "Yeah, and we worked it all out. She's gonna see you tomorrow. At her apartment. She don't get out much anymore. So you're gonna have to cart your cameras and microphones downtown to Irma's."

"I'm really grateful, Granddad."

Jerry raised a palm. "Not my doing. Irma called me herself after your show. Said the reporters were ringing her phone off the hook, but seeing as how you're my granddaughter, she'd give you the scoop. Scoop. Her word exactly." Jerry grinned across the table.

Kate grinned back. "You sure you wouldn't like to come to work for the station? People get paid a lot of money for doing what you did today. They're called advance men."

Jerry laughed. "Sure, sweetheart, that's just what you need, your old grandfather hanging around your TV station. Besides, I put in fifty years with the garment workers. Started work when I was fifteen. Guess I earned my pension and the right to sit on my duff all day."

Here he goes again, Kate thought with a satisfied grin. She got up and carried her plate to the sink, rinsed it and placed it in the dishwasher. Her face averted, she tried to sound casual as she said, "Vaughn's invited me for lunch at his country house on Saturday. But you know, it's just business. We'll talk shop the whole time."

"Well, whoop-de-doo. It's about time you started having some fun."

Kate walked over and kissed Jerry on the top of his head. "I'm glad you approve." And I'm looking forward to it, she realized. "I've got a stack of printouts as tall as the Empire State Building to study for the show tomorrow, so I'd better get cracking."

"Good night, sweetheart. Don't stay up too late."

After she left the room, Jerry muttered to himself, "Business, my eyeball! Still, I'm glad she's goin' out and having herself some fun, but why'd she have to pick a stuffed shirt like Thompson? He's way too old for her!"

In her room Kate lifted a framed picture from her dressing table. In it, she and her best friend Dolly had just skated off the Wollman Rink. Jerry had snapped the picture. She and Dolly had their arms around each other, their faces side by side, pressed cheek to cheek. They were laughing at the cold, laughing at each other and the spills they'd taken that afternoon. They didn't have a care in the world.

Kate and Dolly Devereaux had been best friends since grade school. That was decades before Dolly had become "the copper mine heiress." A distant relative had left her his controlling shares in a profitable copper mining company. But money hadn't changed Dolly. She still made the children in New York Hospital's cancer wing laugh as she cavorted around in her clown suit and makeup. In fact, she'd given most of the money to the hospital. That's my Dolly!

Wonder what she'll think of me arriving at her apartment in a limo? With all her riches, Dolly won't hire one for herself. Says it's a waste of money. And maybe it is.

Kate set the picture back in its place and picked up the one next to it. Her mother had posed for this photo when she was a child. She looked like an angel in her white confirmation dress. She probably *is* an angel now, Kate thought, that's why that private investigator I hired can't find her. "If you are an angel, Mom," she whispered, "watch over me."

Shaking off her gloom, Kate headed for the shower, a wayward thought causing her lips to twitch in mirth. Poor Vaughn. Wait till he gets a load of Granddad. He doesn't know that any man who wants to date me more than once has to go a couple of rounds with a fire-breathing dragon.

NINE

At One Police Plaza, Rick Smith and his partner Joe Mateer sipped strong coffee and tried to remain focused. Like bookends, the two men were tall and muscular, dressed conservatively, and wore their black hair short and neat. Joe was the older of the two. Rick was better looking. His complexion tended toward a ruddy hue, especially when he was excited about a case, and his eyes were a deep warm brown while Joe's eyes were gray. Otherwise, they were frequently mistaken for brothers. By eleven at night, they'd rolled up their shirtsleeves and ditched their ties. Their day had begun dismally at seven A.M. at a Dumpster behind Devon's Irish Pub on Second Avenue in the Turtle Bay section of Manhattan.

Frustrated and tired, Rick rested his forehead in his palms, his elbows propped on the conference room table. The room had been commandeered for the strangler case. Pinned to the walls, like a lunatic's idea of pin-up girls, were lurid photographs of the strangler's victims.

Without warning, Rick jumped up and shoved his chair hard against the wall. "I'm sick of looking at this stuff," he barked as he paced the room's perimeter. "I can't sleep at night because when I close my eyes I see these pitiful creatures. I feel dirty, like I'm some sort of voyeur."

"The dead have no right to privacy," Joe said mildly. "In fact, they have no rights at all. You knew that when you joined the Violent Crimes Division."

"I knew it and that's *why* I joined!" Rick slammed his fist on the table, causing papers to jump and coffee to slosh over rims. "I knew it and I wanted to make a difference, to be somebody to stand up for them. To treat what was left of them with some dignity. What's dignified about this?" His arms swung out, encompassing the macabre gallery.

Joe got up and put a hand on Rick's shoulder. "I know it's getting to you, buddy. Hell, it's getting to me too. But it's a cool head that's gonna crack this case. And I know we can do it. You and me together. If there's anyone who can figure out this psycho's M.O., it's us. We've done it before. We'll do it again."

The senior member of the team, Mateer liked Smith, his partner of several years. Smith was not a bleeding heart but a decent guy who had not developed a crusty exterior like some of the other detectives. I hope he never does, Mateer thought. The respectful way he handles a crime scene preserves evidence, for one thing. Some of those guys go stampeding in like a herd of bull elephants.

"Look at them," Smith said, "they're all innocent, just innocent young women. This one, our gal number one, did you know she slept with a teddy bear? It was on top of her bedspread, and her mother told me she slept with it since she was an infant. After you get to know the details of their lives, these girls are not just corpses anymore, they're real people."

"Hey, buddy, I'm on your side. I agree. But you can't let it get to your psyche, or you won't be effective." Mateer had another thought. Smith was always edgy after a run-in with Kate Callahan. "Did you happen to catch Kate's show earlier?"

Rick slid back his chair. At the mention of Kate's name, his face lit up. "Yeah. She's getting better and better, isn't she, Joe? Someday we're gonna turn on the set and there she'll be, anchoring for one of the big national networks, like Brian Williams or Diane Sawyer. That was always her dream."

He scooted his chair under the table. "Thanks, Joe. I'm under control. Let's get back to work and put all those profiling courses we took to good use. I'm gonna get a handle on this crazy killer if I have to stay here all night."

Mateer settled into his own chair and opened a file. "The costumes are our most important clue, but what's their significance?"

"That's got me stumped." Smith rested his chin in his hand and eyed his partner across the table. "I don't know how long we'll be able to keep the fact that the victims were dressed in period costumes from the media. We've been lucky so far. All the camera crews were able to shoot were the body bags."

He sipped cold coffee, made a disgusted face, slammed the mug down. "Let's call that museum curator first thing in the morning and get her to look at the clothes this latest victim was wearing. Maybe she'll see a pattern this time. Sorry I exploded."

"Don't sweat it. You've got to unload on me and your buddies, otherwise you'll burn out fast. And don't go feeling guilty if you get the need to talk to one of the docs. That's why the PD keeps them on the payroll. The guys who keep this shit bottled up inside are the ones who end up divorced, or worse, start working for the other side."

Rick carried his mug to the coffee tray for a refill. "It's just as well I didn't marry Kate. How would I ever be able to talk to her about this stuff?"

Joe Mateer couldn't help thinking that the reverse might be true. Callahan was a pretty spunky woman. She'd seen a lot of tragic deaths in her line of work. Rick would be better off if he had someone to go home to. He gets emotional every time he bumps into Kate at a scene. Poor guy, he really blew that one, and he's been paying for it for years.

TEN

IN THE DARKENED ROOM, twelve o'clock glowed brightly red on his bedside digital clock. Midnight. The witching hour. The hour when the demons came out to play havoc with men's souls. He couldn't sleep. Today had been much too eventful—far too stressful. Pretending to be nice, putting on a polite face for the world, all the while wanting to scream. He'd felt backed into a corner, and it had taken all of his willpower not to strike out.

He got up, tied a silk robe around his naked body, and turned on a soft lamp. He wandered to the living room to pour himself a brandy. Why weren't the media saying anything about the clothes? All those vintage outfits he had to track down and purchase. The exact accessories so that the costumes would be just right, perfect.

He swirled the brandy in a snifter. The TV reporters and the newspapers weren't saying a word about the clothes, the hairdos, the hair ribbons. Yet, he knew that one day the media would sing his praises. But for now they just didn't get it. They hadn't a clue about what he was doing. Nobody knew. All they cared about were the girls. But the girls were nothing, simply the means to an end, a very desirable end.

One day, perhaps decades from now, after he was gone, the world would recognize and herald his achievements. Wasn't that always the way? Honor a man posthumously.

He sipped the warm brandy, enjoyed its sensuous slide down his throat, its warmth in his stomach. Now Kate

Callahan, there was a happy thought. She intrigued him, with her abundant auburn hair, her pale, oval face. He had honored her by selecting her. He would formalize his commitment to her now. He went to his desk, unlocked a drawer, and pulled out a sheet of crisp paper. Taking up his silver pen, he added a star next to Kate Callahan's name on the list of women's names.

ELEVEN

In the News Division's conference room the next morning, Kate Callahan, Mike Cramer, Evan Wallace, and their assistants were planning the day's schedule.

Kate said, "I'm taking a camera crew to Irma Greenbaum's apartment in an hour. Granddad's meeting us there. He feels Mrs. Greenbaum will be more comfortable with him at her side. I've never met her, although I've heard a lot about her and her husband."

Mike shook his head in wonder. "Rabbits out of a hat, Callahan. Rabbits out of a hat."

"Granddad deserves all the credit, Mike. He and Mrs. Greenbaum arranged everything over the phone. He said she offered to give me the 'scoop.'" Kate smiled, remembering her grandfather's modesty, his delight in giving her something he knew she wanted. She remembered the many times Jerry had given her what she wanted and needed, often before she herself knew what they were.

As the producer, Mike stacked the show. "Right now, Greenbaum's our big story, we'll air her segment tonight. Shipley, who was supposedly giving us an exclusive, is now talking to everyone. He's getting his five minutes of fame. So, we'll schedule his live interview to follow right after Greenbaum's taped one. The art professor from NYU will be tomorrow night's guest."

"Professor Haber," Kate's assistant Dolores Del Fazzio prompted. Dolores was dark, tiny, a dynamo. "Kate, Mr. Shipley called first thing this morning. He's invited a camera crew up to his gallery. But it's got to be at eleven, same time you're interviewing Mrs. Greenbaum."

"Where's Susan? The arts are her beat," Kate asked.

"I thought you knew," Mike said, "Susan went into labor at two o'clock this morning."

Kate gave Dolores a dark look. Dolores shrugged. "Sorry. This place is so crazy I forgot to tell you."

Kate blew out her breath. "Yeah, I know. But please call the florist and send flowers."

"I'll cover Shipley for you," Evan Wallace volunteered.

Kate smiled. "Oh, would you, Evan? That's great. Thanks." Kate regarded the investigative reporter fondly. Wallace was so good at what he did, he had no need to stoop to jealousy and scheming, as other anchors complained their colleagues did. Evan was large boned and solid looking, with a thick thatch of short sandy hair above a high forehead. He had one of those faces that would forever look boyish. But one glimpse of his shrewd hazel eyes and few people made the mistake of underestimating him. Evan didn't miss a thing. His air of dependability matched his personality. He wasn't after Kate's job. He liked his freedom, liked working on the outside, digging up the dirt. He didn't want to be tied down to the anchor desk.

"I don't mind talking to Shipley while the crew tapes his tour of the gallery," he said. "Nothing to it."

"Okay, so that's settled," Mike said, checking off another item on his list. "We'll edit the footage and use a few of the shots for background while Kate's doing the lead-in."

Dolores's cell phone chirped. "See what I mean," she told Kate. Then, "Neil Lorneby for you, Kate." She arched her eyebrows and handed the phone across the table.

Kate took the phone and moved into a corner so the others could continue their discussion. There was never enough time.

Handing the phone back to Dolores, she announced to the news group, "Neil Lorneby wants to appear on the show. He says that as an auctioneer, he can contribute to the topic of stolen paintings."

"I hope you took him up on the offer," Mike said. "We can schedule him for Thursday night."

Kate grinned at her boss. "That's exactly what I told him, Mike. He'd like us to videotape him at the auction house early Thursday morning. I said we'd be there with bells on. Y-e-e-s!" she sang, punching the air with her fist.

The corner of Mike's mouth twitched upward. "Okay, now Evan, let's review your piece on the strangler story. I think we ought to lead with that, Kate. It's the city's hottest number right now."

"I agree."

Evan leaned back in his chair. He couldn't help looking pleased with himself. "Over the past year I've developed a good relationship with two detectives from the Violent Crimes Division: Rick Smith and Joe Mateer. Now, as it turns out, they are the lead detectives on the strangler case. They've agreed to be interviewed. And I've got a surprise for them." He opened a manila folder. "A source at the PD got these copies for me." He fanned out a sheaf of black and white glossies.

Kate leaned over to look, then quickly shut her eyes. Opening them, but staring at the wall, she crossed herself and whispered a prayer for the departed souls. "Dear God, those poor girls."

"We can't show those on the air!" Mike declared vehemently.

"No, of course not," Evan agreed. "The thing is, the strangler's victims were dressed in period costumes. The police have been keeping that juicy tidbit to themselves. Those detectives are going to be mighty surprised when I ask them about it. So surprised, I'm hoping they'll deviate from the script."

"We'd better rethink that one," Cramer advised. "As much as I'd like to break the story, that one could come back to bite us in the ass. We need those detectives' good will or we'll find ourselves out of the loop. See if you can't get them to agree to let you go with the revelation. Or at least strike a deal that you know about the costumes but won't report it in exchange for an inside track on the investigation. Maybe we'll get the Edward R. Murrow award for our coverage."

"What if some other station's got those photos too," Kate said, "and they run with it?"

Evan's eyes narrowed thoughtfully, "I think Mike's right, Kate. I'd rather have the police give me an inside track over the long haul so I can be there when they arrest this psychopath."

Mike stood up and clapped his hands together. "Okay, people, let's go. We've got a news show to put on!"

At her end of the table, Kate seemed to shrink into herself, momentarily withdrawn. Hearing Rick's name bandied about casually was hard, and running into him yesterday had upset her. Thank God Evan's conducting the interview downtown at police headquarters rather than here at the studio, she told herself. I don't want that man invading my territory. It's bad enough when I meet him at the scene. Although how I'm going to avoid him as long as this strangler story runs, I don't know.

"Callahan, you comin'?" Cramer called.

"Be right there, Mike," she said, getting up. Somehow the newsroom didn't seem as sacrosanct as it once did.

KATE GOT INTO the backseat of the station's van with Mike. Up front, the cameraman drove, the audio guy rode shotgun. "I'm riding with you guys," Kate said. "There's no way I'm taking a limo to Mrs. Greenbaum's."

True to his word, overnight Thompson had arranged for a car and driver to meet Kate at her apartment building at nine that morning. Her driver, Marty Sokolov, looked like an ex-prize fighter. Just the sight of him would be enough to make any would-be mugger turn tail and run.

The truck headed south on Twelfth Avenue. As the Hudson River flew by her window, Kate couldn't shake off her sense that the walls of the safe world she'd created for herself were beginning to crumble under the pressure of emotions she couldn't deny. Her pain over Rick had dulled over the years, but it still flared up from time to time, like an old injury.

There must be something wrong with me, she told herself. First my mother rejects me before I'm a year old, just up and leaves me in the middle of the night. Thank you Lord for Granddad and Grandma, otherwise, I'd have been an orphan and who knows what terrible things might have happened to me.

Then, the first and only man I fall in love with rejects me too, just about jilts me at the altar. We were engaged, all the wedding plans were made. But at the last minute he gets cold feet and wants out.

At the time she'd reined in her emotions. She'd lifted her chin and said, I understand, Rick. It's okay. But she hadn't understood and it wasn't okay. No way. No how. He didn't love her. It was as simple as that. But she had her pride, and she'd put up a good front. You learn to do that when you grow up a kid to whom other kids ask: Where's your mother? Why don't you live with her? Who's your father?

No child could have wished for better grandparents than she had. Maybe she was being selfish and ungrateful to still pine for a mother who didn't care enough to stick around for her first birthday. But pining for Rick was an-other matter altogether. Her grandparents had taken her parents' place. No man had ever taken Rick's place.

Kate and Rick had met when both were in college, Kate at New York University, Rick at the John Jay College of Criminal Justice. Rick was two years older than Kate. He'd joined the NYPD straight out of high school. But after the Police Academy, and a stint as a rookie cop, he realized that if he was going to hold a position of authority and importance, he needed a college degree. What Kate liked about Rick was that he knew exactly what he wanted and he went for it, same as her. Rick loved law enforcement. To be an inspector in the Violent Crimes Division was his dream. He graduated college with honors.

They dated for six years, six years of being madly in love and bursting with passion but rarely having a moment alone. In the summers, they managed to borrow a friend's house on Long Island Sound for a few weekends. Those were the happiest days of Kate's life.

As soon as Rick signed up with the PD again, he pro-posed. The plan was to be married in a couple of years. That was okay with Kate, she was struggling with her own career, and Jerry wanted her to be a bit older before she married. Kate, out of college for two years, was working as an associate producer for TNYC Television. Rick kept the streets of the city safe. Quickly he was promoted to plainclothes cop, then he got his detective's gold shield. That was when Rick changed. He let his job consume him. He clammed up. He wasn't ready for marriage, he informed Kate. She let him go gracefully. It wasn't her style to make a fuss.

But the pain never went away. The aching, the loneli-ness, the longing for Rick were there all the time, every day, and it was just something that she lived with, like a

TWELVE

IRMA GREENBAUM'S MODEST apartment seemed crowded with the addition of the crew from TNYC. Kate knew she was in trouble when she caught sight of Mrs. Greenbaum standing in the middle of the living room, handkerchief clutched tightly in a hand pressed to her lips. At her side, Jerry patted her free hand. He glowered at Kate. "Me and Irma weren't expecting the second landing at Normandy."

Mike approached them. "Hi, Jerry," he said. Shaking her hand, Mike said to Irma Greenbaum, "I just want to take a look around, then I'll catch a cab back uptown. I've got a meeting with the head honchos at the station. Once the camera and audio guys set up, you'll hardly know they're here."

Kate led Jerry and Mrs. Greenbaum to a brocade sofa. Spying traditional dining room furniture in the adjoining room, Kate intuitively felt the dignified setting would make an excellent backdrop for the interview. She called to Mike, "Have them set up in there."

Ordinarily, Kate tried to wring every emotion possible from an interview. But Irma Greenbaum was her grandfather's special friend, and she felt an overwhelming urge to protect the fragile lady. Besides, she told herself, Granddad will be disappointed in me if Mrs. Greenbaum experiences any embarrassment as a result of trusting me. And the last thing Kate ever wanted to do was to disappoint Jerry. So, Mrs. Greenbaum can hide her trembling hands under the tabletop, and psychologically she might feel more secure with that large table between her and the camera.

"I'm sorry about all the confusion, Mrs. Greenbaum," Kate apologized.

"This is Kate," Jerry said.

"I'm so glad to meet you, Mrs. Greenbaum. Granddad has spoken to me about you and your husband often and in the fondest terms."

"Thank you. Jerry's the best friend Harry ever had."

Kate took a moment to study Mrs. Greenbaum. Her age, Kate knew, was seventy-eight. By nature she was timid and a mite reclusive, Granddad had clued Kate, but "she knows how to stick up for herself when she has to." There was something serene and comfortable about Irma Greenbaum, the kind of woman men gravitated to. Dressed in a pale blue knit suit, she was perfectly groomed, with not an ash blonde hair out of place. Her nails were polished a soft pink and her diamond and platinum rings twinkled in the lamp light.

The apartment was immaculate, yet comfortable. Chairs and sofa in the Greenbaum household were meant for sitting on not looking at. The coffee table was set with a fine but much-used silver tea service. This home was not a museum.

"Have you lived here long?" Kate asked, hoping to get Mrs. Greenbaum to warm up to her.

"Ever since Harry joined the staff at Beth Israel. That was nineteen fifty-five. The medical center is just across First Avenue, you know, so that made it convenient for him."

"You have a lovely home," Kate said.

"Harry liked it here. I do too."

"Let me explain how we'll conduct the interview, Mrs.

Greenbaum. You and I will sit at your dining room table—if that's all right with you?"

"Yes. That's fine. Wherever you like." She smiled for the first time. "I'm in your hands."

"And they're good hands too," Jerry interjected.

Kate grimaced mockingly. "Granddad's not at all prejudiced."

Suddenly, they were all smiling at each other. The atmosphere had lightened. In the next room, the two-man crew worked quietly, setting up equipment. Thank goodness, peace has been restored, Kate thought. She said to Irma, "Okay, then, I'll be asking you questions and you tell me whatever feels right. We'll take our time and just chat."

Noting that the technicians were standing by, she asked, "Ready?"

Irma Greenbaum smiled. "Ready as I'll ever be."

Jerry cupped a hand under her elbow and assisted her from the sofa. "I'll be right out here, Irma. Rootin' for ya. Don't let that camera faze you. It's nothing."

Kate chuckled. "Look who's talking. I couldn't get him in front of a TV camera for all the cheesecake at Ferrara's."

As the interview progressed, Irma Greenbaum seemed to relax and became very focused. She answered Kate's questions with dignity, and she was natural and calm. She's everybody's grandmother, Kate thought. The viewers will love her.

"Mrs. Greenbaum, your husband's father was a successful dealer of valuable European paintings in the twenties and thirties. Did your husband ever try to find out what became of his father's extensive collection?"

"Oh my, yes. Harry traveled to Berlin and to Paris often." Mrs. Greenbaum looked directly at Kate. It was just the two of them, the camera was forgotten. "My husband was a physician, you see, and any time a medical convention was held in either of those cities, or Frankfurt or Vienna, Harry attended. He used his free time to scour the private galleries and the museums in hopes of finding his father's paintings."

"How did he know what to look for, Mrs. Greenbaum? He was only a teenager when he and his father were sent to Auschwitz. How could he remember which paintings were part of his father's collection?"

"Because of this," Irma Greenbaum said, turning in her chair and reaching into a drawer in the breakfront behind her. She produced a slim volume and handed it to Kate. Kate held it up to the camera.

Irma Greenbaum explained, "That is what is called a *catalogue raisonné*. See the gold lettering on the front. 'The Greenbaum Collection,' it says. And inside, it says it was printed in 1938. That was one year before my father-in-law's entire collection was looted by those thugs. Before they carted him off to the concentration camp. And my Harry with him."

Irma Greenbaum pressed her handkerchief to her lips to stifle a sob. Kate steeled her emotions. She wanted to reach out and hug the older woman. She settled for patting her hand and waiting.

Mrs. Greenbaum spoke, "All his life, my Harry had the worst nightmares. He'd wake up screaming."

"I hear that's not unusual," Kate said soothingly, reminded of her own nightmares.

Irma Greenbaum wiped her brow with her handkerchief. "My, those lights are hot."

"Yes, they are. But it won't be for long." Under her blouse, Kate was sweating too. The studio was kept frigidly cold. But this was a home and overheated at that.

"Explain to us, just what is a *catalogue raissoné*?"

Irma Greenbaum exhaled. "It's an inventory of all the paintings in a collection. My father-in-law had it printed for his clients." She took the book from Kate and opened to a page at random. "It's written in German, so if you don't read German you won't know what I'm showing you. But this first line is the name of the artist. Under the name are his nationality and the years of his birth and death. Below that is the title of the painting. Next comes the date it was painted, and the medium, for example 'oil on canvas.' And last there are the dimensions of the framed size. This paragraph gives a brief history of the artist and a description of the work. So you see, this catalogue proves that all these paintings," and she riffled the pages, "rightfully belonged to my husband's father, Henry Greenbaum. Now," she said resolutely, her eyes locked on Kate's, "they belong to me."

"How did this book come into your husband's possession?" Kate asked.

Irma Greenbaum's face lit up and she smiled. "Why, that was quite a miracle. Harry found it quite by chance when he was browsing in an old bookstore in Greenwich Village. He told me the name 'Greenbaum' jumped off the shelf at him. He could scarcely believe his eyes, and when he held it in his hands and realized what it meant, he cried. Right there in that musty bookstore."

The emotional aspects of Mrs. Greenbaum's story were getting to Kate. She cleared her throat. "And so he began his search," she prompted.

"And so he began his search," Irma Greenbaum echoed. "But he had good help in the last years of his life. Professor Leon Haber of the World Jewish Congress—a wonderful man, a wonderful ally to my husband in his quest—Professor Haber searched too. There is a whole network of people looking for our paintings."

"And now you have the first one back," Kate said reflectively.

"Thanks to that good man, Thomas Shipley. But the other paintings? Where are they?" She clenched her fists. "Someone knows. Someone has them locked away in private rooms, someone enjoys them in secret. Someone enjoys them in shame."

"One last question, Mrs. Greenbaum. Now that you've recovered one of your father-in-law's paintings, what are you going to do with it?"

Irma Greenbaum's smile was rueful. "Well, I'm not going to hang it on my living room wall, Kate. This morning I received two telephone calls offering to buy the painting. One was from a collector. The other was from a museum. Also, Mr. Shipley has offered to buy the painting back. If I sell it to anyone, it will be to him. For the time being, he's holding it for safe keeping at his gallery. I don't have insurance coverage on it and he does."

"It's worth five million dollars," Kate said thoughtfully. "You'll be a rich woman."

"Not me. I have everything I need right here. But I'll be able to set up trust funds for my children and grandchildren, and I can contribute to my husband's hospital, Beth Israel, for emergency room equipment. Giving money away, not hoarding it, that's what makes a person feel rich."

"I have a friend who says the same thing," Kate remarked, thinking of Dolly.

She paused. "That was good," she said, glad that they'd ended on a positive note. To the cameraman, she called, "I'll have a couple of cutaways." The film rolled on for a few seconds.

"Thank you, Mrs. Greenbaum. That was a splendid

interview." Kate started to shake hands, then impulsively put her arm around Mrs. Greenbaum's shoulders and pulled the small woman to her.

Jerry coughed. "What say I take you two lovely ladies out to lunch," he suggested.

Irma looked up at him, admiration shining in her eyes. Kate did not fail to note the look and was pleased. "I've got to get back to the station. You two have fun." Besides, three's a crowd, she thought.

THIRTEEN

EVAN WALLACE HAD grown up poor in a borderline slum neighborhood west of Washington Street. The experience had turned him into a risk taker. What was there to lose? He knew firsthand what poverty and failure were all about; he'd lived in their grip for the first twenty years of his life. He also knew that he'd survived and made a success of himself, and that if he had to, he could survive and succeed again. His attitude of not worrying about job security, of not getting bogged down in the politics at the station or always looking over his shoulder and covering his ass, was what made him a top-notch investigative reporter.

Wallace had no designs on Kate Callahan's job. His dreams did not include the anchor desk at a regional news show. His ambitions were aimed higher, just as he knew Kate's were. Someday he was going to be a regular contributor to *60 Minutes* or *20/20*, exposing the misdeeds of the rich and powerful, exposing corporate greed, restoring balance to a system that favored the rich and powerful and giant corporations.

A man trusted by other men, Wallace knew he could strike a deal with the detectives from the Violent Crimes Division, Rick Smith and Joe Mateer. With an inside track on the strangler investigation, he might just win himself an EMMY and land himself a job offer from NBC or CNN.

But first he had this tour with Thomas Shipley to conduct for Kate while she was interviewing Irma Greenbaum. Technically, it was not an interview. Kate would interview

Shipley this evening live at the news center. All Evan had to do was follow Shipley around the gallery with the camera crew and ask a question or two here and there. Whatever footage they filmed this morning would be edited to approximately a minute and a half of TV air time. He'd let Shipley do the talking as he showed off his gallery.

Thomas Shipley greeted Wallace warmly. "Come in, come in," he called effusively. "Jeffrey," he said, turning to his assistant, "get these gentlemen some coffees. Or would you prefer tea or a soft drink?" he asked the crew from TNYC.

"Nothing for me, thanks," Wallace said.

The lighting technician had already moved into the center of the gallery, his light meter in his hand. "Don't bother about me." The cameraman shook his head negatively. "We'll just set up. Thanks anyway," the audio woman said.

"Light's perfect," the lighting technician said.

"Everything here is state-of-the-art," Shipley said proudly.

Wallace looked around the place. Clean and austere, like the galleries at the Metropolitan Museum of Art, the walls were covered in pale silk. Incandescent ceiling fixtures spotlighted each painting. He complimented Shipley.

"We don't want the background distracting from the art," Shipley said.

Shipley was a little too effeminate for Wallace's tastes, but he didn't think the art dealer was gay. Wallace had done a cursory background check, just as he did on everyone he interviewed, and Shipley had at one time been married to a painter of some renown back in the eighties. She'd dropped out of the art scene after their divorce.

Shipley was of medium height with thinning brown hair and intelligent brown eyes. He likes stripes, Wallace observed. A muted charcoal brown pinstripe suit was worn over a red and white striped shirt with a red and brown bow tie. The clothing looked expensively tailored, right down to the shirt's monogrammed cuffs. It was Wallace's job to notice the details.

"Do you own the entire building, Mr. Shipley?" Wallace asked conversationally.

"All five floors," Shipley replied. The square brown brick building occupied the northwest corner of Madison Avenue and Sixty-seventh Street. "If your crew is ready, I'll begin the tour. I assume you want to keep this low key and informal."

"Anyway you wish, Mr. Shipley," Wallace said, thinking how lucky the dealer was to be getting this free publicity for his gallery. The cost of a sixty second television spot was astronomical. Well, Shipley could probably afford anything he wanted to buy. A man who had blithely given away a five million dollar painting had to have plenty of dough.

"Roll camera," Wallace instructed. Then spotting an oil painting on an easel positioned so that it commanded the center of the room, he asked, "Say, isn't that the stolen Klimt?" The picture portrayed a beautiful pale-skinned, red-haired woman and a tanned man with black hair locked in an embrace under a brilliantly colored coat with gold trim. "It's a beauty," Wallace marveled.

Shipley positioned himself on the other side of the easel. "Many collectors covet this painting. I could have sold it ten times over. But that would have been unthinkable once I discovered its history."

"You're the hero of the day," Wallace remarked without rancor.

Shipley's smile was modest. "Hardly."

Wallace wanted to ask Shipley how he had acquired the painting and how he had discovered its sordid past. But he knew that Kate would be asking Shipley those questions during her interview tonight, so he held his boundless curiosity in check.

Instead, he commented, "This is some layout."

Shipley beamed, his out-flung arm encompassing the gallery. "When I acquired the building, I gutted these first two floors, opened them up to give us a sense of space and light. A perfect setting for my treasures."

Evan Wallace tilted his head back and looked up all the way to the ceiling of the second floor. He knew the camera was panning the scene. The center of the building had been gutted, creating an atrium, with spiraling galleries lining the perimeter walls.

"It's just like the Guggenheim Museum," Wallace observed.

Shipley seemed pleased. "Yes, it is, isn't it? The arrangement allows me to display my paintings to maximum advantage."

As Wallace surveyed Shipley's collection, he was pleased to see that the pictures were painted in a realistic style. "I don't care for those paintings where you can't tell if they're hanging upside down or not. Always makes me feel like the artist is pulling my leg," he confessed.

Shipley chuckled. "I specialize in Contemporary and Impressionist paintings. This," he pointed while glancing over his shoulder to verify that the cameraman was keeping up, "is a very fine Twachtman. I share your disdain for the hit-and-run style of painting that is so prevalent today."

"Say, isn't that a John Singer Sargent?" Wallace asked as he stood before a very large portrait. "I'm no art expert but I do like spending Sunday afternoons in the American Wing at the Metropolitan Museum of Art."

"You've got a keen eye, Mr. Wallace. That *is* a Sargent. Most of his paintings are larger than life. This is a portrait

of his sister, Miss Emily Sargent, whom he painted often."
Shipley seemed to pose as he directed his answer to the
camera. "It is the dealer's job to educate his clientele. If
they're pleased with what they've purchased, they'll remain loyal. I have many long-standing clients. The chairman of your television network, Vaughn Thompson, is one.
Mr. Michael Douglas, the actor, is another. I've helped Mr.
Douglas accumulate a fine collection of paintings from the
Hudson River school."

Shipley mounted the stairs. "I display the Impressionist paintings up here on the second floor."

LATER, AFTER THE tour had been videotaped and while the
technicians loaded the van, Wallace lingered. "Ever had
anything stolen?"

Shipley's brows knit into an angry black line. "As a
matter of fact, I have. A thief had the nerve to walk right
out the front door with a twelve-inch statue by the French
sculptor Gaston Lachaise. I determined then never to stock
any small pieces, and I've eliminated statues from my collection altogether."

"Was the stolen statue ever recovered?" Wallace asked.

"No trace of it. It's listed with the Art Loss Register
at the International Foundation for Art Research. There's
a reward."

"Say, this stolen art stuff is fascinating. Maybe someday I'll do a follow-up investigative piece on it. Would you
be willing to help?"

"Delighted to. May I take you on a quick tour of the
rest of the building. A behind-the-scenes tour for your
own edification?"

"Delighted," Wallace echoed warmly. He was always
pleased when he established a rapport with a professional
who might be useful to him on future investigative pieces.

Glancing at his watch, he noted that he had plenty of time before his meeting at One Police Plaza with Detectives Smith and Mateer. "Lead on, Macduff," he quipped.

Shipley clapped him on the back and steered him onto the elevator. They descended to the basement. "I had these storage rooms with specially-designed racks installed," he said, referring to huge bins where paintings were arranged in rows.

A man of about seventy advanced slowly around a corner, bent under the weight of a heavy wooden frame he carried. He nodded respectively as he passed.

"My workrooms are down here. That's Marco," Shipley said. "Marco's an artist in his own right. He constructs stretchers for canvases. Occasionally, a canvas arrives in poor condition, frayed at the edges, loose on the stretcher. Marco's a genius."

They entered the elevator again. "We'll bypass the third floor. My offices are there. Let me show you my personal collection." They rode up.

The elevator doors opened. "These are my private quarters. I have a duplex apartment up here on the fourth and fifth floors. I don't like to leave all of my treasures below. I prefer to surround myself with beautiful things."

The walls were painted stark white, the carpet was gray, and the place felt chilly to Wallace. Spotting another colorful painting of a redheaded woman, Wallace asked, "Say, isn't that a Klimt too?"

"You do have a collector's eye, Mr. Wallace. If you ever decide to collect, I hope you'll let me assist you with your purchases."

I think I'm being snowed, Wallace told himself. Anyone can see this picture looks just like the painting downstairs. "Well, it reminds me of the painting you're giving to Irma Greenbaum. That's how I recognized it," he said modestly.

FOURTEEN

"THESE GARMENTS ARE VINTAGE," Phyllis Stern said with assurance. "They are not copies of antique clothing. They are the real thing."

"How can you be sure?" Detective Rick Smith asked.

Stern regarded the doubting detective with a flinty eye. "It is my business to know such things, Detective. I can tell by the way they are constructed. By the thread and the stitches. And by the cloth, itself. I've been authenticating antique clothing for sixty years."

"I'm glad you're sure of yourself, Ms. Stern. Makes my job that much easier."

There was nothing pretty about Phyllis Stern, nothing soft. She did not remind Smith of his grandmother, although Stern was at least eighty. Yet she was striking and compelling to look at with her crisp black and white outfit, her bobbed steel gray hair, her black-framed half-glasses that perched on the tip of her hawk nose. Yet she carried herself with assurance and authority.

Comes from running the Metropolitan Museum of Art's Costume Department for decades, Rick thought.

Joe had printed out an old feature article on Ms. Stern from *Town & Country* magazine. Phyllis Stern, the features writer had written, was a trend setter. At an early age, she realized she wasn't much to look at so she set about to acquire her own special style and aura. Over the years, she'd become a magnet for myth and rumor. She was always immaculately turned out, the article said. Ms. Stern even went so far as to polish the soles of her low-heeled black patent leather trademark pumps.

Rick had regarded his own brown tasseled loafers. "Forget the bottoms," he laughingly told Joe, "the tops could do with a shine."

"Tell me what you can about these garments," Smith asked Ms. Stern.

Phyllis Stern reached out and lifted the white dress by its shoulders, holding it out in front of her. "The Dumpster," she said, wrinkling her nose and eyeing slimy food stains. She shook her head. "Those poor girls. What is he doing with them? Why these costumes?"

"If we knew the answer to that," Joe Mateer commented, "we'd be on our way to discovering what's driving this psychopath."

Rick Smith warned, "This aspect of the case is still confidential, Ms. Stern. We appreciate you not talking to the media."

"Oh, the media," Stern said in a disparaging tone. "What have they ever done for me? Fabricated ludicrous stories, that's what." Gently, Phyllis Stern lowered the dress to Rick Smith's desk, smoothing the fabric with her hand. It was all right for her to touch it; forensics had been all over it.

"Very well, Detectives, this is what I can tell you. This dress was made at the turn of the century, anywhere from 1900 to 1905. Clothing was made to order for the client's measurements in those days. In today's retail market, this dress would be equivalent to about a size 14 or 16. The fabric is a fine cotton called mull. The workmanship is superb and the dress was made by Fortuny."

"Fortuny?"

"These tucks in the bodice are the famous Fortuny pleats. In 1905 shoulder lines in ladies' garments dropped a bit, and the silhouette narrowed. The style of this dress predates 1905. It would have been worn by a society lady as summer sportswear."

"Do you mean sportswear as for engaging in sports?" Smith asked.

Phyllis Stern peered over her half-glasses. "That's exactly what I mean, Detective. She would have worn it to play croquet or a gentle game of lawn tennis. The shoes bear out my assessment. They are a feminine adaptation of the man's evening pump with a flat, grosgrain ribbon bow, intended to be worn in warm weather."

"I'm impressed," Mateer said. "The underwear looks like today's stuff," Mateer commented.

"It is. The underwear must have belonged to the dead woman," Stern agreed.

"Where would a person find an old dress like this?" Smith asked.

Stern shrugged her shoulders. "Why, many places. Vintage or antique clothing stores in New York or London, for one. A costume house that rents to theatrical companies, for another."

"We'll send some plainclothes guys to check the vintage clothing stores and costume rental places again," Smith told Mateer.

Stern continued, "As well as the Smithsonian. My museum. Your grandmother's attic. And last, but certainly not least, the Internet: eBay, for example."

Mateer said. "We made the rounds with the clothing from the other victims. Nada." His expression was grim.

"What about the stockings?" Smith asked.

"You can buy stockings like these in any department store." Stern began pawing through the pile of clothing. "Is this everything?"

"Yes. Why?"

"Then where are the garters?"

"There weren't any."

"Pendant garters weren't invented until 1907 when they were attached to corsets. The round garter held up stockings for centuries, for both women and men. So how did these stockings stay up? When she moved around, the stockings would have worked their way down her legs. Were the stockings up or down when you found her?"

"Up," Smith replied.

Phyllis Stern's somber brown eyes met Rick Smith's tired ones. A flash of knowledge leapt between them. They were thinking the same thing: Unless for some reason she was unable to make a run for it. Like the victim was already dead when the clothes were put on her.

"One last thing, Detectives," Stern said as she gathered up her jacket and purse. "That dress is worth thousands of dollars. So unless it was stolen, whoever this killer is, he is not poor."

"DID YOU FIND any fingerprints on the victims?" Evan Wallace asked.

"You know we can't tell you that, Evan," Rick Smith said, but thinking to himself: No. We did not find prints on the victims' skin. If we had, we might have a handle on his I.D. right now.

Evan Wallace weighed his options. "I think I should show you what someone leaked to me." He pulled the manila envelope from his inside pocket. Dramatically, he shook the black and white photos out onto Joe Mateer's desk.

Mateer, who'd been lounging in his swivel chair, sat up with a lunge. "Where'd you get those?"

Evan smiled. "You know I can't tell you that."

Smith scrubbed his face with his hands. Jeez, he was

tired. Working this case, dawn till midnight, day after day. Unable to sleep well at night. Existing on coffee and sandwiches on the run. Now he was going to have trouble with a wise-ass reporter, although up until just now he'd always thought Evan Wallace was a pretty straight shooter.

"What do you want?" Smith asked Wallace. "If you were going to go public with what you have, you'd have done it by now, so you must want something. Are you asking for our blessing? Because if you are, we aren't giving it."

"Why? Why are you holding back the stuff about the crazy outfits?" Wallace asked. "Look, I'm not going to report anything without your okay. But what's all the secrecy about these costumes?"

"It's always useful to hold back something from the public in cases like these. Helps us separate the crank calls from the real thing. Might prevent copycat killings." Smith gave Wallace a level look. "Might even save innocent lives."

"Okay," Wallace replied, "I take your point. But I can't guarantee that some other reporter hasn't got copies of these pictures too. It's my job to report the news, but more than that I want to be there when you collar this S.O.B. How about if I tuck these photos away for safekeeping, and maybe you'll let me tag along on the case."

Smith and Mateer exchanged looks. Mateer said, "You can't report what you overhear unless we give you the go-ahead."

Wallace stuck out his hand. "Same deal we've always had. I'll keep my eyes and ears open and my mouth shut. Who knows, I might be able to help."

I hope we're not making a mistake, Rick Smith thought.

Wallace continued, "So back to my original question. Did you find fingerprints on the skin or any of the clothing?"

"Nada," Smith said. "The perp must have worn gloves when he handled those women." Although four women had been strangled, collars and ribbons around their necks would have absorbed fingerprints if the perp had been barehanded.

"I assume you've got someone helping you identify these costumes."

"We do. Phyllis Stern of the Metropolitan Museum of Art."

"Oh, yeah, I've heard of her. She's a legend. So what's the significance of these outfits?" Wallace fanned out the photos. "Here, this first girl. Ashley Fuller, lived with her folks in Scarsdale, came into the city by train several times a week to attend ballet classes. She was found dressed up like a ballerina, yet there's something old-fashioned about these clothes. The black velvet ribbon around her neck, the big bow on the back of her dress."

"That's because they are genuinely old. Over one hundred years old, according to Phyllis Stern," Smith said.

"Well, if she's a dancer, and he gets his jollies by dressing her up like she's in the corps de ballet, maybe the guy you're looking for is someone connected with one of the ballet companies or ballet schools," Wallace suggested.

"We've questioned everyone Ashley Fuller came in contact with at that ballet school: the instructors, her fellow students. She was well liked. Had made no enemies. There are no rejected lovers." Smith spread his hands. "No suspects. From everything we've been able to learn, Ashley Fuller was a sweet, innocent kid who just loved to dance."

"Did she go on auditions? Maybe she met some weirdo at one of them."

"We're looking at everything. We're getting to know these girls like they were our kid sisters," Joe Mateer volunteered.

"That must make it rough," Wallace said.

"Very rough," Rick Smith said. "I can tell you one thing, Wallace. We're dealing with a clever, resourceful killer. He's blending in, acting normal, and when we catch him, his neighbors will look incredulous and say, 'Who? Mr. Joe Nice Guy? But he was so quiet and polite. Why he carried my groceries in for me. He liked to help.' That's always the way with these serial killers. On the outside, they look normal; on the inside, they're monsters. This guy knows how to exploit a situation. He's cunning and he's bold, and he's relying on other people being so absorbed in their own lives, they don't notice the clues he's bound to be dropping."

"Are you telling me you don't have any suspects?" Wallace asked.

Smith shook his head. "We're looking hard at the relatives, but, no, no one we can tie to all four victims, or even to one. But the thing that links all our victims is the costume angle. That's why it's so important that we keep this information to ourselves for as long as possible."

"You can count on me," Evan Wallace said sincerely.

FIFTEEN

KATE CALLAHAN SAT in her office admiring her new brief-case. Only minutes earlier, her assistant Dolores Del Fazzio had brought in the elegantly wrapped gift box from Mark Cross. Kate had lifted the lid to see a shiny leather brief-case.

"Wow! Mark Cross. That thing cost a bundle," Dolores quipped. "Who sent it? There's no card."

Kate smiled to herself. "I think I know. Will you excuse me, Dolores."

Alone, she picked up the phone and tapped in the chairman's extension. Mrs. Russo put her through immediately. Kate thanked Vaughn for his thoughtfulness, but explained that she could not accept an expensive gift from him.

"But it's not a gift," he chuckled. "It's a business necessity. Like your desk and your computer." His tone softened. "I feel badly about what happened to you last night, Kate. Please let me try to make it up to you."

"You already have. There was a limo waiting for me this morning."

"I'm looking forward to Saturday," Vaughn said. "Got another call. Gotta go."

Kate went back to preparing for her interview with Shipley. Occasionally, she'd look at the briefcase and smile. So his interest in me is not all business, she told herself. Is that a crime? I'm single. He's single. We're both over twenty-one. Let's just see what happens next.

AT FIFTEEN MINUTES before five, Dolores buzzed Kate on the intercom. "There's a Ryan MacPeterson on line one for you, Kate."

With a trembling hand, Kate picked up the handset. "Mr. MacPeterson? I thought you were in San Francisco."

Ryan MacPeterson, a New York State licensed private investigator for over thirty-five years, sucked in his breath before saying, "I am in San Francisco, Ms. Callahan. I thought I should call you right away."

Kate blinked back the tears that were already forming under her lashes. She knew by the gravity of the investigator's tone that he did not have good news for her. Still, she asked in a hopeful whisper, "Have you found my mother?"

"In a sense, I have, Ms. Callahan. I'm sorry to be the one to tell you that your mother is dead. She died thirty-four years ago. I've seen her grave with my own eyes."

"Oh, dear Lord, no," Kate cried.

"Ms. Callahan, I am so sorry. Are you alone? Perhaps you should call a friend to be with you," Ryan MacPeterson suggested sympathetically.

"Hold on, hold on," Kate said. She dropped the handset on her desk, and fumbled in a tissue box. Doubling over in her chair, she thought she was going to be sick, and she put her head between her knees. Okay, okay, she told herself, pull yourself together. Take deep breaths. This is not coming as a surprise. This is what you expected all along. You hired MacPeterson to confirm your darkest suspicions.

Picking up the handset, she said, "I'm all right, Mr. MacPeterson. Please. Tell me what you've learned."

"I have an old friend out here with the San Francisco police department and we help each other out. He spent some off-duty time searching the PD's old records back to 1978, the year you said Anne Callahan first moved to San Francisco. On June 20, 1980, the police dispatcher got an anonymous call that a woman had overdosed on drugs and that she needed help because she wasn't breathing. The police sent an ambulance to the address given and went there themselves. The woman was alone. The police were with her when the paramedics arrived and when she was pronounced dead. From a soup kitchen card and a clinic card, they identified the woman as Anne Jeanne Callahan. No address. The woman was approximately twenty years old, undernourished, about five feet four, with light auburn hair. The autopsy revealed that she had borne a child about a year earlier.

Kate took a deep breath. "That sounds like a description of my mother. Where is she buried?"

"I've got the address for you, and I'll include it with my written report. It's a city-operated cemetery for the indigent. They'll cooperate if you decide to have your mother's remains transported to New York and interred in a family plot."

Kate shuddered. Although she'd doubted that her mother was alive, she'd never gone so far in her imaginings as to consider things like a memorial service and interment. "Thank you, Mr. MacPeterson. You've been most kind. I'll wait for your written report."

Maybe by then, I'll have worked up the courage to tell Granddad that I've found his daughter, my mother.

Kate dialed a number she knew by heart, praying that she'd catch her friend before she left for the hospital. "Dolly, I have to talk to you. Please tell me you're free tonight."

"Kate, what's wrong?"

"I don't want to talk about it now. I've got a show to do in two hours. But I have to see you. Alone."

"Sure. Of course, Kate. I was just on my way to the

hospital but I'll leave there at eight. What say I meet you at my apartment at eight-thirty? Is that okay?"

"Perfect. You're a pal. Love you."

"Love you," Dolly said, hanging up and wondering what had upset Kate.

JERRY CALLAHAN'S LARGE wrinkled hand seized and pumped Thomas Shipley's small smooth one. "It's an honor to make your acquaintance. I sure appreciate what you've done for Irma. She's a good friend of mine."

"Yes, I know of your association with Mrs. Greenbaum. But regarding the return of the painting, it was the right thing to do," Shipley said modestly.

"Sure it was, but how many people do the right thing these days? Darned few."

They were in the Green Room at the TNYC-TV station. That morning, Jerry had called Mike Cramer and said he'd like a chance to meet Thomas Shipley. Cramer had not hesitated to invite Jerry to the station. Jerry Callahan was a popular figure wherever he went. Now he and Shipley were waiting for Evan Wallace's lead piece on the strangler story to be reported and for the associate producer to come backstage to escort Shipley out onto the set.

Jerry had stuck his head into Kate's office when he arrived, but she'd been busy at the computer, typing up the questions she planned to ask Shipley. She acted funny, not meeting his gaze, sniffling and saying that she was behind schedule and thought she was coming down with a cold. Well, she worked too darn hard, that was for sure, and if he didn't take care of her, she wouldn't take care of herself. No wonder she'd caught a cold.

I hope she finds some decent guy and gets married before my time comes, he thought, so she'll have someone to remind her to take her vitamins and to get eight hours of sleep a night.

Shipley's question interrupted his musings. "Did Mrs. Greenbaum tell you that I offered to buy the painting from her at market value?"

"Yeah, she sure did, Mr. Shipley. And I think she's gonna take you up on your offer. What's she gonna do with a famous painting like that? It'd just attract burglars. Why the insurance premiums alone are more than she can afford. She lives on a pension, you know. I do know one thing, she ain't gonna sell that picture to nobody else."

Shipley smiled broadly. "I'm pleased to hear that."

"Irma and me think you're tops. I ain't no art collector, but if there's ever anything I can do for you, just pick up the phone. You've restored Irma's faith in mankind. Mine, too."

Shipley grinned. "I think you might be exaggerating."

KATE TOOK SOME aspirin and pulled herself together. The show must go on.

"What have you been doing to yourself," Sophie the makeup girl complained. "It's going to take a pound of makeup to conceal those red eyes."

Kate gave Sophie the same excuse she'd given Jerry. "I'm coming down with a cold. You're a miracle worker, Sophie. You'll make me look good. You always do."

Sophie snorted. "Flattery will get you everywhere."

KATE MANAGED TO get through the first thirty minutes of the show. Again, the lead story concerned the strangler case. The New York City coroner answered Evan Wallace's questions and stated that the victims had not been dead long before they were found. In all cases, less than twenty-four hours had elapsed. "He wants us to find them," he said. "He's not trying to hide them." Wallace honored his agreement with the detectives; the costumes were not mentioned.

Ten minutes of the first half hour were devoted to Irma Greenbaum's taped interview while Kate got a break from the camera which magnified everything. A minute of Thomas Shipley's intro was used to run the footage from Evan Wallace's tour of Shipley's gallery.

Then Kate and Thomas Shipley were seated on either side of a coffee table in a studio set that was a replica of Kate's own living room at home. "Mr. Shipley, your gift of a valuable painting to Irma Greenbaum, its rightful owner, is being heralded as an act of supreme unselfishness. You've just watched my interview with a grateful and emotional Mrs. Greenbaum. Can you explain for me and my viewers how so many paintings were stolen and kept secret for all these years? Did Adolph Hitler have a direct hand in their theft?"

Shipley sat a little taller. "Adolph Hitler had a direct hand in everything that went on in Nazi Germany. Yet, the doctrine of Hitler's Nazi party condemned Impressionist and Modern paintings as the decadent and impure scribblings of degenerate would-be painters. That included the works of Gustav Klimt. So no, Hitler was not sending his jackboots out to steal pictures in order to hang them on his bunker walls." Shipley smiled at his own joke.

He continued, "But among Hitler's top echelon, there were generals eager to profit from the sale of the 'impure' Impressionist and Contemporary paintings.

"In the beginning, the thefts and transfers were one colossal conspiracy. Later, after paintings had changed hands several times without fanfare, buyers believed they were acquiring works of art in good faith. If, indeed, they entertained any suspicions that they were buying stolen works, they rationalized that they themselves were not the thieves. They convinced themselves that they were innocent bystanders. And besides, what were they to do? They had no way of knowing who the original owners might have been. Most of those unfortunate people had perished in the holocaust."

"But isn't that exactly the purpose of establishing provenance, so that a painting's ownership can be traced?" Kate asked.

"You may not be aware, Ms. Callahan, but there are no laws requiring that provenance be provided with the sale of a painting. None whatsoever. Yet, a reputable dealer will always provide provenance with his sales. Any time a dealer, or a museum for that matter, buys or sells a painting without a provenance that can be traced back to the artist, there's always the possibility that somewhere along the line, theft—and maybe even murder—might have occurred."

"Was it the lack of provenance that made you suspicious about *The Embrace*?" Kate asked.

"On the contrary. It was the existence of a particular provenance that made me suspicious. *The Embrace* was painted in 1910. Yet its provenance was traceable only to 1939. Nothing prior. I suspected that I was being offered a painting that had been stolen before the war. And because the painting could not be offered for sale on the open market, I was able to acquire it for considerably less than its real worth."

"Who did you buy it from, Mr. Shipley?" Kate asked.

"I'm afraid, dear lady, I cannot answer that question. Let me just say that the person who sold it to me professed that he had purchased it some years previously, quite innocently and largely ignorantly. I made up my mind that an example had to be set, so I bought *The Embrace* and set about finding its rightful owner. Now I'm prepared to buy it back from Mrs. Greenbaum, if she'll sell it to me."

"And what will you do with it this time?" Kate asked. "Will you resell it?"

Thomas Shipley passed a hand over his thinning hair. "I haven't reached a decision at this time."

SIXTEEN

"WELL, WALLACE KEPT his word," Joe Mateer said, clicking off the TV. "He didn't go public with the information about the costumes the dead women were wearing. Maybe we can trust him, after all."

"We can trust him to act in his own best interest," Rick Smith said cynically.

Smith was out of sorts. Watching Kate on TV was tough on him. And something had been bothering her tonight. She had that hurt look in her eyes, the same look that he'd put there six years ago when, stupidly, he'd called off their wedding. Whatever had possessed me? he asked himself. I loved her. She's capable of handling the down side of my job, just as she is capable of handling the down side of her own. She's proved that. But I was arrogant and elitist, and maybe a little sexist thrown in for good measure. I thought what I was doing was more important than us. I thought she'd never be able to cope with my mood swings, my total involvement with my cases, my silences.

How many times did I dial her number, only to hang up when I heard her voice? Some tough detective I am, I didn't have the nerve to ask her to take me back. I judged her without ever giving her a chance. And I'm the loser. We both lost.

The phone rang sharply, interrupting his brooding. "My turn," he said. "Probably another crackpot. But with four girls dead, someone must know something.

"Detective Smith," he said, punching the speakerphone button with more force than was necessary.

"Detective Smith, this is Elsie Hoover. They told me you're in charge of the strangler case."

"Yes, ma'am, that's right," Smith said, wondering if this was a real lead or another crank. The woman sounded nervous which was par for the course, yet her voice held a note of sincerity. She seemed both troubled and desperate. "What can I do for you?" Smith asked.

"I'm a buyer for Lord & Taylor," Ms. Hoover explained, "and I was in Los Angeles all last week. I returned to New York on Sunday night. My daughter Regina and I share an apartment. Well, Regina wasn't at home when I arrived, but she *is* twenty-four and she does sometimes stay over with her boyfriend. Usually, though, when she does that, she leaves me a note so I'll know where she is. There was no note this time."

Smith and Mateer sat at attention, their eyes and ears riveted to the speakerphone. "Bet this is the one," Mateer mouthed to Smith.

"Ma'am, this is Detective Mateer. I'm working the case with Detective Smith. Are you saying your daughter has been missing since Sunday?"

"No, Detective Mateer. Regina hasn't been answering her cell phone but then she'd been having some trouble with it so that did not alarm me. But I've just learned she's been missing since Friday. You see, I assumed Regina was staying at her boyfriend's apartment, and that the reason I couldn't reach either of them was because they were out when I called. But I've just learned that Bill—that's Regina's boyfriend, Bill Lockhart—hasn't seen her since Friday either. Bill flew home to Cincinnati on Friday to attend a class reunion. He took yesterday off so that he could have a long weekend with his folks. He arrived back in New

York this morning. When he couldn't reach Regina today, he called me here tonight. The last time he saw Regina was Friday morning. We've called her friends and they haven't seen her either. Detective, I'm terrified that the murdered girl is my daughter!"

SEVENTEEN

ROSALIE RUSSO, EXECUTIVE Assistant to Vaughn Thompson, arrived home from a hectic day at the CEO's offices at TNYC-TV. Changing into casual clothes, and sipping a Diet Coke, she relaxed on the porch steps of her tiny cottage. It was the hour before dusk when the rabbits came out, and in a far corner of the courtyard, a cottontail was happily nibbling Dr. C's tender lettuce leaves. Rosalie did nothing to stop him. He's gotta eat too, she told herself.

Is this heaven or what? she asked herself. It was a question she'd asked herself often over the past fifteen years. Overhead a patch of cerulean sky slowly deepened to violet. The May days were warm with cool nights, but enclosed as it was on all sides by buildings, the courtyard captured and retained the sun's warming rays. She could sit out until nine if she wished before the night air cooled things off.

Rosalie Russo could count on one hand the number of lucky days she'd experienced in her lifetime. Some people believed you made your own luck. If that was so, Rosalie would still be living in the streets. No, good fortune had intervened in her life on few occasions, and while she got credit for turning her life around, without those fateful interventions, she would have been incapable of reaching deep down inside herself to make things change. She just didn't possess the internal fortitude. External events had to kick-start her into action, lucky breaks that gave her the incentive to aim for something better.

One of those lucky days had happened fifteen years ago. She'd just started her first job and was telling herself that now she could move out of her drab room at the YWCA on Lexington Avenue and start looking for a studio apartment. But she'd done nothing about it for weeks, preferring to drift because that had always been her way of handling life.

She had no social life. Summer evenings were spent walking the streets where once she'd slept, exploring new areas of the city. On that fateful evening, she was strolling through the West Village, wandering down narrow twisting streets in residential neighborhoods, staunchly avoiding Bleecker Street and Greenwich Avenue with the tantalizing smells that emanated from their bars. She turned a corner into quaint Greenwich Street. How many people know there's a Greenwich Avenue and a Greenwich Street? she had mused idly until her attention was caught by a man affixing a sign in the first floor window of a lovely old Federal style townhouse.

APARTMENT FOR RENT, the sign read. Rosalie waved to the man, pointed at the sign, then to his front door. He met her on the tiny stoop and quickly explained to her that the rental apartment wasn't actually an apartment at all, but a very small house.

"A house?" Rosalie echoed, looking up and down the street at the well-tended homes. "If it's a house there's no way I can afford it."

"Well, have a look now that you're here and I've opened the door. What can it hurt?"

She scrutinized him closely. Years on the street had taught her to gauge a man's character by his eyes, and this man's eyes were kind and decent. He stuck out his hand. "I'm Ren Christopher. I live here." His free hand indicated the four-story gray stucco Federal house behind him. Rosalie introduced herself.

"Come on in, Rosalie," he said, leading the way into a dimly lit hallway. On the right, an open door offered a view of his living room. Straight ahead, at the far end of the hall, another door was closed and bolted.

"What do you do?" he asked as he unlocked that rear door. Rosalie told him she was a secretary at a television station. Actually, she was more like a gofer for an assistant producer, but she didn't tell Christopher that.

"I'm a biochemist," Christopher offered. "I run the lab over at St. Vincent's."

Rosalie started to comment but at that moment Dr. Christopher swung the rear door outward, and her mouth dropped open. There before her eyes was the prettiest garden she had ever seen. A courtyard, really, walled in on all sides, with beds of flowers and vegetables and sunflowers that were six feet tall and surrounded by birds.

Smack dab in the middle of this green oasis, like a fairy tale Gingerbread house, a tiny cottage stood. It was a wooden structure, unusual for New York. "We aren't really sure what it was used for originally, maybe a laundry, or a workshop," Dr. Christopher explained. "The people we bought the property from had already converted it into a rental apartment. It's really quite small."

He unlocked the cottage door, pushed it open, and they entered. The ground floor consisted of a room about fifteen by fifteen with an efficiency kitchen tucked into a corner and a small bathroom that could accommodate only a stall shower. Up a freestanding, circular, wrought iron staircase, there was a bedroom and two closets.

Rosalie fell in love, painfully in love. There was no way she could afford this house.

"We're forced to rent it out," Dr. Christopher explained.

"The kids would like to use it for a playhouse, but we need the money. One of them got trapped in the old root cellar once, so we've had that sealed up, and when we've got a tenant, the kids know to stay away." Through the open doorway, he glanced back across the cobblestone walkway to his own house. They were being watched. Rosalie counted five heads at the windows.

"They're all mine," Christopher beamed. "My wife Jane is an artist who designs book jackets for a publishing house. It's a good thing she can work at home, otherwise I don't know what we'd do."

"You must like children," Rosalie observed with a chuckle.

"We love children." His open palm indicated the tiny house. "You like it?"

"I love it. How much rent did you have in mind?"

Christopher named a figure that was almost two hundred dollars more than Rosalie could afford. Her heart sank into her stomach. Then inspiration struck. She had an idea.

"To tell you the truth, that's about a hundred and seventy-five dollars more than I can afford. But how about if I babysit for you and Mrs. Christopher to make up the difference? I'm free evenings and weekends and I'm crazy about kids. And I can give you references." The references she could provide were those of her new employer, the director of the secretarial school where she'd recently graduated, and the minister who had counseled her. Still they were solid references.

Christopher narrowed his eyes, weighing her suggestion. Suddenly, he grabbed her hand and shook it. "It's a deal. Jane will be thrilled. She likes to eat out evenings after a day of juggling work and children. Come on in. Meet Jane and the kids, and we'll sign a lease."

The arrangement had worked out famously for everyone. Rosalie was a gentle soul and the children loved her. Now, fifteen years later, the older three were away at college, the younger two still in high school. Dr. C needed the rent more than ever. And now, as executive assistant to the CEO of TNYC-TV, Rosalie could afford to pay Dr. C double what he'd originally asked.

She rubbed her arms and lifted her gaze skyward. The stars came out one by one in a sky so soft and velvety it made you want to cry. Rosalie Russo realized with a start that she was happy. Cool breezes stirred the treetops. She got up and went inside her cozy little house, nicely furnished now, and spotless. She picked up the latest issue of *Architectural Digest* from her coffee table. The magazine fell open to the feature on Kate Callahan and her grandfather. Lately, it seemed like her boss Vaughn Thompson was obsessed with Kate Callahan, always wanting to see her schedule, planting himself in front of her show every night. At least he's not chasing around with those bimbos anymore, Rosalie told herself.

But why did he have me call her car service yesterday and change the pick-up time from ten-fifteen to ten-thirty when Miss Callahan's got a secretary of her own to handle that sort of thing?

EIGHTEEN

THOMAS SHIPLEY FLIPPED a light switch and his secret room sprang to life. His private gallery was located in the northwest corner on the third floor of the Shipley Galleries building. As he'd informed Evan Wallace, the third floor housed his offices. In them, he and his assistant, Jeffrey, recorded the gallery's acquisitions and sales. Once logged in by hand, the records were now computerized. Shipley had embraced the Internet age enthusiastically, having established a Shipley Galleries Website.

The northwest corner of the building faced an air shaft that separated his building from a neighboring apartment house. During renovations, he'd had the windows in the secret gallery, and those in two private rooms on either side, filled in with brick. The whitewashed room with its bare oak floor and recessed lighting was his *sanctum sanctorum*. No one had a key to the three rooms but he.

Lovingly, he transported *The Embrace*, his hands grasping either side of the ornate frame. Just minutes ago, after getting her call, he had arranged to have five million dollars wire-transferred to Mrs. Irma Greenbaum's bank overnight.

Carefully, Shipley hung the cherished painting on the wall in the empty space that had been reserved for it. The pictures in the room all complemented one another. There wasn't a jarring theme or color to be seen.

My collection is magnificent, he told himself, as he uncorked a bottle of champagne and prepared to celebrate.

He filled a fluted glass and toasted his latest acquisition. "To Gustav Klimt," he said aloud. "With this addition, my holdings can compete with those in any museum."

On a serious note, he reflected that people had died to make this unique collection possible, and for that he experienced a short-lived pang of regret. Yet, he acknowledged that there were those in the art world capable of killing him to get their hands on his collection. He'd never let that happen.

Irma Greenbaum had been right about one thing: around the globe there were collectors with hidden rooms such as this, and in those rooms the collectors enjoyed their treasures in seclusion. But Greenbaum was naive. She didn't know the true nature of the people she spoke of when she said that they admired their collections in shame. Thomas Shipley felt no shame. He regarded his gallery of priceless pictures with fierce pride. He was content to experience this pleasure alone. He had no need to share his pictures with anyone.

Shipley smiled to himself, and his usually chilly eyes twinkled merrily. The *coup* he'd just pulled off had been a stroke of genius. All New York was singing his praises, and in the salons of London and Paris, he was being touted as the most ethical of dealers. From now on, his reputation would be above reproach. No one would ever question him. No one would ever again look at him with jaundiced eyes. He was home free.

Just today, the Editor-in-Chief of *Art & Antiques* had personally telephoned to ask him if he would consent to a feature article. Shipley had responded with appropriate humility, "I'm honored to have been selected."

His glass in his upraised right hand, he executed a spry little soft-shoe as he circled his private gallery. Among his prize pictures were a few that he had painted himself. They

NINETEEN

WHEN KATE ARRIVED at Dolly's apartment at Fifth Avenue and Sixty-second Street, Dolly had already removed her face paint and her clown suit, but she was still in a robe. "Give me a minute to jump into a pantsuit," she told Kate, after checking Kate's face for signs of tears and giving her a warm hug and kiss.

While she waited, Kate looked around her friend's living room. Dolly collected pottery. She made frequent forays into New England and Pennsylvania in search of little-known potters from whom she bought jugs and vases, bowls and platters. The fruits of her foraging were arranged in backlit glass display cases around the room.

During grade school and high school, Dolly had lived in this apartment with a maiden aunt. The place had been dark and dreary, and during the school week Dolly counted off the days until Friday when she could make her escape. Every weekend was spent at Kate's apartment with Jerry and Babs.

"Will you be my grandparents too?" Dolly used to ask them. And of course they'd always put their arms around her and assured her she was as dear to them as their own.

Poor Dolly, Kate thought, she never had a family life like I did. The aunt had done her duty by Dolly, but nothing more. Dolly had never wanted for food or clothing, but she had been starved for affection and someone to take an interest in her. When Dolly was nineteen, the aunt died, and within a year, that woman's brother, Dolly's Colorado uncle, whom she'd seen only on Christmas breaks when he had come to New York, died too. The uncle had been the major shareholder in a prosperous copper mining concern. He left his shares and his wealth to his only relative, Dolly.

One of the first things Dolly did was banish the gloom from her apartment. Now it was decorated in creams and blonde woods, and flooded with light, even if most of that light was artificial.

"I'm not going to bother with makeup," Dolly said as she rejoined Kate in the living room. "I wear enough of that when I'm Posey the clown. Would you like a glass of wine? We can talk now before we go out if you want."

"Oh, Dolly," Kate cried, unable to control her tears a moment longer, "my mother is dead. Mr. MacPeterson found her grave."

Dolly embraced Kate and let her cry on her shoulder. "I was afraid of this," she told Kate. "Oh, Katie, I am so sorry. So very very sorry. What can I do for you?"

Kate gulped, "You're doing it. Just hold me for a while."

EVENTUALLY, THEY WALKED around the corner to Arcadia, a small restaurant that was carved, cave-like, into the deep recesses of a building tucked mid-block between Edwardian mansions and commercial Madison Avenue. Kate's limo was double-parked across the street. Marty would stay with the car and wait until she was ready to go home. Kate wondered if she'd ever be comfortable with that. The evening was spring soft and mild, inspiring the restaurant's management to increase their seating capacity by setting up small tables and folding chairs on the sidewalk. Kate and Dolly chose to sit outdoors.

"I'll have the chimney-smoked lobster," Dolly told the waiter.

"Just a small salad for me," Kate said. "I'm not hungry."

Dolly added, "And bring us a bottle of chardonnay." She looked at Kate. "This is not a night for sobriety."

"I don't know why I'm taking this so hard," Kate confided. "It's not like I knew my mother, but…well, I guess I always thought that someday, God willing, I'd be reunited with her. Now, that's impossible."

"Well, of course, you're upset," Dolly commiserated. "How could you not be? For all that hotshot reporter image you try to project, you've got the most tender heart of anyone I know."

Tears glistened on Kate's eyelashes, but she managed a brave smile. "Look who's talking. No, my friend, you're the one with the most tender heart. And you put your money where your mouth is. And your time and your talents. You make those little kids over at the hospital forget their troubles and laugh. And we both know what an elixir laughter can be."

Dolly's expression grew sad. "Kate, there's the most precious child. Little Kevin Brown. He's such a trouper, always cheerful. The cancer's just eating him up. You know, I'd willingly change places with him if I could, just so he could have a chance. I've had thirty-three happy years. Kevin is only eight years old and he's seen his last Christmas. One of the nurses confided that he'll be gone by the Fourth of July. It just breaks my heart. I wish there was something I could do."

Kate covered Dolly's hand with her own. "You're doing everything you can, and more than most people. You give to cancer research, you donate huge sums to the peds unit, and most important, you spend time with those kids, quality time—entertaining them, listening to them."

Dolly gave her long dark hair a shake. "What's wrong with me? Here I am wallowing in self-pity while you're the one who's just had your darkest fears come true. And I know you well enough to know that you're worrying about Jerry and what this news will do to him."

Kate sighed. "You're right, Dolly. I can't bear to tell him and yet he has a right to know. He needs to have closure."

"Your granddad's a strong man, Kate. All these years, he's been wondering, hoping for the best, expecting the worst. Now he'll know for sure. He'll be able to say good-bye."

Kate sipped her wine thoughtfully. "I'll tell him, but not right away. It's been more than thirty years since she left. The news can wait a few more weeks. Next Friday is Granddad's eighty-sixth birthday, remember? I don't want to spoil a happy occasion by giving him such bad news. Circle your calendar for next Friday night, Dolly. And put on a party face." Kate's spirits lifted as she thought of the surprise birthday party she was planning for Jerry.

"We're still on for this Friday night, aren't we?" Dolly asked.

"Same as always. Friday night's our special night. Has been for the past twenty years. We'll meet you at ten at Cafe Carlyle. Granddad's really looking forward to hearing Bobby Short," Kate replied with a tight smile.

AT THE REAR of the restaurant a man sat watching them, his gaze locked intently on the fascinating view offered by the two young women leaning companionably toward each other, murmuring their secrets into each other's ears.

He couldn't take his eyes off them. One a redhead, the other a brunette. Both young, healthy, striking. Most New Yorkers recognized Kate Callahan. He noted that other men in the restaurant were staring at her too, to the chagrin of their female partners.

He'd been an admirer of Kate Callahan's for some time. Her face was etched into his consciousness. Ravishing

Kate Callahan. Hers was the starred name on his list. Save the best for last, he thought. Then the Herculean task he had set for himself would be complete. But who was the woman with Callahan?

He had a good view of her profile. Everything about her evoked pleasurable responses. Her skin, clean and shining. How refreshing. All that dark hair, so alive and warm. Dark eyes that flashed as she talked. Heavy black brows. A generous mouth, wide and full-lipped. A mouth like that could give a man a lot of pleasure.

The woman changed position in her chair. As she recrossed her legs, the outline of her thighs showed through her trousers. Round and firm. Her jacket fell open casually, and he noted with satisfaction the small mound of a tummy.

She's a divine odalisque, the image of men's fantasies, with her sensuous limbs and sultry expression, he thought. A series of pictures came to mind as he visualized the classical odalisques, in particular Manet's *Olympia*. Yet, the woman before his eyes was more perfect that any of those lifeless creatures. She'll be breathtaking naked, he thought. Forgetting where he was, he extended his arm and raised a thumb. Closing one eye and squinting through the other, he fixed his subject in perspective.

"Will you be ordering dessert, sir?" the waiter inquired.

Startled, he jumped. "What?"

"Dessert, sir. Will you be having dessert?"

He glanced up at the waiter's eager face, then back at the two women. The waiter followed his eyes. "That's Kate Callahan," he said importantly. "She's a regular here, she and her friend."

"I believe I've seen the friend here before," he said casually. "Does she live in the neighborhood?"

"Oh, sure. That's Dolly Devereaux, otherwise known as Posey the clown."

"Clown?" he repeated. What was this kid yammering about?

"She's an heiress who dresses up like a clown and entertains the kids at New York Hospital. Everyone in the neighborhood knows all about her. She lives in that big building on the corner of Fifth. Shall I bring the dessert cart, sir?"

He favored the young man with an appreciative smile, suddenly quite hungry for sweets. "Yes, do. And a decaf cappuccino."

Thank you, young man, he said silently to the waiter's back. You've just earned yourself a handsome tip.

TWENTY

"ONE GOOD TURN deserves another," Rick Smith told investigative reporter Evan Wallace. "Joe and I appreciate your keeping those pictures under wraps."

Last night, he and Joe had escorted Elsie Hoover and Bill Lockhart to the morgue. Elsie Hoover, he observed, treated Lockhart like a son, leaning on him, relying on his judgment. Shaken and in shock, they'd both positively identified the strangler's latest victim as their beloved Regina. When shown the clothing she'd been wearing—the old-fashioned long white dress, the equally antique slippers—they were dumbfounded. "Those aren't Regina's clothes," Elsie Hoover declared adamantly.

Finally, Rick had been able to go home to catch about four hours' sleep. He met Joe back at headquarters early in the morning. They'd strategized and come up with an idea, then decided to include Evan Wallace in their plans. Waiting until eight o'clock, Rick called Wallace, waking him from a sound sleep. He and Joe were working around the clock. If Wallace wanted a scoop, he'd have to keep their hours.

"I have to admit at first my motive was self-serving," Wallace said, "but the more I thought about it, the more I realize you guys are right. Saving this information for just the right moment ought to help you make the collar, and it might also save some lives. Now, what can I do for you fellas? Why'd you call me down here?"

Evan had dressed quickly but well. His camel's hair

jacket was obviously expensive. Rick had done a background check on Wallace and knew about his lower-class background. He's overcompensating, Rick thought, by buying expensive clothes. Still, he's made something of himself and I've got to hand it to him for that. Wallace had taken a fast subway downtown to meet with them; his sandy hair was still damp from his shower.

Joe Mateer pulled his chair a little closer to Wallace. "Our victim number four was ID'd late last night. We got the captain to give us twenty-four hours before he breaks the news. And the girl's mother and boyfriend are cooperating."

Wallace perked up, smelling an exclusive.

Smith jumped in and Wallace's head swung in his direction. "What we have in mind is this. We'd like you to have me and Joe, and the mother and boyfriend, on a live interview on your show. This girl was missing since Friday and her body was found early Monday morning. Maybe somebody saw or heard something during those three days."

"You said boyfriend," Wallace said. "Any chance he did it?"

"Airtight alibi," Mateer volunteered. "He flew to Cincinnati for his high school reunion early Friday morning and returned to New York yesterday. Surrounded by friends and family the entire four days. His folks met his plane and took him to the airport yesterday morning."

"Just a thought," Wallace said.

"Don't worry. He was the first one we checked out. Even checked out the mother. We verified that she was in L.A. as she claimed to be. So what do you think about our going on your show?"

Wallace could barely contain his enthusiasm. "We *are* talking about tonight, aren't we?"

"Sure are," Smith answered. "It's gotta be right away.

You can interview the mother and boyfriend. They'll be good for a special interest angle. I happen to know they'll do anything to get this murder solved. We'll show the girl's picture. Offer a reward. It'll be kinda like *America's Most Wanted* except you won't be dealing with a cold case."

Wallace stood up and pumped their hands. "I know my producer will go for it. Just give me a minute to call him and give him a heads-up. Kate's interviewing an art expert, but I'm sure she'll cooperate and move that to the second segment." He left them to step out into the hall to call Mike on his cell phone.

At the mention of Kate's name, Rick felt his face flush. He turned away from Joe but his partner saw everything.

In a minute Wallace was back, giving them the thumbs-up. "Mike Cramer from the station will be in touch with you to work out the details. We'll want you at the studio early. He'll tell you when. I'll meet you there." He shook hands again. "Man, I sure do appreciate this."

TWENTY-ONE

THAT WEDNESDAY WAS one of those rare crystal clear days that tempt New Yorkers out of their buildings and into the streets and parks. At four-twenty P.M. he parked his black van on the Central Park side of Fifth Avenue, across from Dolly Devereaux's apartment house. Tender green leaves on the trees along the park wall shaded the sidewalk from a late afternoon sun. He lowered his passenger-side window. The Children's Zoo was two blocks back and squeals, laughter, and calliope music drifted into the van on the fresh spring breeze.

Barely comprehending the beauty of the spring day and incapable of partaking in ordinary pleasures, he remained vigilant, his attention riveted on the entrance of Dolly Devereaux's building. A uniformed doorman held the door open for a woman with a poodle on a leash. On another day, the man in the van would have noticed the resemblance between the woman and her pet, for he was an ardent observer of his fellow man's foibles. In her mid-sixties, the woman's stark white hair hugged her scalp in a cap of tight curls, and her long, pointed chin jutted forward. The dog's owner seemed to be the human twin of her white standard poodle. On another day, the man would have chuckled derisively as he considered how absurdly predictable people could be.

But not today. Today he had a more important issue on his mind. Suddenly, the object of his obsession appeared. A clown, dressed in a white clown suit with red harlequin designs, face painted chalk white with a broad, red, exaggerated smile, and wearing a wig that looked like it was made of orange yarn. Quickly, he raised the window and turned the key in the ignition.

The doorman hustled out onto the curb, blowing his whistle sharply and repeatedly at a cab that approached but did not slow. The doorman stepped out into traffic and waved his arms but to no avail. The cab sailed past, its OFF DUTY sign blazing, almost as if the driver was thumbing his nose at those in need of transportation. The doorman turned back to Miss Devereaux and shrugged his shoulders. You know it's hopeless at this hour, his shrug said.

What was the clown name the waiter had called Dolly Devereaux? Ah, yes, Posey. Posey the clown.

Now Posey was saying something to the doorman. The doorman gestured, seemed to be appealing to her to wait. But Posey was in a hurry, he observed. Between four and five, many cabdrivers went off-duty, he mused, and Posey was in too big a rush to wait until five when an on-duty cab might come along.

Restlessly, she paced back and forth. Through the dark-tinted window, he watched her, knowing she could not see him nor his intense scrutiny of her every movement. He frowned. Whatever possessed the woman to conceal her voluptuous figure inside a baggy clown suit? But then women were enigmas, were they not? And wasn't it the irrational, fathomless quality they all possessed that was the source of all his problems?

Posey said something to the doorman, fluttered her white-gloved hand, and took off at a trot around the corner into Sixty-second Street. He put the van into gear and careened recklessly across three lanes of traffic to cut into the side street after her, ignoring the horns that blared in his wake. Luck was with him for Sixty-second was a one-way eastbound thoroughfare.

Posey hurried along on the sidewalk on his left. Some pedestrians stopped to stare at the ludicrous sight she made, others apparently knew her and called bemused hellos. She caught up with the woman from her building walking the standard poodle and gave the dog a quick pat on the head. Hurriedly, she crossed Madison Avenue. He followed closely. Crosstown traffic was heavy and his progress was no faster than her own.

At Park Avenue, a cab drew up in front of the Colony Club and deposited two women. Posey jumped into the cab. Keeping the yellow cab in sight, he trailed it east all the way to York Avenue, then north to Sixty-eighth where it turned in to New York Hospital's private driveway.

Looping around the circle behind the cab, he watched through the passenger-side window as Posey got out. A gardener planting mixed flowers in circular beds called to her cheerfully and staff members waved hello. It was clear to him that Posey was a well-known and popular figure here.

There was a rap on his side panel. He lowered the window just as Posey disappeared through the revolving door. "You can't park here," a guard in a blue uniform growled.

"I'm just leaving," he said, giving the man a salute and one of his winning smiles. "Was that a clown I just saw?" he asked, seemingly incredulous.

The question disarmed the guard and he mellowed. "Yeah. That's Posey. She entertains the sick kids up on the cancer floor. She's a fixture around here. Sorry, but you'll have to keep moving. You're holding up traffic."

"I've got a delivery," he said. "Where can I unload?"

"Take York up to Seventieth Street and pull around. You'll see a loading dock next to the ambulance bay."

"Thanks," he called as he raised the window and drove off.

Everything was going his way. Luck was with him. Fate was on his side, he reassured himself.

Hospital security was lax as to be almost non-existent. No one questioned him when he left his van parked at the loading dock. He climbed the side steps, clipboard in hand, attracting not a whit of curiosity.

Inside, the corridors formed a maze and he had to ask for directions. "Follow the blue line," a maintenance man pushing a broom instructed him.

The blue line that ran down the center of the vinyl floors led to the main elevator bank and to the medical center's directory which he consulted. Getting out on the oncology floor, he was able to stroll unchallenged past the nurses' station and numerous patient rooms.

He followed the sound of children's voices to a playroom. Posey was juggling fruit: an orange, an apple, and a peach. A few nurses crowded in the doorway, as enthralled with her antics as the children. One of the nurses was a man, he noted approvingly. Glancing at the man's hospital I.D. badge, he quickly memorized the nurse's name: Randall Herman. Bet Posey knows you as Randy, he speculated.

He watched over their shoulders. Posey beckoned to one little boy who seemed to be in worse shape than the others. "Come on, Kevin. Want to give it a try? I'll show you how."

Quickly he walked back to the elevators. In less than forty-five minutes he had learned everything he needed to know about the daily habits of Miss Dolly Devereaux.

TWENTY-TWO

RICK SMITH WORE his best navy suit. He had stopped at a barbershop for a haircut and even got a professional shave and manicure, something he rarely did. But how often was he on TV? If he was honest with himself, he'd have to admit his attention to his appearance was motivated by more than being in front of the camera. Kate worked here; he was hoping to run into her.

Mike Cramer, the producer, gathered them all in his office: Evan Wallace, Rick and Joe, Elsie Hoover the dead girl's mother, and Bill Lockhart her boyfriend. Cramer was the quintessential pro; he had staff writers put together the scenario and script, and now was going over the logistics with the guests and the staff. Technicians were busy on the set, installing a bank of eight-hundred number telephones. Cramer was hoping their lucky break would happen during the show. So was everyone else.

Bill Lockhart started to speak, then lowered his head. His shoulders slumped forward and heaved; gurgling noises bubbled up as if they came from deep within his soul. Elsie Hoover reached for his hand, tears streaming down her cheeks. Mike Cramer came around his desk, a box of tissues in his outstretched hand, just as Evan Wallace jumped up and moved to Lockhart's side.

Wallace patted Lockhart's shoulder. "Don't be ashamed to break down. In your place, we'd all do the same. It's this kind of raw emotion that will elicit a sympathetic response from the audience. Anyone with knowledge about Regina's abduction will be anxious to call in and help you and Mrs. Hoover when they see how badly broken up you are."

Lockhart looked up, eyes swimming. "It's just so hard to accept. And when I do accept it, the pain is more than I can bear. You didn't know Regina." He squeezed Elsie Hoover's hand. "She was an angel. Wasn't she, Elsie?"

Mrs. Hoover mumbled something inaudible and nodded her downcast head.

Rick Smith said, "Excuse me," but no one seemed to notice as he slipped out of the room. He had to get away from this scene of heart-wrenching grief. It was okay for Lockhart and Mrs. Hoover to display their emotions but he and Joe never could. The minute they let down their guard and became personally involved, they would lose their perspective. And as his wise partner had warned him only recently: it would take a cool head to catch this psychopath who was destroying so many lives.

Blind with rage, Smith stumbled to the watercooler. Not until they collided, did he realize another person was headed in the same direction. "Sorry," he mumbled.

"It was my fault," she said.

The voice was one he knew well. The sweetness of it played in his head like music late at night when he was trying to sleep. It was a voice he'd never forget, and one he often heard when he caught the news.

"Kate?" he said.

She looked cool and self-possessed. Her lips were curved in a small smile but her eyes were wary and watchful. "How are you, Rick?"

He breathed her in. "Kate…you look wonderful." She looked better every time he saw her. Watching her on television, or glimpsing her at news conferences, was no match for seeing her up close like this. The years had been good to her, sculpting her face from that of a pretty girl to a beautiful woman. Her body too was more defined, thinner and firmer, yet somehow more womanly. The dark cinnamon suit she wore brought out the ginger in her hair, and caused her amber eyes to look almost green. Those eyes, once trusting and loving, regarded him now with caution. I destroyed her trust, Rick thought. And right now, as much as I want to, I don't have any idea how to restore it.

Kate stood absolutely still, saying nothing. He's uncomfortable, she thought. Some small part of her took pleasure in that fact.

Rick felt clumsy, like he had suddenly grown too large for his skin. "I'm here for the interview with Wallace. We got an I.D. on the last dead woman."

"Yes, I know," Kate said calmly.

She's not calm, he thought, she's on fire. She's that angry. I know her so well I'm probably the only person who can see it. It's like the past six years have never happened. She's as icily reserved as she was when I made the dumbest mistake of my life and told her I had second thoughts about our engagement. But underneath that reserve, she's as mad as hell and she'd like to hit me. If it would help get us back together, I'd let her.

"I've meant to call you," he said, although the many times he'd lifted the receiver and dialed her number, he immediately hung up. "Just to see how you are. To congratulate you on your new show."

Kate's expression remained impassively frozen. He was disconcerted by the way she was not focusing on him, not listening hard, not picking up their rhythm.

"How's your grandfather?" Rick thought to ask.

"He's well," she replied, and her expression softened. "He's getting older. He'll be eighty-six a week from Friday."

Rick smiled. "He's a great guy." God, I've missed you, Kate, he wanted to say.

Far down the hall, a small dark woman stepped out of an office. "Kate!" she yelled. "Telephone."

Kate turned. "I've got to take this."

Rick said, "Sure. Well…it was nice seeing you again." Don't go, he wanted to say. What can I do to square things with you? he wanted to ask.

"Bye," Kate said softly.

She sounds as sad as I feel, Rick thought.

PROFESSOR LEON HABER sat across from Kate on the studio set. The mahogany butler's tray table with its crystal bowl of fresh lilies was identical to the one Kate had in her living room at home. Both she and Haber sat in comfortable, chintz-covered club chairs. Haber knew from the feature article on Kate's apartment in *Architectural Digest* that the set was a replica of Kate's own living room with its rosy marble fireplace, cream walls, and floral chintzes. Her producer must want the audience to think she's interviewing her guests from her home, he thought.

"Welcome, Professor Haber. And thank you for being here," Kate began.

"My pleasure," Haber said formally. He tried to smile but the bright lights irritated his eyes. He had shaved only two hours ago yet he could feel the bristly beginnings of the five o'clock shadow that perpetually plagued him. On the monitor he came across as dour, heavy-jowled, brooding. He tried to make up for his lack of good looks by smiling a lot, but that only made him look nervous.

Kate began the interview. "Professor Haber, this week we've been learning about the good work you do for organizations whose mission is to recover art objects and other treasures that were stolen from the European Jews during the war. Mrs. Greenbaum, in particular, gave you special credit for the recovery of her father-in-law's painting, *The Embrace*, by Gustav Klimt."

"Yes, I worked with Mrs. Greenbaum's late husband for many years to locate the painting. But Thomas Shipley was the one to find it."

Kate's expression was guileless. "And you're glad of that, aren't you, Professor?"

"Why, yes of course," Haber said, nonplussed. He'd have to be careful. He'd have to guard his tone of voice against revealing the resentment he felt at being upstaged by Shipley. Kate Callahan missed nothing, and she wasn't afraid to call him on what she might perceive as his duplicity. His admiration for her soared even if her style might put him at a disadvantage. At last, an intelligent female, he thought.

Kate leaned forward. "Professor Haber, I wonder if you could explain to me and my audience how so many famous paintings remained hidden for the last sixty-five years." She shook her head. "That fact simply amazes me."

Haber smiled. "It amazes me too. But the answer lies in human nature, Kate, for don't we humans possess the ability to demonstrate great goodness and also great evil?"

"Was there a conspiracy, Professor Haber?"

"Indeed, there was. A dark web of secrecy surrounded the theft of paintings by many famous artists: van Gogh, Cezanne, Matisse, Picasso, Braque. In the thirties, Hitler's regime condemned the works of such artists as Grosz, Kandinsky, Salvador Dali, to name a few, as degenerate. Those artists fled Europe and immigrated to America."

"How did the conspiracy work?" Kate asked.

"Goering looted art for himself and for Hitler. When the Nazis invaded France, collections there were also confiscated," Haber replied.

"But how were the paintings kept secret and why didn't

collectors know they were buying stolen works? Thomas Shipley said on this show that many collectors bought in good faith, unaware that they were acquiring stolen goods."

"That explanation insults my intelligence," Haber declared hotly. "And it ought to insult yours and your viewers, as well. Shipley's a nice guy. He's just trying not to accuse anyone."

"Explain what you mean, Professor Haber," Kate persisted. "How would an ordinary person know that a painting was stolen?"

"The lack of provenance, for instance. And, one very important distinction, Kate. The Nazis were great record keepers, very methodical. Stamped on the back of every stolen canvas is a small swastika, followed by the first two letters of the surname of the original owner, then a number. Those paintings are tainted. Wouldn't finding a swastika stamped on the back of…say, a Picasso you were thinking of buying arouse your suspicions, Kate?"

"It certainly would, Professor. I see your point."

"All his adult life Harry Greenbaum searched for his father's collection, but the pieces had vanished into thin air. He couldn't find record books or the original inventories either. That is, until he stumbled upon that *catalogue raisonné* in a Greenwich Village bookstore."

"If you saw my interview with Mrs. Greenbaum, Professor Haber, you saw for yourself how happy she was to have one of her father-in-law's paintings returned to her."

Haber had been waiting for an opening to drop his bombshell, and Kate, unknowingly, handed it to him. "The fact is, Kate, *The Embrace* is one painting of a three-part set painted by Klimt. There are two others, *Lover's Touch* and *Ecstasy*, that are still unaccounted for."

Kate controlled her surprise. "And they've been so well

hidden over the years, they may never be found. Is that
what you're telling us, Professor Haber?"

"We can only hope. One has surfaced. Let's hope the
others do as well."

As soon as the show was over, Kate hurried off the set. For
the second night, she was skipping Mike Cramer's postmortem. She'd see Mike in the morning and apologize.
Maybe she'd tell him the truth, that she just couldn't run
the risk of bumping into Rick Smith again. Maybe she'd
even ask him to help her avoid Rick. But, no, that was impossible. And unprofessional. What kind of reporter was
she if she was trying to avoid the lead detective in a serial-
killer murder case she was covering? Better get yourself
under control, Callahan, she told herself. You're losing it.

She locked the door to her office behind her and sank
into her chair. The interview with Leon Haber had gone
well, but it had taken all of her training and experience to
concentrate on her script and not let her mind drift back
to her brief encounter with Rick. She'd been shaken by it,
although she thought she had concealed her feelings well
while she was with him. She was still hurt and resentful by how he had dumped her, yes, but standing so close
to him in the hall made her realize that what she wanted
more than anything was for him to put his arms around
her. If he had done that, her resistance would have melted
and all her pent-up longing for him would have erupted.

But he hadn't taken her in his arms. He hadn't told her
that he missed her, that he'd never stopped loving her. He'd
been nervous. Probably feels guilty, she thought. I hope
he's miserable. As miserable as I've been.

Her musings returned to the show. She was pleased
with the outcome of Evan Wallace's segment. The revelation that the victim was Regina Hoover, the impromptu

appeal to the public, had made for a stunningly successful show. The telephones had started to ring, and it was all
they could do to keep up with answering them. And then,
as Kate watched from backstage, the crucial call came
through. Early Monday morning, an insomniac had seen
a black van drive into the alley alongside Devon's Irish
Pub. In a matter of minutes, the van had backed out. The
sleepless man had watched from his third floor apartment
window across Second Avenue. Unfortunately, because he
was looking down on the top of the van, he could see neither the front nor the rear license plates.

By contrast, Kate's interview with Haber had been anti-
climactic, with the exception of his last revelation. But
that's the way it goes in this business, she thought. You're
the star one day, a supporting actor the next. The important thing is to be a solid team player. Once I unleash my
ego and it gets out of control, I'm done for, she reminded
herself. I've seen it happen too many times to too many
good journalists. The staff starts to resent you, they adopt
a passive-aggressive mode, and you find yourself isolated.

Thinking of being lonely brought her full circle back to
Rick. Oh, Rick, she cried to herself, why did you have to
come back in my life? I was okay without you. A cripple,
yes, but limping along pretty good. Now that I've seen you
again, how can I ever settle for less than you? How can I
ever settle for less than *us*?

There was a knock on her door. Kate jumped. Oh God,
don't let it be Rick, she thought. Her prayer was quickly
amended to: Oh God, *please do* let it be Rick.

She pulled open the door to find Professor Leon Haber
standing there. Kate forced a welcoming smile. "Professor, Haber. What can I do for you?"

Haber was relaxed now that he was off the set. He'd removed the powder they'd put on his face, and had brushed

TWENTY-THREE

PROFESSOR HABER TOOK Kate to Greenwich Village, or rather he directed her driver Marty Sokolov to Greenwich Village. As they turned right off Fifth Avenue onto Waverly Place, Haber pointed out his dignified townhouse to Kate.

"I've always had a secret desire to own a townhouse," Kate confided. "But…well, they're expensive, and not easy to find."

"There's no way I could have bought this on my professor's salary," Haber protested. "It's been in my family since about 1910. I can barely keep up with the maintenance and taxes."

"Don't get me wrong," Kate said, "I love my apartment. It suits me and my grandfather just fine. We've got plenty of room and we don't have to worry about whether the roof is going to leak. And I like the security of a twenty-four-hour doorman."

"After that article in *Architectural Digest*, everyone knows where and how you live, Kate," Haber remarked with disapproval. "Did it ever occur to you that letting the world know where you live isn't the smartest thing to do? Women in your position attract stalkers. You hear about it all the time."

I don't like the direction he's taking this conversation, Kate thought. He might mean well, but he's crossing the line, getting too personal. She managed a soft laugh. "Don't pull your punches on my account, Professor."

Haber turned in his seat to face her. "Call me Leon," he invited.

In the front seat, Marty Sokolov didn't like the direction of Haber's conversation either. In a loud intrusive voice, he called over his shoulder, "Where to now, Miss Callahan?"

Haber leaned forward. "Turn left around the square, then take your first right. Mid-block, you'll see a restaurant called Marta's. Stop there." Sitting back, he said to Kate, "Best Italian food in the City."

KATE GOT THROUGH dinner by concentrating on the food—Haber was right about that—and by steering the conversation away from herself. She regretted accepting his invitation. He asked too many personal questions and they made her uncomfortable. Was she seeing someone special? Had she ever been married? She changed the subject. "What do you think became of the two other paintings that were part of Klimt's triptych? Do you think the trio was broken up?"

"Well, naturally it was broken up," Haber replied with asperity. "Otherwise how would one, *The Embrace*, have surfaced alone?"

"Of course," Kate said. "I stand corrected."

Haber wanted to kick himself for the misdirected pedantic criticism he had leveled at a woman he wished to impress. She's not one of my dimwitted students, he told himself.

"Sorry," he said, "I've lived too long in my ivory tower. I've forgotten what it's like to be in the company of an intelligent, mature woman." He pointed to Kate's empty wineglass and the hovering waiter hurried to refill it.

"You must be a regular here," Kate said, glad their talk had shifted to neutral ground.

"I come here at least twice a week," Haber replied.

"Neighborhood restaurants are the best, don't you think? Speaking of my neighborhood, the Greenwich Village art association is holding its annual sidewalk art show this weekend. Why don't you consider coming? Of course, there will be the usual tacky leopards on black velvet, but there will also be some nice surprises. I like discovering new talent, and I may even exhibit a few of my own small efforts. Call me if you decide to come."

"Ah, so you paint as well as authenticate paintings and teach and search for stolen treasures," Kate said, deliberately flattering the man in the hopes of deflecting his attention away from her. "What is it? Why are you looking at me that way?"

Haber steepled his fingers against his lips thoughtfully before speaking. "Kate, I'm an expert on the art nouveau period. In fact, I'm writing the definitive history on that period. Gustav Klimt was an influential figure on the art nouveau scene. How familiar are you with his work?"

Kate set down her wineglass. "I'm familiar with *The Kiss*. Most everyone is. And now I know *The Embrace*. I'm afraid that's the extent of my knowledge on Klimt's work."

Haber said, "*The Kiss* and *The Embrace* are both fine examples of Klimt's 'golden style' and exemplify his passion for the mosaic pattern. A forerunner of his 'golden style' was his painting of Pallas Athene, the mythical patroness of the arts, whom Klimt believed took a personal interest in his work. Most painters go through a series of styles. But I'm wondering if you've ever seen the portrait of Emilie Floge that he painted in 1902?"

Kate smiled. "No. You must have a particular reason for asking. What is it?"

Haber returned her smile. Finally, he was getting through to her. "Because you bear a striking resemblance to Emilie Floge. Your hair is ginger-brown like hers. You have the same level gaze. The same striking amber eyes. But your eyes change to green when you're excited."

He arched his brows. "As you are now. I refer to intellectual excitement, naturally. And you have the same determined chin."

Kate lifted her chin slightly, and raised her wineglass to her lips. "Who was she?"

"Emilie Floge was the love of his life and his favorite model. She was a person in her own right, however, a sophisticated Viennese fashion designer. The original painting hangs in Vienna. But I could show you a plate in an art book I have in my library. We could stop at my house on your way home."

"As much as I'd like to see the plate, Leon," Kate said, "I'll have to do it at another time. I've got preparations to make for tomorrow's show. Actually, I should be leaving soon."

Haber grunted but said nothing. Nicely rejected, he thought to himself.

As they waited for the check, Kate returned the conversation to Haber. "What kind of pictures do you paint, Leon?"

"Oh, I'm not very good. My work is much too constricted, far too self-conscious to be any good." His expression grew dreamy and his voice faraway. "Once I knew a lovely young woman who possessed an enormous talent. You remind me of her. You have the same spirit. The same fierce determination. Rebecca painted with a virtuosity that comes only when one is born with the gift. She showed promise of becoming truly great."

Inexplicably, Kate felt chilled. "And did she become a great painter?" she asked, instinctively knowing this story did not have a happy ending.

Haber's expression darkened. "Unfortunately, no. Like so many promising young women, she got involved with the wrong man."

TWENTY-FOUR

AT A FEW minutes before ten, Thomas Shipley pulled his van into his basement parking garage. He got out and opened the van's rear doors. Ordinarily he used a bonded courier to pick up and deliver merchandise. But this was no ordinary painting. Lifting a carefully padded and wrapped rectangular package out of the van, he carried it to the elevator and pushed the button with his elbow. Reaching the first floor, he unwrapped the elaborately framed canvas and displayed it on the easel in the center of his gallery. He was alone; his assistant had left at his usual time, seven. Shipley snapped on the overhead spotlights and stepped back. The painting was good, very good.

EARLIER IN THE DAY, Kate Callahan had telephoned him. "Mr. Shipley, I've been thinking about your offer to assist me with an art purchase, and I'd like to take you up on it. Next week is my grandfather's birthday and I'd like to give him something special."

"Of course, Kate. I'll be glad to help. What do you have in mind? What kind of pictures does your grandfather like? I met him yesterday in your green room. A delightful gentleman," Shipley said, thinking to himself that Jerry Callahan was a little too rough around the edges to suit him.

"Grandfather's favorite painter is Winslow Homer," Kate replied.

"Ah, a man of refined tastes," Shipley said.

Kate continued, "I know a real Homer is out of the question, but I thought a picture in Homer's style would please Granddad. I'm afraid five thousand dollars is my limit."

Yesterday, after his television interview when he'd made the offer of assistance, Shipley had told her that he had his fingers on the New York art scene's pulse. If he didn't have a particular picture, he could usually find it.

"You're in luck, Miss Callahan. A colleague of mine happens to specialize in pictures that were painted in Homer's studio by students working under the master's direct supervision. Many are quite good and their cost falls within your budget. Tell me, does your grandfather like seascapes?"

"Yes, they're his favorite," Kate replied.

"Then we really are in luck. I happen to know that my friend has an excellent seascape available. That is, if he hasn't recently sold it," he cautioned.

"Let's hope not. I'll keep my fingers crossed," Kate said, feeling excited.

"Well, then, let's say that I'll have the seascape here for you to examine later today unless you hear from me to the contrary. What time may I expect you?"

"I would like to settle this soon, Mr. Shipley. But most nights I can't get away from the station until ten. I suppose that's too late."

"I'll be glad to open the gallery for you at ten. I have a dinner engagement at eight so ten suits me well."

"I'm grateful, Mr. Shipley."

"Kate, I like to think that we've become friends. I'm happy to help you. And by the way, my friends call me Ship. So I'll see you at ten tonight then."

She had agreed and said goodbye.

Now, it was almost ten. She'll be here at any minute, Shipley thought. He adjusted the painting on the easel.

It was unsigned, but then Kate would not be expecting Homer's signature.

The doorbell rang and Shipley verified through a glass panel that it was Kate before admitting her. A black limousine waited at the curb; a burly chauffeur leaned against the car. He looks like a prize fighter, Shipley noted. I wonder if she's been threatened. Television personalities like her frequently attract stalkers. The bodyguard took him by surprise. He'd assumed she'd be arriving by cab.

Once inside, Kate clasped her hands in pleasure. "What a beautiful seascape! If I didn't know better, I'd think Winslow Homer painted it himself." She turned to Shipley, glowing.

Shipley beamed. "It is good, isn't it? And it's well within your price range. Only twenty-five hundred."

"Granddad will love it. Could you keep it here for me until next week?"

"No problem. I'll keep it safe. Just call me when you're ready to have…"

The doorbell rang, startling both Kate and Shipley. "I'm not expecting anyone. Must be your chauffeur."

But when he peered through the glass panel, Thomas Shipley saw two men on the sidewalk. Behind Kate's limo, a second car was parked, a sedan with a flashing blue light on the dashboard. Oh, no, Shipley thought. What an inconvenient time for the police to come calling. He opened the door and greeted them curiously.

"Mr. Shipley, I'm Detective Rick Smith and this is my partner Joe Mateer. We'd like to ask you a few questions if you don't mind."

Shipley controlled his apprehension but his moist hand slipped on the door handle. "Can't it wait until morning?" he managed to protest.

From behind Shipley, Kate called, "Rick?"

The detectives stepped inside. "What are you doing here?" Rick Smith asked angrily.

Shipley closed and locked the door.

Kate was taken aback by the hostility in Rick's voice. She responded indignantly, "If it's any of your business, I'm buying a painting."

"At this hour!" Rick exclaimed.

Kate's chin shot up. "If it was two in the morning, it still would be none of your business. Unless, of course, I'm a suspect."

"Now you're being silly," Rick snapped.

Kate glared at him. "What's this all about?" She looked from him to Shipley. Her newswoman's antennae vibrated. "It's about the strangler case, isn't it?"

Rick was about to retort, but Joe Mateer stepped in. "Kate, it's police business. I'm sorry but I've got to ask you to leave."

Kate narrowed her eyes at both of them. "Ship, thanks for all you've done. I'll call you next week." She shook hands with him and he let her out. From her car, she called Evan Wallace on her cell phone. Reaching his voice mail she left a message describing this latest development in the strangler case. "Evan, they're questioning Thomas Shipley now!"

Rick Smith watched her car pull away from the curb. Now why'd I have to go shooting off my big mouth? he asked himself. But he was here to question Shipley about the strangler case. Shipley might be implicated. Seeing Kate here alone with him was disconcerting and worrisome. She acts like there's not a killer on the loose in this city. He squared his shoulders. More immediate matters to attend to now.

Thomas Shipley got out a handkerchief and mopped his brow. "Should I call my lawyer?" he asked.

"That's your constitutional right," Joe Mateer responded. "But how about if we just tell you what we want to know. Then if you feel you need a lawyer before you answer, call one."

"All right. Let's get this over with."

"Kate was right. We're here about the strangler case, Mr. Shipley."

"What's that got to do with me?" Shipley shook his head. "I don't understand."

Smith explained, "The strangler's latest victim has been identified as Regina Hoover. Does that name mean anything to you?"

Shipley shook his head, a puzzled expression on his face. Then he did a double take. "Actually, it does, but I can't remember the context."

"According to Elsie Hoover, the dead girl's mother, the deceased had an interview with you about a job on Thursday."

Shipley responded with relief, "So that's it. Yes, now I remember. There was a young woman named Regina Hoover here last Thursday. My assistant Jeffrey Biggers conducted the interview. I just stuck my head in to have a look at her and be introduced. We're trying to hire a data entry clerk to help with the computerized inventory and sales records because business is booming and I need Jeffrey on the floor." He knew that he was saying too much but couldn't seem to control himself.

"Did you offer Miss Hoover a job?" Joe Mateer asked.

"No, we did not."

"And why was that?" Smith asked.

"Jeffrey said she was over-qualified and wanted more money than we'd budgeted."

"Do you remember what time she left, Mr. Shipley?"

"No, I can't say I do. It was some time before noon,

I think. Jeffrey may remember. Why don't you speak to him?"

"That's exactly what we will do," Smith replied. He glanced around the gallery. "Nice place you have here."

"Thanks," Shipley said. He exhaled and relaxed. Then he shrugged. "Look, I'm sorry about those wretched girls. And I'm sorry I can't be more helpful."

"You have helped," Smith said. "You're helping us to reconstruct her last days."

Walking to the car, Mateer said to Smith, "Shipley sure is nervous about something."

Rick replied, "When a self-contained man like Shipley loses his composure, it's because he's guilty of something. I'd like to know what."

TWENTY-FIVE

RICK SMITH IS the most infuriating man I've ever met, Kate thought as she let herself into her apartment. What did I ever see in him?

And Professor Haber? There's something strange about him. He's snobbish, yet at the same time insecure. I could almost feel sorry for him. Some woman broke his heart, that's for sure. And I, for one, can relate to that.

The thought of Marty sitting in a cold car while she was comfortably inside the Italian restaurant dining on delicious Italian food had made her feel guilty, no matter what Vaughn said. Some night I'm going to invite Marty up here for one of Granddad's homey suppers.

"Hi, Granddad, I'm home," she called.

"Back here in the den," he yelled.

Kate couldn't help smiling to herself. If she and her grandfather lived in a thirty room mansion, they'd still shout to each other across the rooms. We're just peasants at heart, she thought, and I wouldn't have it any other way.

She found him in his favorite recliner, feet up, sipping dessert wine. "Pour one for yourself," he said.

Kate threw her coat on a chair and helped herself to a glass of wine. Jerry had turned on the gas logs in the fireplace. That seascape will look perfect hanging over the mantel, she reflected. At least this night has not been a total loss.

Kate looked around. She loved this room with its dark paneled walls, teal sofa and teal patterned rug. One wall was bare, unfurnished. She'd been waiting for the right piece of furniture. She could imagine a breakfront there. Something old and interesting. She pictured Jerry's collection of books lining the shelves behind the breakfront's glass doors. She'd always thought of this room as his. She had saved five thousand dollars for his birthday present. He might not be having many more, and she wanted this one to count. Now, thanks to Thomas Shipley, she had twenty-five hundred dollars left for a breakfront. Shipley's such a good guy, she thought, bet he's not making a dime off that seascape. What did Rick and Joe want with him? There's no way a respectable man like Shipley could be involved in the strangler case.

She lowered herself onto the hassock in front of the fire. "Have you had dinner?"

"So now you think about dinner," Jerry groused, "and me. But you couldn't find time to call to let me know you weren't eating at home tonight. I had to call the station. Somebody saw you leaving with Haber so I figured you were going out to eat with him."

"Oh, Granddad, I'm so sorry. I should have called. I don't know where my brain is these days."

"I do," he commented.

Kate didn't challenge him. She didn't want to get into it with him tonight. "I had a hectic day," she remarked, rubbing her temples.

His voice softened. "I can imagine." He sipped his sweet wine. "I watched Wallace's segment of the show. That was high drama. That poor Mrs. Hoover and that nice young boyfriend. Lockhart, that was his name. So why hasn't Joe Friday caught this psychopath?"

"Joe Friday?"

"Yeah, Joe Friday. Alias Rick Smith. He's sure as

wooden as Friday. Didn't bat an eye when that nice Mrs. Hoover broke down and bawled on TV."

"Granddad, if Rick gets emotional about this case, he's not going to be objective and solve it. He has to put his personal feelings aside. I saw him out in the hall and he was devastated by her grief and by those girls' deaths." Now why am I defending him? Kate asked herself.

Jerry flipped a lever and his chair shot upright. He got up to pace the room. "Well, I sure as hell am glad you got Marty Sokolov to look after you. He's one hell of a guy, I can tell ya. Me and him had a good talk when he drove me over to the station yesterday. Two men with a single mind, far as you're concerned." Jerry raised an eyebrow meaningfully.

"Uh oh," Kate said.

"By the way, thanks for sending him to pick me up today. I felt like a real swell being chauffeured around town in that swanky limo."

Kate got up and kissed him on the cheek. "You are a real swell. So does this mean I'm forgiven?"

Jerry grinned. "Yeah, but don't let it happen again. When you're goin' out to eat, let me know."

"Did you eat out?" Kate asked.

Jerry averted his face. "Yeah," he mumbled. "Me and Irma went to Smith and Wolensky's for steaks."

"Oh? And how is the fair Mrs. Greenbaum?" Kate asked, a teasing lilt in her voice. No matter how low her mood, ten minutes with her grandfather fixed it.

"Irma's just fine. In fact, *she* took me to dinner. She's feeling flush since she sold that painting back to Shipley. That guy's all right. Giving her that painting, buying it back for a cool five million. He must be loaded."

"I think he's done well," Kate commented. "I'm glad you like Marty. I have to admit Vaughn was right about him. I feel safer having him drive me around. Seeing how Mrs. Hoover and Regina's boyfriend are suffering brings those murders closer to home. They're more than a hot story. Those were flesh and blood people and their relatives must be going through hell."

She looked up at Jerry. "Granddad, I'd like to ask Marty up for supper one night soon when he brings me home."

"I was having the same thought myself. How about tomorrow night I fix lasagna? You make sure he comes up with you. Waitin' around for you all day in that car, bet he lives on fast food. We'll give him a decent meal."

"You're the best, Granddad," Kate said simply.

Jerry returned to his recliner; Kate curled up on the velvet sofa. "Dolly sends regards. She's looking forward to going out with us on Friday night to hear Bobby Short."

"That girl's like another granddaughter to me. She's spent every Friday night with us since you girls were in the third grade. That's how many years? Twenty-five? Didn't we have fun in those days?" He gazed at the fire. "Nights like this, I sure do miss your grandma."

"Yeah. Me too, Granddad." Kate sighed.

"See you licked the cold you was coming down with," Jerry said. "That was fast."

"I took a lot of vitamin C," Kate replied. It made her uncomfortable to tell white lies to Jerry. But after her talk with Dolly last night, she had decided to definitely delay the news about her mother's death until after her grandfather's birthday. She's been dead for over thirty years, another week won't matter. Anyway, Granddad probably attributes my sniffles to Rick Smith being around the station.

As if he read her mind, Jerry said, "So you bumped into Smith out in the hall, did you? Hope he didn't upset you."

"It wasn't as hard as I thought it would be," Kate lied. She didn't mention seeing Rick again at Shipley's gallery.

"Good," Jerry said. "That Haber's an odd duck. What's he like? You had dinner with him."

"He's an odd duck," Kate laughed. And perhaps it was as simple as that, she reasoned. Haber was a misfit. Leave it to Granddad to help me put events and people in perspective. I think I've just got too much going on these days: Vaughn's attentiveness, my run-in with that drunk, the detective I hired calling with the news that my mother died thirty-some years ago. And tonight bumping into Rick twice and knowing that this case is going to throw us together.

And this serial killer thing. It makes everyone uneasy just knowing he's out there, stalking the city streets, looking for his next victim. In all fairness, it must be hard on Rick. I know it's harder than he lets on. I used to know Rick better than anyone, and he's decent and kind-hearted. I know this is just tearing him up on the inside.

"So tomorrow you're interviewing that big auction house tycoon?"

"Yes, tomorrow we'll be filming at Lorneby's Auction House. Think I'll turn in, Granddad. Don't fall asleep in your chair. You know you always get a stiff neck when you do."

"Yeah, yeah."

TWENTY-SIX

VAUGHN THOMPSON TOSSED and turned in his bed. A scene that was indelibly imprinted on his brain played and replayed itself like a videotape on forward and rewind. After Kate's show he'd taken the elevator down to the news floor to personally congratulate Evan Wallace on his coup, and to shake hands with Detectives Rick Smith and Joe Mateer. He had intended to offer the services of the station in whatever way the police might want to make use of them.

As the elevator doors opened, there stood Kate with Leon Haber. Kate was wearing her coat and Haber's hand was under her elbow. The two stepped onto the elevator together as he stepped off. Kate gave him a jaunty wave and called goodnight. Haber bade him a formal good evening.

Vaughn had felt his temper flare. He'd ducked into a men's room and splashed cold water on his fiery face. What was Kate doing with Haber? Where were they going? Vaughn knew Haber, had met him through Thomas Shipley. And Haber, in his estimation, was an oddball and not to be trusted. Sure, he was on the President's Commission and the World Jewish Congress. And he taught at NYU's Institute of Fine Arts. And every once in a while, he was quoted in the *New York Times* Arts and Leisure section. Still, there was something seriously wrong with the man. Vaughn didn't like the idea of Kate spending any time alone with him.

He punched his pillow. What he really resented was that Haber seemed to be all wrapped up in Kate. He's after her,

Vaughn told himself. He wants to get her in bed. The nu-
bile students he sleeps with must be boring him. But Kate's
going to be my wife. She's not some piece of arm candy,
like those show girls I used to run around with. I intend to
marry her, to make her the mother of my children. No one
else can have her. Not Haber. Not Rick Smith.

Vaughn had found Mike Cramer. "Great show with the
detectives. Tell the staff: TNYC will cooperate fully with
them. Offer them air time. Anything they want."

Cramer had seemed surprised but agreed it was the
right thing to do.

Vaughn walked away satisfied. He knew he might be
throwing Kate and Rick Smith together. But they would be
on his turf. On his terms. He'd always followed the strategy
of keeping one's friends close, but one's enemies closer.

Fully awake now, he complained aloud, "I give up," and
climbed out of bed. He switched on a soft light. In its circle, Vaughn Thompson stood nude. He caught a glimpse
of himself in the mirror. I'm a good-looking man, he reminded himself. His shoulders were broad, his waist slim.
The hair on his head was full and black with attractive
silver streaks at the temples. Springy black curls covered
his chest and groin.

All my life women have chased me, he thought. Now
the tables are turned. Who would have thought? The great
Vaughn Thompson has to resort to subterfuge to get a date
with a woman. But Kate's different, and worth whatever
effort it takes. I'll get her no matter what I have to do or
how long it takes. The Rick Smiths and Leon Habers of
this world have nothing to offer her. They're no match for
me. She'll see that.

He lifted a soft cashmere robe off the foot of the bed
and put it on. Then he turned on the hall lights and went
down two flights of stairs to the kitchen.

Thompson lived in a renovated five-story townhouse on Sixty-eighth Street between Fifth and Madison avenues. The street floor of the narrow building housed a formal entrance and an adjoining garage where Thompson kept two vehicles. His kitchen and a dining room were located on what was called the first floor. On the second were the rooms where he entertained. His bedroom suite, a small home office, and his private gallery comprised the third. The fourth and fifth floors were off-limits to everyone but himself; not even the maid went up there.

His pantry was well stocked. On weekends Vaughn liked to indulge his passion for preparing Northern Italian food. He filled a teakettle and while he waited for the water to boil, clicked on a contact on his cell phone.

The man he called was asleep and answered groggily.

Thompson demanded, "Why didn't you call me? You know you're supposed to let me know where she goes and what she does."

Yawning, the man offered a sleepy apology. "Sorry. I forgot."

"I'm not paying you to be forgetful!" Vaughn snapped. "I saw her leave the station with Haber."

"Yes, sir," the man said, "they went to a Greenwich Village restaurant. They had dinner. Then Marty dropped him off, and took her uptown to Shipley's art gallery. She left when the police arrived. Sorry I didn't call, Boss, guess I nodded off."

The teakettle whistled and Vaughn turned off the gas jet. "What do you mean 'when the police arrived'?"

The man cleared his throat. "Two detectives came to see Shipley. Miss Callahan left. Marty drove her straight home."

What did the detectives want with Shipley? Vaughn wondered. "See that there's not a repetition of this. If you want your money, you'll keep me informed. Daily. If you don't want this job, there are plenty of others who do." He clicked the off button.

While his tea steeped, Vaughn dropped two slices of rye bread into the toaster. On Saturday, he would drive Kate to his country home. His man servant there would prepare lunch for them. He'd show her the house and the grounds, breathtaking now with flowering dogwoods. He'd show her what she'd be getting when she agreed to marry him. The key is her grandfather. Next time, I'll invite the old man. Maybe take him out to one of the putting greens. A little male bonding. Two men who love Kate with all their hearts.

Then in the evening, before the party at the Met, she'll be here, he reminded himself, attending my pre-gala cocktail party. I'll make sure she meets all the right people. Then I'll take her aside and give her a private tour of this house. I'll show her my art collection. That ought to impress her.

Vaughn had worked hard since the age of eighteen to acquire these luxury items. Now he wanted to share them. With Kate.

At the kitchen table, he ate his midnight snack without tasting it. Chamomile tea was supposed to be good for the nerves. He drained the cup, then put the dishes into the sink for the maid to wash in the morning.

Back in his bed on the third floor, he acknowledged that he felt relaxed now, drowsy. Today he had offered Thomas Shipley six million dollars for *The Embrace*. But Shipley had turned him down, saying the painting was not for sale.

"Let me have it, Ship," he'd pleaded. "I'll pay you whatever you ask, but I've got to have that painting." Ship hadn't asked why and Vaughn hadn't explained that he wanted it for a wedding present—his wedding present.

As Vaughn drifted off to sleep, the painting floated before his closed eyes. The breathtakingly beautiful ginger-haired woman with the pale opalescent skin was locked in the embrace of a black-haired, strong-jawed man. A gilt-embellished, multi-colored blanket covered them. He imagined that the model was Kate. The blanket slipped off her shoulder, revealing a bare upper arm and full breasts that shone like alabaster. The first stirrings of arousal plunged Vaughn into a pleasant, erotic dream. In it, he and Kate lay together under a radiant, jewel-encrusted blanket. He reached for her and pulled her to him, and she came: soft, yielding, eager. In his sleep he cried out with pleasure.

TWENTY-SEVEN

"RICK, WE'VE GOT to talk." Kate burst into Rick Smith's and Joe Mateer's office without waiting to be announced.

Surprised, Rick Smith set down the pen he'd been making notes with.

Joe Mateer summed up the scene instantly, got up and excused himself. "I've got to check on something in the Evidence Room. Good to see you again, Miss Callahan."

Rick stood up too. "Hello, Kate. I guess you're right. We should talk. Here, have a seat." He removed a stack of file folders from his guest chair. "Can I get you some coffee?"

Kate produced a white paper bag. "I brought us Starbucks. You used to prefer it."

"Yeah, I still do," Rick said softly. "Thanks."

Kate reached into the bag and handed him a cardboard container. She took the remaining one for herself and held it as she sat down in the available chair.

Rick was glad for something to do with his hands. He pried off the container's lid, threw it away, then held the cup in both hands. He looked at Kate. He'd never expected to see her here, across the desk from him in his office. She looked fresh and pretty in her tailored green suit. Her only jewelry was pearl earrings and a watch. He remembered her aversion to necklaces and scarves, to anything around her neck, and he wanted to ask if she still suffered from that phobia. But he didn't know how she'd take a personal question. And she seemed so business-like this morning. "What can I do for you, Kate?" he asked instead.

"This isn't easy, Rick, so hear me out. I lay awake most of last night, thinking about my run...encounters with you yesterday and the day before. Until this strangler case is solved, we're going to be thrown together. There's no way around it. You're the lead detective; my station has an interest in covering this story. So do I. And now it seems you're giving Evan an inside track."

Rick started to speak, but Kate held up an open palm. "Let me finish, please. I've rehearsed what I have to say.

"I'd like us to come to terms with each other and our past. Let's not let whatever personal feelings we once had for each other influence how we handle what should be a perfectly straightforward work relationship. We're both professionals. Let's act like it. Starting now, we'll put the past behind us."

Rick hesitated, then said kindly, as though he was trying to spare her feelings, "Kate, I already have."

Kate blinked. She was quiet for a moment, digesting the import of his words. Was she the only one their brief encounters had affected? Was she to believe they'd meant nothing to Rick?

Her chin shot up. "So have I. It just seemed to me that last night you treated me with a certain amount of hostility that was unwarranted under the circumstances. I'm here to tell you that I will not tolerate that kind of hostility toward me when circumstances bring us together again. Let's get this off the personal plain."

Rick dumped the empty coffee container in his wastebasket. "I apologize if that's the way I came across, Kate. I bear you no hostility." He shrugged his shoulders. "This case gets to me. Makes me impatient and grumpy. I want to get this guy so bad, sometimes I lose my sense of perspective."

Kate reflected, trying to be fair. "I can understand that. It's got to be awful. Until I got to know Elsie Hoover and Bill Lockhart, this was just a story we were covering. Now that I know the people involved, I want to do something to help them. Which brings me to the second reason I'm here."

Rick rested his elbows on his chair arms, steepled his fingertips thoughtfully. He didn't want Kate involved in a case as ugly and dangerous as this one. But he had no right to stop her.

His body language was saying he'd resist whatever she said. Despite that, she made her pitch. "Vaughn Thompson, our CEO, has offered the station's resources and services in any way you want to use them. Evan and I discussed this latest development early this morning. My series on stolen paintings is almost over. We'd like to devote a segment, maybe even several entire shows, to the strangler case. Last night's show with the dead girl's loved ones gave me an idea. Why not have the relatives of all four victims on our show? Repeat the call-in format."

Kate leaned forward, intent on pleading her cause. "I've called all the relatives. They say they're cooperating with Detective Smith and that Detective Smith has asked them not to give interviews."

"Because they might say something that could jeopardize our case. Something we don't want the public to hear, that we don't want the perp to know that we know," he said defensively.

"There's a way around that. You and your partner can appear on the show with them. We'll use a loose script. Television is a powerful media, Rick. Let us help."

"I'll run it by my partner," he agreed reluctantly. "And the captain."

Kate stood up and stuck out her hand. "Thanks. You were always fair. I'd like to work with you. Strictly business."

Rick took her hand in his. Its cool softness flooded him with memories. "Good-bye, Kate."

Joe Mateer stood in the doorway during their last exchange. Strictly business? he thought. Uh oh. I can feel the chemistry all the way over here. When those two get together, even the atmosphere gets charged.

KATE GOT INTO her limo, smiling to herself. So, he's already put us behind him, huh? You forget, Rick Smith, that I used to know you better than anyone. There's that little nerve in your cheek, right in front of your left ear, that jumps when you get emotional, nervous…or are lying!

AT TEN A.M. Phyllis Stern strolled through the Costume Department's exhibition rooms at the Metropolitan Museum of Art. Her department had been closed all week as she and her staff prepared for a special exhibit that would open on Sunday. The exhibit was titled *Party Animals: Formal Wear through the Ages*. Exhibits such as these, with their fancy ballgowns and pretty party clothes, were always popular with the public, and Stern knew that her department would draw record crowds this weekend. On Saturday night, the museum would host an extravagant gala so that the press and the New York social set could preview the exhibit.

The mannequins were arranged in casual groupings as guests would have naturally assembled at dances and parties. On the walls behind them, enormous blown-up photographs of the former owners of the party clothes were on display. In this case, the very sophisticated and elegant

Duke and Duchess of Windsor danced together. They made
a handsome couple.

Consternation clouded Stern's face as she observed one
of the dressers trying to fit a beaded dress on a mannequin.
"No, no, no!" Stern cried, springing on the girl. "You'll
have to find a smaller mannequin. Wallis Simpson was a
tiny woman. She weighed less than one hundred pounds.
Don't you dare rip that dress!"

"Sorry, Ms. Stern," the young woman mumbled, close
to tears. "This is the smallest female mannequin I could
find."

"Then you'll have to find a child-size one," Stern
scolded. "The Duchess had the figure of a pubescent girl
so a child mannequin will do nicely. Go down to the mannequin room and select several; bring them to me and I'll
select one. I'll wait right here until you return." She tapped
the toe of her patent pump, showing her impatience.

Rattled, the young woman scurried away, taking the of-
fending mannequin with her, but dropping the blue beaded
dress in a heap on the floor.

Stern's thick dark brows knit together in a frown. "Tsk,
tsk, tsk," she clucked, shaking her head. Every art student in this city wants to work here, she thought, but they
haven't got the sense of a newborn kitten. At least the male
mannequin is correctly dressed. She stepped back to admire the midnight blue tuxedo that King Edward VIII, later
the Duke of Windsor, made famous back in the thirties.

Stern picked up the tiny dress from the carpeted floor
of the dais and held it out by the shoulders. She recalled
that she'd held the white mull sports dress the last dead
girl had been wearing in just this way when she'd been at
police headquarters on Tuesday morning.

I wish I could understand the significance of those var-
ied costumes the strangler is putting on his victims before

he kills them, she thought. Those poor girls. I really want to help detectives Smith and Mateer. They are so sincere about wanting to catch this killer. But what do the clothes mean?

Studying the blue beaded dress, she reminded herself, once this very dress covered the back of a woman who caused a king to abdicate his throne. Is that what this is all about? Are the strangler's selections somehow related to history? Does he hate the people who once wore the clothes he puts on his victims? But how could he hate them? He doesn't know them. Some of the costumes he used are over a hundred years old.

The tiny duchess's dress and their problems in finding a mannequin small enough to wear it reminded her of the large size white mull dress she'd examined on Tuesday. Regina Hoover, the victim, had been a large girl, probably a size fourteen. In fact, all the costumes she'd identified for the police had been in appropriate sizes for the deceased girls who'd worn them. "He's acquiring specific outfits for specific girls," she said out loud. I've got to call Detective Smith as soon as I return to my office. Those dresses fitting was no accident!

Oh, all this pressure is giving me a headache. She draped the blue beaded dress over her arm and tapped her toe impatiently. Where is that simpering idiot? she asked herself.

Mentally, she reviewed the costumes the victims had been wearing. A ballet dancer's costume about one hundred and twenty five years old. A common Parisian street outfit from the turn of the century. The Fluffy Ruffles look from 1906. And lastly an upper-class ladies' sports dress. The costumes dated from about 1875 to 1910. They represented no one particular class. But what did it all mean?

The dresser appeared at last carrying two mannequins.

TWENTY-EIGHT

KATE AND HER crew entered Lorneby's International Auction House through the Park Avenue entrance. The austere, imposing white marble seven-story structure presided over half a block on the Upper East Side. Colorful flags over the entrance, representing the world's great industrial powers, snapped crisply in the wind.

Neil Lorneby was waiting just inside the doors, surrounded by several dark-suited directors. "Kate. Welcome," he said, his hands outstretched to clasp both of hers, a large smile on his face.

He introduced her around. "Each of my directors is a specialist in his or her field. Come, let me give you the grand tour. Oh, but what am I thinking? You've been here before. You're a client."

"Yes. You were nice enough to invite me to lunch in your penthouse here when I was furnishing my apartment. And that reminds me, my grandfather's birthday is a week away, and I'd like to give him something special for his den. A desk or a breakfront to hold his books. Granddad is an avid reader of biographies and owns quite a collection."

"Well, we have more than our share of desks and breakfronts. Do you have any particular period in mind?" Lorneby asked. His associates remained silent, evidently preferring, or having been instructed, to let him do the talking.

"Not period so much as country of origin. Granddad's Irish, you know. His father emigrated from County Cork when he was a boy. Granddad's gone back to his family's village many times. I think he would prize a piece of furniture that had been made in that region."

One of Lorneby's directors stepped forward and started to speak, but Lorneby silenced him with a raised hand. "I'll personally review our inventory and call you myself, Kate. Now let's have a look around."

One by one Lorneby's directors excused themselves, telling her what a pleasure it was to meet her, and drifted away, apparently returning to their own departments. He rules with an iron fist, Kate thought, as her technician wired Lorneby for sound. He clipped the lavaliere to Lorneby's lapel, then guided the wire down Lorneby's suit jacket and clipped a miniature transmitter to his waistband. Kate preferred to interview using the lav. Thrusting the stick, as the hand-held microphone was known, into interviewees' faces made them self-conscious.

For the better part of an hour, Lorneby guided Kate through the auction house as the cameraman filmed the interior and the microphones recorded their conversation. Strolling through public and private rooms, and vast storage rooms, Neil Lorneby explained, "As with every other industry these days, auction houses have been forced, due to the sheer volume of their holdings, to reorganize into highly specialized departments. We've got departments for paintings, for tapestries and rugs, for furniture. We've got a European department and an Asian department, and a department that handles only silver."

They were in an enormous room that seemed to contain nothing but chairs; chairs of every shape and size were lined up in rows from wall to wall and from floor to ceiling.

"Where do all these things come from?" Kate asked.

"I'm glad you asked. I think I can take the mystery out of what auction houses do."

Lorneby's eyes were aquamarine and they seemed to change from green to blue, depending on his mood. At the moment, he seemed charged by his subject, and his eyes responded by gleaming brilliantly blue. He is a consummate showman, Kate thought.

"Most of the time, we acquire a 'lot' when a person of property passes away and his, or her, executors or heirs must settle the estate. We are asked to appraise and sell the goods at auction, and naturally to get the best prices possible for the 'lot.' For your viewers' information, a 'lot' is an item or group of items. Most everyone remembers the sale of the late Jacqueline Onassis's jewelry and memorabilia."

"A most impressive collection," Kate responded.

"The auction house and the seller establish a minimum price for the 'lot' that is called the reserve. The amount is confidential, of course. The house agrees not to let the items go for a sum that is lower than the reserve. Most sellers would rather hold onto a piece than to sell for a sum that is too low. In a year or two, the value of that particular item might go up, and they can realize fair market value for it if they wait."

Kate forged ahead, asking the question she'd been wanting to ask, but without mentioning Thomas Shipley and the Gotham Group's suit by name. "There's been a lot of talk recently about auction houses charging fees that are unreasonable. How do you respond to that charge?"

Lorneby remained cool and focused. "Perhaps if I describe the life of a lot, you'll see that our commissions are more than fair. A truck arrives loaded with the furnishings of a deceased person's home or homes. The items are unpacked and receipted. They are inspected by an expert, appraised, and photographed. The photographs are used in our catalogues along with descriptions written by our experts. Then the items are assigned to the appropriate storage area where they are stored free of charge."

He paused for a second and Kate waited.

"Preparation for exhibition could involve cleaning and minor repairs, again free of charge. Then the items are moved out of the storage rooms and into the exhibition areas where they are put on public display. Next they are moved to the auction room itself where they must be shown off to advantage."

"With all that moving around, does anything ever get broken?" Kate asked.

"Never," Lorneby said firmly. "Our movers handle antiques as if they were crates of eggs."

He continued, "The actual gavel to gavel sale is the easy part. We've devised a revolving stage that is stationed near the auctioneer's rostrum. As one item is being sold, the next is being set up. Of necessity, we must ascertain in advance that all bidders have the wherewithal to pay should their bid bring down the hammer. We require payment within three days and we're responsible for collecting New York state sales tax or verifying a tax-exempt resale number. After the monies are received, the items are moved to the shipping area, packed, signed out, and sent on their way."

He raised his eyebrows. "Does that sound like we are providing a valuable service?"

"It does to me," Kate said. "I was very pleased with the way my furniture arrived in good condition."

"For all of the services I've just described we get ten percent of the sales price. And, as you know, we also add a premium of another ten percent to the bid price that is payable by the buyer. And it is that premium that is in dispute."

"Well, I for one, didn't mind paying it. I got some really

lovely, original pieces of furniture here." Kate looked around. "Mr. Lorneby, I don't see any guards. And I didn't see any at the entrance either."

Lorneby beamed, his eyes bluer than blue. "Our guards don't wear uniforms. They are dressed like you and me, and they mingle with the crowds in the exhibition rooms. We want our patrons to feel free to touch and examine the merchandise."

"But wouldn't someone be tempted to pick up a small object and tuck it into a purse or a pocket?" Kate asked. "Then just walk out the door."

Lorneby replied, "Every object at Lorneby's is tagged with a plastic chip. It sets off a silent alarm if it is removed from the public viewing areas. The guilty party is discreetly escorted to one of the offices. If we decide to press charges, the police are called. There's no public scene.

"And after hours there are no guards here at all. We have a highly sophisticated, state-of-the art electronic security system consisting of cameras, automatic doors, silent alarms, heat sensors and motion detectors. When we close for the day, all entrances to this building are sealed with steel-reinforced sliding doors. And up in the penthouse, where I live, there's a security command center with monitors that show every inch of the place. If there is an attempted break-in, alarms summon me to the command center and simultaneously summon a private security force."

"May we continue our interview in your office, Mr. Lorneby," Kate said.

"That's an excellent idea, Kate." Lorneby led her and her crew to his executive suite on the sixth floor. They stopped a minute at the opposite end of the building to peek into an enormous room where rare rugs and tapestries hung in rows. Then Lorneby directed them down a long hallway, past an unoccupied office, another eleva-tor, and finally into his own magnificent corner office. Behind Kate, the cameraman followed with the steady-cam. Sound and light technicians ensured the quality of voice and picture.

"Ah, this is perfect," Kate cried, clasping her hands to-gether. "Just what our viewers would expect an auction house chairman's office to look like."

The room was square, paneled in oak with elaborately carved moldings, and the floor was made of herringbone parquet. Lorneby's furniture was from the neo-classical period, glossy black surfaces featuring classical designs of pale inlaid woods. Egyptian artifacts provided decora-tion. In particular, a sleek bronze cat on Lorneby's desk, and in one corner, an upright stone sarcophagus. Rich, crimson brocade draperies fell in deep folds at two tall windows that overlooked Park Avenue. The ceiling was at least sixteen feet high and decorated with plaster cher-ubs and mythical creatures.

"Bet you could shoot baskets in here," the cameraman commented.Lorneby smiled. He'd heard that one before. "Shall I sit behind my desk?"

"I think that would add to your authority, Mr. Lorneby," Kate answered. "And I'll draw up a chair next to yours."

When everything was set up, Kate advised him as she had advised Irma Greenbaum. "Feel free to say whatever you wish and take as much time as you need."

"How long will this segment run when you air it to-night?" Lorneby asked.

"Total, about twenty minutes," Kate replied. "And the twenty minutes will be divided between clips from the tour we just made and sections of this interview. The tour will be our lead-in and I'll introduce you as it runs."

Lorneby seemed anxious. "I don't want to be misquoted or quoted out of context," he said.

"I won't do that, Mr. Lorneby. If I didn't play fair with my guests, I'd never get anyone to agree to appear on the show. My reputation is precious to me, just as yours is to you. Now are you ready?"

Neil Lorneby settled back in his chair, rested his clasped hands in his lap, and lifted his chin. His charcoal gray suit was fashionably cut. Under it he wore a silk shirt in a deeper shade of gray, almost black. His silver hair and silver jewelry flashed in the bright lights.

Kate began, "Mr. Lorneby, all week we've been featuring art experts and talking about stolen paintings. As the head of one of the world's largest auction houses, you are the intermediary between buyer and seller. Have you, perhaps unwittingly, ever sold a stolen object?"

Lorneby appeared earnest as he answered, "I can say with certainty that we have not, Kate. With art objects and memorabilia bringing the astronomical sums they do, I cannot afford to traffic in any piece that is suspect. My reputation would be ruined. And, after all, in this game, if I lose my good name, I lose my livelihood."

After Lorneby's earlier explanation about the buyer's premium, he had given Kate permission to bring up the lawsuit. "It's all over the papers," he had said. "If we don't talk about it, people will wonder what I've got to hide."

Now Kate broached the subject. "Earlier in the week I interviewed Thomas Shipley, owner of Shipley Galleries. Mr. Shipley and his associates in the Gotham Group are suing Lorneby's for price fixing. Would you care to comment on that suit, Mr. Lorneby?"

Lorneby smiled, relaxed. "I welcome the opportunity to get this matter out in the open. It is not the auctioneers who are driving up the prices, Kate, it's the dealers themselves. I can give you a perfect example."

Lorneby leaned forward intently, his arms on his desk, his fingertips touching. "Let me tell you about the sale of Vincent van Gogh's famous painting, *Sunflowers*. On March 30, 1987—coincidentally van Gogh's birthday; he would have been 134—there was a landmark auction at Christie's in London. It was attended by collectors, dealers, and wealthy socialites. A special easel had been constructed to show off *Sunflowers* to its very best advantage.

"The auctioneer opened the bidding at five million pounds. Much to his surprise, the bidding quickly escalated to twenty million pounds. There followed what can best be described as a duel between two dealers. When it was over, *Sunflowers* had been sold for 22,500,000 pounds. Adding the buyer's premium to that, the total was a staggering 24,750,000 pounds. That's 39.9 million dollars in American money. The successful dealer had been bidding for a private collector, the president of a huge Japanese corporation.

"So you see, Kate, it's not the auction houses who are driving up the prices—we're as amazed as anyone by some of these astronomical bids—but the dealers who represent very, and I mean to say, very, deep pockets."

Kate said, "You mentioned the premium, Mr. Lorneby. That seems to be a bone of contention between dealers like those in the Gotham Group and auctioneers. Please tell our viewers why a premium is charged to buyers."

Lorneby replied smoothly, "As it is the auction house that brings the seller and the buyer together, who supplies the product and acts as an intermediary, the auction house provides a service to both parties. It is only sound business practice that we should be compensated by both participants."

"And this practice of adding a buyers' premium is standard in the industry, Mr. Lorneby? All the auction houses do it?"

"All the auction houses do it, Kate. In Europe it had been the custom for decades before it caught on here in America. And in England, where I was born and where Lorneby's originated, it was standard practice in my father's day and in his father's day." Neil Lorneby allowed himself a satisfied smile.

He's vindicated himself with the public, Kate thought, and he's used my show as his forum. A lawsuit like the one the Gotham Group filed is intended to be tried in the media. Shipley's out to destroy Lorneby's reputation. Wonder what their feud is really about? After tonight's show, I wouldn't be surprised if Thomas Shipley and his associates dropped their suit.

Kate did not resent being used by Lorneby. It was a dynamic interview and with all the hedge fund brokers flocking to the big auction houses, people would be talking about it for days. My interview will make page one in tomorrow's *Wall Street Journal*, Kate predicted.

TWENTY-NINE

THE MAN TOOK a key out of his pocket and unlocked his studio. Flipping a switch, incandescent lights that closely resembled natural daylight flooded the room. The windows had been bricked over. He couldn't take a chance that someone in an adjoining building—a voyeur with binoculars or a telescope perhaps—might stare with prying eyes through his windows and into this room.

He walked to his supply cart and verified that all the colors he would need were carefully arranged on the shelves. He tested the tubes of paint; none had dried out. His sable brushes stood upright in glass jars on his worktable, clean and soft and arranged according to size. He took up his position behind his easel and practiced reaching for a brush. The brushes were precisely an arm's length away. His palette was clean and his palette knives lay ready on a tea towel. On the easel a blank white canvas awaited the genius he would bring to it.

Propped on an adjoining easel was the masterpiece he planned to copy. But he would bring an originality to his own masterpiece that would rival Matisse. His model would inspire him to heights Matisse had never known.

He crossed a short distance and surveyed the setting. The portable wall that served as the backdrop was covered in vibrant wallpaper—Turkish cinnamon, turquoise blues, exotic red flowers—the lush and opulent motifs and colors of Morocco. On the wall hung a Moorish mirror which, to his added amusement, would reflect him as he worked at the easel.

To his right a veined marble-topped table sat atop a pile of oriental rugs. The tobacco plant in the blue and white Chinese *jardinière* was placed to his left. In the foreground, an empty blue bowl rested casually on the rugs. Tomorrow he would fill the bowl with fresh oranges. Every detail was important; no detail was too small.

Behind him on a peg on the real wall hung his painter's smock. Next to it, a long scrap of white silk fluttered under the air conditioner vent.

He cupped his chin in his hand and reflected with satisfaction that this time he had been spared the necessity and trouble of locating the authentic garments, of hunting down the correct period accessories.

All was in readiness: his quiet, private studio which no one but he entered, about which no one even knew; the setting; his painting supplies. All awaited his magic touch. The only item that was missing was his subject. But by nine tomorrow night she would be here with him. He'd have the long weekend to immortalize her. He'd work night and day, and by early Monday morning he would have executed his own interpretation of Henri Matisse's *Decorative Figure*, the lush, nude, odalisque Henri Matisse had painted in an artificial Moroccan paradise in 1925.

THIRTY

In Manhattan, where Rick Smith lived, most residents did not own automobiles. But in Brooklyn where he'd grown up, every kid had wanted a car. Rick's brother, Mark, got his first car when he was eighteen. He loved that convertible, a ten-year-old red Thunderbird with whitewall tires and chrome hubcaps. Late one Saturday night, Mark took his friends and Rick out for a ride. Somehow things got out of hand, with Mark's friends daring him to do seventy, then eighty. Careening around a curve on the wrong side of the road, a truck came roaring at them in the lane. Mark jerked the steering wheel to the left. The car flew off the road and crashed into a telephone pole.

Mark died instantly, the paramedics said. The boy in the front seat with Mark was not wearing his seat belt and was thrown fifteen feet from the car. He died of internal bleeding in the ambulance on the way to the hospital. In the backseat, Mark's friend Bobby, the real instigator of the high speed joy ride, suffered a ruptured spleen which had to be surgically removed. Only sixteen-year-old Rick, who'd been called a wuss by the others because he'd strapped himself in, survived with minor injuries. Rick hated Bobby from that day on. Years later when Rick joined the PD, he tracked Bobby's criminal record. He didn't grieve when Bobby died in a prison hospital from an infection that his crippled immune system could not fight off.

Rick couldn't understand why the first officers to arrive on the scene had treated him with cold fury, questioning him, making him feel worse than he already did. Only years later when he was a cop himself did Rick understand that they weren't angry with him, but with the total waste of precious young lives.

Rick's parents were smart enough to get him counseling. He was suffering from survivor's guilt, his therapist told him and them. There were ways of coping with the guilt, but Rick was never very good at employing those coping strategies.

At about the same time, the movie *Ordinary People* came out. Rick went to see it again and again, identifying with the surviving younger brother. Like him, Rick only began to heal when he fell in love. But that wasn't until years later when he met Kate Callahan at a party.

It wasn't just her prettiness that attracted him. There was a goodness about Kate that he'd never known in any other woman except his mother. Rick could talk to her for hours because she listened with her heart; she heard the emotions behind his words. She was the best thing that ever happened to him.

So why did I destroy it? he asked himself over lunch. Do I think that because Mark died I don't deserve to be happy? And whatever possessed me to treat her with hostility last night, and then so coldly this morning? To pretend that my feelings for her were over and that I was so indifferent to her presence that working with her would be a snap? It won't. It'll hurt like hell. Every time I see her, I'll be wishing we were back together again. What the hell's the matter with me? I need you back, Kate. You were good for me.

"More coffee?" his waitress asked, giving him a big smile.

"No thanks," Rick answered. "Just the check." His plate

was empty but he had no memory of eating his cheeseburger. He paid the check and tip, returned the waitress's smile, and left Hamburger Heaven.

BEHIND THE COUNTER, the two waitresses, hands full, bumped hips. "Did you see that dimple when he smiled?" one asked the other.

"Yeah, he ought to smile more often." She laughed. "In my direction."

"What's that old saying? He can park his shoes under my bed any night?"

"Yeah, you got it. Ditto for me."

"Did you see his big gun?"

"No. But I'd sure like to."

"You dope. No, I mean a real gun. He must be a cop."

"Maybe we'll get mugged. And he can come to our rescue. Maybe we'll need mouth-to-mouth."

"We should be so lucky."

The two women laughed and went back to serving their customers.

RICK TOOK OFF on foot for East Fifty-sixth Street. He had an appointment with Celeste Parker's parents at Celeste's apartment. Celeste had been murdered on April 2nd, but had not been identified until April 11th. The police had searched her apartment, dusted for prints which they would hold onto to compare with any future suspect, and sealed the door until they were through.

Rick had met Mr. and Mrs. Parker when they came to New York from Wisconsin to identify the body. That was almost two weeks after Celeste's death, but no one had reported her missing. It had taken a couple of weeks for the parents to contact the authorities. They'd been concerned, they said, but not seriously worried. Celeste was twenty-five and both parents were busy high school teachers.

Celeste usually called home once a week. But she had an extremely full schedule. She worked in a coffee shop on Lexington Avenue and Sixty-seventh Street for the breakfast and dinner shifts. Afternoons were spent making the audition rounds and attending acting, singing, and dancing lessons. A small trust fund from her grandmother paid for the lessons. The coffee shop tips and an allowance from her parents paid the rent on a studio apartment on Fifty-sixth Street between First and Second avenues.

After a week and a half of not hearing from her, Mr. and Mrs. Parker left several messages on her answering machine. When that didn't result in a response, they called the coffee shop and learned that she hadn't been to work since March 28th. In reply to Mr. Parker's questioning Flo, the owner, about her lack of concern, she'd said, "These actresses come and go. If they land a part, they think nothing of leaving me high and dry. They don't know what it means to give notice at work. Although I must say, I've never had one not come back to pick up her wages."

"Are you telling me Celeste didn't pick up her last paycheck?" Paul Parker asked. "She needed every dime she could get her hands on."

"No. Like I say, I haven't seen her since March 28th. Look, I'm sure she's all right. These waitresses come and go. But I do miss Celeste. She was a real good worker, a real nice girl. Hey, but I'm no babysitter for actresses, you know. Don't worry. She'll turn up."

And she had. In the city morgue. Mr. and Mrs. Parker boarded the next plane for New York, and after a discussion with Detective Rick Smith, that's where they found their daughter.

THE DOOR TO the apartment stood ajar. Boxes filled the hallway outside of the apartment. Rick tapped on the jamb and called hello. Mrs. Parker straightened up from a box filled with excelsior. Mr. Parker was standing near the window, a framed photograph in his hand. The apartment was small and Rick took in the total disarray at a glance.

When Elaine Parker had come into Rick's office looking for her daughter, the first thing he'd noticed about her was how much she looked like the Jane Doe they were trying to identify. Just one look at Elaine and he knew the two were related and that Jane Doe was about to get a name. Now as Mrs. Parker straightened, Rick was reminded of the girl whose photographs covered the wall in his conference room. He noted her long lean torso, her long shapely legs. She was about five-ten, the same height as Celeste. She had thick orange hair, almost as bright as Celeste's. The hair color was the real thing, the coroner had told him, no bleach, no dye job. An unusual color. Bright orange, like a newly minted penny. Even Elaine's face was shaped like Celeste's, long and narrow.

Mr. Parker shook hands with Rick. His face was pinched with grief. It's always harder on the dads, Rick theorized, because they won't let themselves cry. Just like my dad held back his tears over Mark. These guys think they have to be strong for everyone, hold everything inside, then they have coronaries. This is a wicked business I'm in, he told himself.

The picture Paul Parker was holding was of Celeste, dressed as a prom queen. In the postmortem pictures of Celeste on Rick's office wall, she was wearing an odd outfit. A long drab green, black, and mustard yellow flounced skirt, green bodice, black stockings and shoes, long black gloves, and a floppy hat with a black plume. Her face had been garishly rouged. Rick had never heard the term 'strumpet' used outside of movies, but that was the word that came to mind the first time he saw Celeste's dead body.

"Our older daughter works for the Peace Corps in Guatemala," Paul Parker said. "She's often in such remote places we can't reach her. We were only able to tell her of Celeste's death yesterday. She's flying to New York as soon as she can get to an airport."

Elaine Parker wiped her dusty hands on a dish towel, then took both of Rick Smith's in her own. "Paula tells us that Celeste had a lover. Celeste wrote to her about him about six months ago. Celeste did not tell Paula his name but she said that he was a very powerful man in the television business and that he was going to help Celeste get a part on a soap opera. She never mentioned him to us. We wondered if he was married, and she was ashamed. Do you know who he is?"

"This is the first I've heard of him," Rick said, but felt his heart beat faster. A lead. A clue.

Paul Parker said, "We thought you might have discovered his name in Celeste's address book. Or found some evidence of his existence in this apartment."

"We checked every name and number listed in your daughter's address book, Mr. Parker. We subpoenaed her recent telephone records and assigned a detective to check out every number. We didn't come up with anything out of the ordinary. Certainly no television executives. And we haven't found any leads from her emails so far."

Elaine Parker's face fell. "Celeste had a wonderful memory for numbers. She probably memorized his number."

THIRTY-ONE

As was his custom after Jeffrey left and he had closed the gallery, Thomas Shipley poured himself a glass of chilled chardonnay and took it with him into his secret room. Generally, admiring his private collection soothed him. Just being in the presence of his beautiful pictures was panacea for the day's pressures. But not so tonight. Tonight he was sorely troubled.

He'd just watched the telecast of Kate Callahan's earlier interview with Neil Lorneby. Shipley was smart enough to recognize that Lorneby had skillfully defended himself against the Gotham Group's charges. He's vindicated himself with the public, Shipley thought, and he's restored his reputation. Although the Gotham Group had asked the New York State Consumer Affairs Department to investigate Lorneby's business practices, deep down in his heart, Shipley knew that Lorneby hadn't done anything illegal, and that he did not engage in business practices other auction houses did not engage in as well. He slammed his wineglass down on a table. "Where do we go from here?" he asked out loud. "I'm through with paying these outrageous prices!"

In the quiet studio at his house on Waverly Place, Leon Haber applied oil paint to canvas. Usually, the act of painting relaxed him. The items for his still life were arranged on a damask cloth covered rectangular table. There was a gleaming copper pot, a bunch of purple grapes, a bowl of lemons, and a dead young rabbit. The rabbit lay limp near the edge of the table. Haber had found it early that morning under a bush in nearby Washington Square Park. Its neck had been cleanly broken. Canine or humankind, whichever was responsible, Haber told himself, this is just another reminder that the world is comprised of predators and their prey.

His painting wasn't going well. The paint stuck to the canvas in thick globs. He took a clean brush and tried to smooth the globs out. That resulted in a clump of paint being transferred to a place where it should not be. He picked up his palette knife and scraped away the excess paint. Frustrated, he screamed, "I hate you!" Gripping the palette knife, he slashed the painting to ribbons.

In a fit of rage, he strode to the table and began stabbing the dead rabbit. The dead animal did not bleed, but Haber succeeded in creating a pulverized mass of fur.

His arm froze mid-air and he stepped back, horrified, to agonize over the mutilation he had caused. I have nothing against that poor dead rabbit, he told himself. It's Neil Lorneby I hate. The way he finessed his way out of the lawsuit, taking his case to the public. And, unwittingly, Kate Callahan helped him to do it.

I have to admit I moved too fast with Kate the other night. She's so pretty and spunky. She challenged me whenever I said anything she didn't like. She put me in my place. When do I ever get a chance to meet a woman like that? I'm surrounded by simpering art students all day long. Bet Callahan is hot in bed. Bet she knows what she wants and how to get it, makes a man crazy wanting to please her. The image he created excited him.

Wonder who she's knocking boots with these days? he asked himself. He'd picked up the coarse expression from the dull-witted but curvaceous student he was dallying with this term. Well, he'd call the girl later. She was flattered by his attentions; she'd come right over.

Years ago he'd loved a woman who excited him in the same way Kate Callahan did now. The girl had been a student at the Art Institute; she'd been extraordinarily gifted, smart and talented. He invited her into his home and she stayed. In the evenings they'd set up their easels side by side, paint the same subject while listening to chamber music. Rebecca's paintings were always better than his. Much better.

And then he'd lost her to *him*, with all his money and good looks too. She'd moved out of Haber's home and into his. Months later they were married.

All these years I've pretended I didn't mind, just so I could do business with him, Haber thought. But I've never found any woman to equal Rebecca. With the possible exception of Kate Callahan, that is. And with Kate, I'll have two advantages. She doesn't paint so she won't compete with me in the studio. And because she's a dead ringer for Gustav Klimt's model, she can pose for me.

The telephone rang. He dropped the palette knife on the floor and lifted the telephone receiver. The man calling didn't bother to identify himself. He didn't have to. Haber recognized his voice instantly and had been expecting his call.

"I suppose you saw Lorneby's interview," Shipley said.

Haber replied, "I saw it. We can kiss that lawsuit goodbye. He's come out smelling like roses, as if he's the injured party."

"I guess it's time to put Plan B into effect," Shipley said.

Haber asked, "With the original art dealers from the Gotham Group?"

"The original members plus our one very silent partner, art expert Professor Leon Haber. Yes, it'll be the same players but a different game."

Haber felt the tension in his neck and shoulders ease. He liked this approach much better. "The idea of forming a consortium is a good one."

"Well, you deserve all the credit," Shipley said. "We made a mistake in thinking we could destroy his reputation with a lawsuit. Explain to me how this works again."

Haber smiled. His evening had just gotten much better. "Be glad to," he said. "With this scheme, we'll drastically reduce his commissions and we'll make money in the bargain. The dealers in the ring will agree not to bid against each other. That'll keep prices down. You'll take turns making the buy, then we'll hold a knockout among ourselves. Our own private auction, with us splitting the proceeds."

Thomas Shipley felt quite cheerful now. "Sounds like a plan!"

THIRTY-TWO

DETECTIVE LORI MARTIN needed the extra money. The Chief had authorized overtime pay for any detective who'd been assigned to the task force to assist Rick Smith and Joe Mateer with the strangler case. With a Master's degree in Psychology, and seven years on the PD under her belt, Lori worked the Sex Crimes Division. She had a comfortable way about her that put victimized women and children at ease so that they opened up and confided in her.

"She's a good one to help us interview the grieving relatives," Joe Mateer had told Rick. Three evenings a week, Lori Martin did legwork for the lead detectives.

Her own children were ages four and six and Lori would much rather be spending her evenings at home with them instead of out talking to parents whose daughters' bodies had been found in Dumpsters around the city. It's only for a month or so, she rationalized. It was hard making ends meet these days. There were school expenses for both children, their co-op mortgage, and since the first of the year the maintenance on their co-operative apartment had gone up by twenty-percent. Lori's husband, Max, was a successful psychiatrist, but even so, money was tight. Max fully supported Lori's work on the strangler case, saying that for the month or two she'd be working, he and the kids would miss her but they'd get to know each other better. But that was Max for you, she thought, always putting a positive spin on troublesome situations. No wonder she and the kids adored him.

Tonight she was interviewing Ashley Fuller's parents for the second time. "We've told you everything we know," Mrs. Fuller had said over the telephone when Lori scheduled the appointment for eight o'clock in the evening, after Mr. Fuller got home from his office in the city.

"I know, Mrs. Fuller," Lori had said sympathetically, "but sometimes just talking about the details with a trained professional will cause some forgotten memory to surface." That was a line she'd borrowed from Max.

It was dark on Maple Street but the Fullers' half-timbered Tudor-style house was lit up like an airport runway. They know only too well about the monsters who walk among us, Lori thought, as she parked on the street under a tree. She engaged her door locks with her remote control and walked up the sidewalk to the front door. Mrs. Fuller opened the door before Lori had a chance to ring the bell.

This was the second time Lori had been to the Fuller's residence but she took time to look around and absorb details as if she had never been there before. Nancy Fuller poured coffee from a silver carafe into dainty china cups. Samuel Fuller sat waiting, resigned. Both Fullers had aged since the last time she'd seen them. How hard this must be for them.

As if reading her mind, Samuel Fuller said, "Ashley was murdered right before Christmas. It's been five months now. Our lives will never be the same. In a sense our lives are over. Yet occasionally we manage to achieve a certain degree of peace and tranquility. Every time that happens, someone from NYPD calls us and wants to rehash the whole thing again, to dredge up our pain all over again."

He leaned forward, his hands on his knees. "It's not that we don't want to cooperate, Detective Martin, we do. We just want this ordeal to end. Ashley's gone, she's not coming back. No matter what we do or don't do."

"Our goals are the same, Mr. Fuller. We want this to be over too. We also want to apprehend this perpetrator so that no more girls like Ashley will die at his hands. And I'm sorry if it seems like we're intentionally shattering your peace of mind. I can assure you we're not."

"I know you're not," Mrs. Fuller said. "We're just so tired. We can't take any more."

"I understand Mrs. Fuller. I wouldn't be asking you these questions if I had any other way of learning about Ashley's habits. You knew her better than anyone."

Lori sipped her coffee, giving them time to reflect. They were good people and she knew they'd come around. She was glad to see that they had not removed Ashley's photographs from the tabletops where'd they'd been prominently displayed on Lori's last visit. Sometimes, grieving relatives had to put away pictures of their deceased loved ones because seeing their faces was too painful. The Fullers' home was furnished with fine antiques, the kind she and Max hoped to collect one day when the children were older.

Pictures of Ashley from dance recitals filled the room. In one adorable picture, Ashley couldn't have been more than five. Ashley could be described as cute, with light brown hair and a pixie face. In her grown-up pictures she looked very much the same as she had as a child, but as if someone had stretched her. At the time of her death, she'd been nineteen years old, she'd weighed 102 pounds and was five feet two inches tall. Lori had committed the details to memory.

"I'd like you to talk to me about Ashley as if I were a friend and not a detective," Lori invited. "Tell me about the things she liked to do."

"Lori loved her dancing," Mrs. Fuller said.

"We've been over this and over it," Mr. Fuller complained, setting his coffee cup down in its saucer with a clink.

Mrs. Fuller patted his hand. "Sam. Please. Maybe something will come up that we haven't thought of before. Something that will help the detectives to find this man."

Mr. Fuller sighed, but relaxed.

Mrs. Fuller continued, "Ashley loved the ballet. She ate, slept, and breathed for the ballet. Four days a week she took the train into the city to attend her ballet classes. Often she and her fellow students would take in matinee performances of the New York State Ballet at Lincoln Center. Just a few days before she died, she'd been to see the *Nutcracker*.

"About once a week, I'd meet Ashley after her classes and we'd go shopping. Then we'd meet Sam for dinner. We made an outing of it." Nancy Fuller twisted her hands. "We are…we were a very close-knit family."

"Tell me about Ashley's eyesight, Mrs. Fuller. She was wearing glasses that day when…" Lori didn't finish her sentence. There was no need to.

Sam Fuller said, "Ashley was myopic. She wore contact lenses. Naturally, she couldn't wear glasses when she danced; they'd fall off. But she always kept her glasses with her."

Nancy Fuller volunteered, "She carried one of those big bulky duffel bags like all the dancers do. In it she'd have her leotards, her toe shoes, as the girls called them, sweaters, hairbrushes. Ashley's glasses were always in that bag too."

"The coroner says she was wearing both prescription glasses and contact lenses," Lori said.

"That never made sense to me," Samuel Fuller said,

agitated. "Ashley would never wear both. There was no reason to. She carried the glasses for back up. In case she lost a contact or her eyes got irritated."

"I understand," Lori said, soothingly. "I know you've said that the clothing Ashley was wearing was not her own."

"They were not," Nancy Fuller said positively.

"In fact," Lori said, "the clothes were vintage. We've had them authenticated by Phyllis Stern."

"I know of her," Nancy said. "She's an expert. She ought to know. But what does that mean?"

Lori shook her head. "That's what we're trying to piece together. Before I go, one more thing. Kate Callahan, the television anchorwoman, has offered her show as a forum for the police to appeal to the public for information and call-ins. Ms. Callahan would like to have all the deceased girls' relatives on her show."

"No way!" Samuel Fuller declared.

Lori asked, her voice neutral, "Did you happen to see her show last night?"

"We did not," he answered. "We make it a point to avoid the news these days."

"I'd probably do the same myself," Lori said. "The latest victim's mother and boyfriend appeared on the show with investigative reporter Evan Wallace and detectives Smith and Mateer. We got two call-ins with new and important information about Regina Hoover's case as a result of that show. That's why we think that Ms. Callahan's idea is a sound one."

"But if people have information, why don't they simply come forward without our having to be put through the ordeal of talking about our loss in public?" Samuel Fuller demanded.

Lori shrugged. "Human nature, Mr. Fuller. They think

the information they have is not important enough to warrant involvement with the police and later with the courts. Let's face it, being a good citizen these days can be a real hassle. But we think that once they see and connect with the relatives, real people like themselves, they'll come forward. That's what happened last night. Something good could come of it. Please consider being on the show."

As the Fullers walked Lori to the door, Lori said, "One last thing, you haven't discussed the antique clothing with anyone, have you?"

"No," both Fullers responded at once.

"Good. It's an important clue and the fewer people who know, the better. And it's one clue that won't be mentioned on the show either. Please consider joining the other families and appearing on the show. It'll be tomorrow night. Kate Callahan will call you in the morning. Good night."

Wonder what I'd do in their position? Lori asked herself as she walked to her car. She couldn't wait to get home to Max and the kids and their wholesome life. Tomorrow she had to start all over again interviewing Ashley Fuller's friends at the dance studio. The answer is there, somewhere, she thought as she put the car in gear. There's no way he could kill all those girls without leaving a trail.

THIRTY-THREE

MARTY SOKOLOV LIVED with his mother and sister in a rent-controlled apartment in Yorkville on East Eighty-sixth Street between First and York avenues. Marty's mother Irene was a nurse at New York Hospital. Irene thought the world of Dolly Devereaux, alias Posey the clown. "She's an angel," Irene often told Marty. "She makes those dear children laugh and forget their troubles."

It's a good thing Mom's a nurse, Marty always said. His little sister Debbie had been born with a congenital heart defect that was inoperable; she would probably not live to see her sixteenth birthday. Marty's wish for Deb was that she would pass peacefully in her sleep. She'd been hospitalized too many times, and Marty couldn't bear the sight of her being hooked up to all those machines.

Marty's dad had flown the coop after Deb was born. Marty felt only contempt for a man who would abandon his family when they needed him most. Mom sure has had her hands full, Marty thought, as he steered the limo into the Seventy-second Street Transverse and drove it uptown and across Central Park to the East Side. Until recently I've been one of her burdens. Well, that's all changed. I've changed.

He glanced into the rearview mirror. Kate Callahan had her head back, her eyes closed. I can sure understand why's she's tired, he thought. She's been going non-stop since eight-thirty this morning, was on live television from seven to eight, and here it is almost ten-thirty.

He checked his side mirror. Recently Marty had the feeling they were being followed. On Tuesday night when he was driving her home after her dinner with Dolly Devereaux, a black van had stayed with them all the way to Kate's building. He'd walked Miss Callahan across the sidewalk until the doorman took over. When he returned to the limo there was no sign of the van.

He wasn't going to let anything happen to Kate Callahan. That's what he'd been hired to do. But now he'd look out for her for nothing, if it ever came to that. She was a nice lady and he liked her. She was always polite to him and took a genuine interest in his life. You can tell when people are sincere and when they're just being phony, he thought. Kate Callahan asked about Deb every day. "I hope Debbie never has to return to the hospital, Marty," she said just yesterday, "but if she ever does, let me know. I'll make sure she has lots of flowers and I'll tell Dolly about her so Dolly can be sure to visit her often."

On Tuesday, Miss Callahan had asked him to pick up her grandfather and drive him to the studio and then back home. Jerry Callahan was some guy! He'd insisted on sitting up front with Marty. "I ain't no swell," Mr. Callahan had told him. "Don't go thinking I'm gonna sit back there all by myself when you're up here alone. I'm sitting up here with you so we can shoot the breeze."

All those old veterans are dying off, Marty thought. And taking their exciting stories with them. He remembered his mom's father telling them his war stories, about heroes and battles and important generals, before the old man succumbed to the malaria he'd contracted in the Pacific. Bet Jerry Callahan's got some stories of his own to tell. I'd sure like to hear them, Marty thought.

Marty stopped for a red light on Fifth Avenue. Maybe if there'd been a big war on when I was coming up and

I'd'a had a chance to go off and fight and become a hero, I wouldn't have got in so much trouble, Marty reflected. But hanging around the house, watching Deb suffer, seeing how hard Mom had to work to take care of Deb and support us, well, I just took to the streets. Started cutting classes, hanging out with the wrong crowd.

One thing led to another, and before I knew it I was doing a juvie stint at Spofford. If it hadn't been for Tony Mastriani I'd never have survived that hell hole. But Tony took me under his wing, liked me for some reason. He got me into boxing and I was good at that. Now they tell me I look like a prize fighter, that I scare away the bums with just one look. Hell, I was a golden gloves champ. Yeah, he thought derisively, the golden gloves champ of Spofford. Big friggin' deal.

I owe Tony big time. After Spofford, Tony looked out for me. It wasn't so much that he kept me from getting into trouble, he kept me from getting caught. Showed me how to survive on the street, and not attract the cops' attention.

Then Tony got a good job driving for Mr. Thompson, and protecting him too. Soon's this job came up, he recommended me to Mr. Thompson. And I sure like driving Miss Callahan around. But as grateful as I am to Tony, I don't like reporting to him on where Miss Callahan goes and who she sees. And, heck, what is there to report? It ain't like Miss Callahan's a bimbo who's sleeping around. All she does is go to work and then back home to her grandfather. One night she goes out to eat with Dolly Devereaux who's her best girlfriend. Another she goes to a restaurant with that dope Haber.

I sure didn't like the way that professor was talking to Miss Callahan, trying to scare her about stalkers, Marty thought and felt his temper flare. It's just like Tony always says: a man can have brains and a shitload of degrees, but without common sense he's worthless. I wish I could get my hands on that Haber; I'd shake some sense into him.

The light turned green and Marty pulled into the one-way traffic headed south on Fifth Avenue. He drove past the Metropolitan Museum of Art, all lit up with flood-lights. Maybe he'd hire a sitter for Deb on Sunday and bring his mom to the museum on Sunday afternoon. A special exhibit on party clothes was opening in the Costume Department. Mom loved pretty clothes, not that she owned any. When was the last time she had an outing? Now that he was earning a decent salary he was helping with the bills. And in the afternoons when Miss Callahan didn't need him, she insisted that he go home for a few hours and keep Debbie company while his mother worked. It sure feels good to be doing something useful for Mom and Deb these days, he told himself.

I don't ever want to lose this job. But I sure as hell hate being a rat. Well, I've reached a decision about that: if Miss Callahan ever does anything out of the way, like she gets a new boyfriend or something, Tony and his boss will never hear about it from me. And they won't hear it from me that this morning she had me drive her to One Police Plaza so she could talk to that detective, Rick Smith, either.

Kate Callahan's voice brought him out of his musings. "Marty, Granddad would like you to come up and have a late supper with us. My grandfather happens to be a fabulous cook and he's fixed his special lasagna just for you."

THIRTY-FOUR

THE VICTIMS' RELATIVES congregated in Mike Cramer's conference room. Kate and Evan were there, as were Detectives Rick Smith and Joe Mateer. Kate's assistant Dolores poured coffee and handed out creamer packets. A tray on the credenza was piled high with assorted Danish pastries. Although he was on Cramer's turf, Rick Smith was clearly in charge. Rick stood at the head of the table, thanking everyone for cooperating, and assuring them that something good would come of their going on Kate's show. Eight-hundred number telephones were being installed on the set. Rick hoped they'd get some real leads.

Once the grieving relatives started talking to each other, there was no stopping them. They had so much in common, they easily understood what the others were going through. They began to interact like a support group.

Elaine and Paul Parker, Celeste's parents, had stayed overnight at a hotel, delaying their return to Madison, Wisconsin so that they could participate on tonight's show. Mrs. Parker was sitting with her head inclined, listening intently to what Elsie Hoover, Regina's mother, had to say. On Elsie's other side, Bill Lockhart, Regina's boyfriend, sat stoically, looking like he was holding himself together through sheer willpower.

Ashley Fuller's parents, Sam and Nancy, the couple from Scarsdale, sat a little to one side, aloof from the others yet holding hands under the table.

They all look shell-shocked, Kate thought. Mike Cramer was just about to explain the segment's format when Ray Dixon started to speak. The Dixons, Jolene and Ray, had taken an early morning flight from Mobile, Alabama. Their daughter, twenty-one-year-old Courtney, had been victim #3, murdered on April 15th, found in a Dumpster dressed up like a Gibson girl.

Ray Dixon was an unsophisticated man, but prosperous. He owned and managed a chain of automotive spare parts service centers throughout the Deep South. "I didn't approve of Courtney's comin' up here. I've never liked New York City." He surveyed the assembled group. "No offense to you folks who live here. Guess you can't help where you were born.

"But my Courtney was born in the South, and she should've stayed there. She didn't have city smarts. I always knew this would come to no good end." He covered his face with a large hand.

Jolene Dixon seemed to feel she had to explain for her husband. She's been smoothing over his rough edges all their married life, Kate thought to herself. Jolene Dixon was blonde and plump, soft in appearance and soft spoken, yet tough under her ladylike veneer. I've met my first steel magnolia, Kate told herself.

Mrs. Dixon said, "What Ray means is that Courtney was a friendly, trusting girl. That's the way we do things down home. It would never occur to Courtney to be suspicious of a stranger.

"I agreed with her daddy. I didn't want her to come up here either. But when she turned twenty-one, she said, 'I'm of age now, Mama, and you can't stop me. I'll pay my own way, but I'm going to graduate from NYU's Institute of Fine Arts because it's the best. It's always been my dream to work at the Metropolitan Museum of Art, and I'll get an internship there when I'm a senior.'"

"And was she able to support herself?" Kate asked, suspecting that the real story was that Jolene sent Courtney money without telling Ray, and Ray sent Courtney money without telling Jolene.

"Yes, ma'am, she sure did. Truth be told, I'm right proud of that little gal. She supported herself by working as a model." Mrs. Dixon got a faraway look in her eyes. "If you ever saw Courtney, you'd understand why. She's the prettiest little thing you ever laid eyes on. Ain't that right, Ray?"

Ray Dixon swallowed his emotions. "Pretty don't begin to describe our Courtney. And that girl had grit. She never asked us for a cent."

"But I flew up here about once a month," Jolene Dixon said. "I took her shopping and saw that she had warm clothes." She shook her head. "How y'all live through these winters, I'll never know. She wouldn't take money from us but she did let me furnish that closet she called an apartment. We did that together. Fixed it up right nice." Tears spilled from her eyes.

"I'd give anything to have one more shopping trip with my Regina," Elsie Hoover wept.

"Oh, me too," Nancy Parker agreed, finally opening up. She smiled. "Ashley and I hit the stores twice a week. We were the original 'shop till you drop' girls."

Kate scribbled a note and passed it to Rick Smith. He read: Did Professor Leon Haber know Courtney Dixon?

He wrote back: According to her class schedule she was not registered in any of his classes. We questioned her instructors, but had no reason to question Haber. Why?

Kate turned the paper over and wrote: He was on my show on Wednesday night. Just thought he might have known her.

Rick read the note, gave Kate a sideways glance and a tiny smile. It's so nice having him near, she thought, being friends again. First and foremost, we *were* friends.

THIRTY-FIVE

THE TRAFFIC ON Fifth Avenue at four-twenty P.M. was bumper to bumper. Buses came in bunches, slow and lumbering, blocking the center lanes. The few cabs he saw were occupied.

Unlike Wednesday when he'd watched Dolly Devereaux's building from inside his van on a beautiful spring day, the weather today was not pleasant. Gloomy skies and dark clouds threatened a rain storm. The impending rain added to the doorman's difficulty in assisting his many tenants. The man had his hands full. This was the hour when women hurried home from their lunches out and their shopping excursions, arms filled with shopping bags. To add to the general air of confusion, a Federal Express truck was double-parked at the curb, the driver hastily delivering envelopes to the over-burdened doorman.

He had planned his arrival well. Even the white-haired older lady with the standard poodle was right on schedule, exiting the building and starting her walk around the block.

At any moment Dolly Devereaux, dressed as Posey the clown, should come dashing out, he thought. But he couldn't take a chance that this evening might be the one time she had other plans. He had to have her this weekend. He'd filled the blue bowl with fresh oranges this afternoon, then given the set a last once over. Everything was ready and waiting.

He retrieved his cell phone and dialed Miss Devereaux's number. Although her telephone was unlisted, he'd managed to find it on the Internet. Every bit of information was available on the Internet, provided one knew how to access it. He did.

The phone rang inside Miss Devereaux's apartment. "Hello," she said.

"Miss Devereaux, it's Randy Herman at the hospital. Little Kevin has taken a sudden turn for the worse. He's been calling for Posey. I knew you'd want to come right away."

"I'm on my way, Randy. And thank you for letting me know. I'll be there soon if I have to run all the way."

You won't have to run, he thought, as smiling to himself he pushed the END button.

The Federal Express truck pulled away from the building and he had an unobstructed view of the entrance from his vantage point across Fifth Avenue. Posey did not disappoint. Within minutes she came rushing out of the building. The doorman was helping a young mother maneuver a stroller with two crying toddlers through the door. He saw the doorman gesture for Posey to wait.

Posey stopped on the sidewalk, took one look at the heavy traffic, and started off around the corner at a trot. Waiting for the light to turn red and the avenue's traffic to come to a halt, he whipped away from his place at the curb and cut in front of three lanes of traffic. The clown was running along ahead, on the sidewalk adjoining Sixty-second Street. She passed the old lady with the poodle, but this time did not slow to give the dog's head a pat.

Just as she stepped off the curb into Madison Avenue, he intercepted her. Turning left at the corner, his van blocked her way. Before she could walk around the van, he jumped out and grabbed her arm.

She didn't resist. He had the element of surprise on his side. She seemed not to know what was happening to her.

Or perhaps she was distracted by her concern over little Kevin and was too preoccupied to feel threatened. She merely looked into his face, her expression concealed by the painted-on smile, yet her eyes asking, Don't I know you from somewhere?

As he pushed her into the van, she came out of her trance and began to struggle. She cried out, but by then it was too late. He had already jammed her inside, and was scrambling in after her. "Stop!" she screamed. "What are you doing? Let me go."

But no one could hear her. The windows were up and locked by the master lock on his side. He punched the DOOR LOCK button before he pulled the hypodermic needle out of his shirt pocket. The windows were tinted black so no one could see her fists pounding on them. No one saw when her fists stopped beating and her head hit the window.

Jaywalkers flowed in front of his van. Horns honked behind him. If anyone had noticed a man pulling a clown into a van, they had either ignored it or thought it was a stunt, just another New York Minute. New Yorkers are so jaded, he thought. He relied on their indifference to let him get away with a multitude of sins. And they never let him down. They didn't want to get involved. They hadn't seen a thing.

ELLA HESTER AND her poodle reached the corner of Madison and Sixty-second just as the black van was pulling away. "This is as far as we'll go, JoJo. It's about to pour." She turned to retrace their steps but the dog stubbornly refused to budge. "Now come on, JoJo, don't be like that," she urged, tugging on the leash until the dog let himself be led back toward Fifth Avenue. She had seen Posey the clown hurry by. Everyone in the building knew Dolly Devereaux and liked her. They especially admired her dedication to entertaining the children at New York Hospital. "I thought we'd catch up with Dolly at the corner," she said aloud to JoJo. "I know how much you like her." The intelligent dog gave her a worried look. "She must have caught a cab on Madison. Wasn't she lucky with this storm brewing?"

A growl rumbled low in the poodle's throat.

THIRTY-SIX

HEADS TURNED WHEN Kate preceded Jerry through the street entrance into the Cafe Carlyle at ten P.M. The rain had let up and she was wearing a simple black crepe dinner dress with a V-neck and long sleeves. Her hair fell around her shoulders in loose waves.

She's oblivious to the attention she attracts, Jerry thought, or maybe she's just used to it. At fourteen, Kate had blossomed, and each year she got prettier. At thirty-three her face had developed character, its contours were defined, and some of her fierce determination shone through. And that's far more attractive than youthful blandness, Jerry reflected. She doesn't know how much she resembles my mother: the way she cocks her head when she listens, the way she looks when she gets mad. Ma, all over again. And my ma was a knockout, even in her faded cotton housedresses.

Jerry shook hands with the *maitre'd*. "How ya doin, Mr. Callahan?" the man asked. Jerry had friends all over town, in every walk of life.

"Couldn't be better, Timmy. Listen, me and Kate are meeting Miss Devereaux here, so be sure to bring her to our table when she comes in. You got yourself a nice crowd here tonight, Timmy."

Bobby Short was playing the piano and singing a medley of Cole Porter tunes. Seeing Kate, he launched into *You're the Top*, a tribute to Kate that he sang when she was in the audience with her grandfather. Written by Porter in

1934 for the Broadway show, *Anything Goes,* the song lists favorite people and Short professed publicly that Kate was one of his favorite people.

At a small round table, Kate ordered a dry Martini. "Glenfiddich, for me," Jerry said. "Straight up."

"You're looking pretty spiffy tonight, your nibs," Kate told Jerry. "I like you in navy. Brings out your blue eyes. You're still a handsome man, Granddad." She grinned. "And I know someone else who thinks so." Her voice conveyed a teasing lilt.

Jerry draped an arm over the back of his chair and turned to survey the room. "I don't know what you're talking about," he said, his face averted.

"Oh yes, you do," Kate teased.

Short sang, "When Katie died at eighty, they buried her in state. Cause Katie loved her Haiti, and prac-tic-a-lly all Haiti loved Katie!" The drummer rolled into a staccato finale.

Short gave Kate a salute, and Kate bowed her head, acknowledging the tribute. Short segued into another Porter tune. Kate looked at her watch, then at the door. "Dolly's late."

"She'll be here."

The waiter brought their drinks. "Here's lookin' at you, kid," Jerry said, then swallowed appreciatively. "Your show tonight was a real tearjerker, Kate. And when that call came in from the guy who ate his supper every night at the coffee shop where Celeste Parker worked as a waitress, I was on the edge of my seat. Said she was popular with the regulars and had a real following. Suggested that maybe one of them tried to get cozy with her and she rebuffed him, and maybe the guy didn't take it so good. Now I think that's worth looking into."

"Rick thinks so too. He and Joe are getting descripti⬤ and names if they can, of the regulars at Flo's coffee sh⬤

"So how's that going? You and him working togeth⬤ Jerry asked.

"Okay. It was *I* who approached *him* about teaming with me on this show, not the other way around." Ka⬤ Martini was cool and smooth in her mouth. If I dr⬤ enough of this stuff, she thought, bemused, I could ⬤ out a song like Bobby. It was good to put work behind ⬤ to celebrate the start of the weekend with Jerry and D⬤ For as long as she could remember, she'd been celebra⬤ the end of, first, the school week, and later the work w⬤ and the start of a fun weekend with them. She glance⬤ the door, expecting Dolly to enter at any moment.

Without warning, Jerry announced, "You know, ma⬤ we've been too hard on Rick Smith."

Kate gulped, almost choking on her drink. "What ⬤

"I've been giving this a lot of thought. I never s⬤ anybody as in love with a girl as that boy was with y⬤

"Granddad!" Kate declared. "He dumped me."

"Well, you know what I think?"

"No. And I don't want to know."

"I think that he had some misguided idea that he ⬤ sparing you from a lifetime of worry and fear." Jerry li⬤ his eyebrows emphatically and nodded his head. "Yes. that's just what I think. Crazy kid probably saw the ⬤ divorce rate at the PD and decided he was gonna save ⬤ heartache and a rocky marriage."

Kate set her glass down with a thump. "I don't v⬤ to talk about this. Where's Dolly? She's already an l⬤ late." Kate picked up her handbag from the extra en⬤ chair and pulled out her cell phone.

"If you're gonna go talking on that thing, take it ⬤ the ladies' room," Jerry said grumpily. "I've had it v⬤

all these people screaming in their idiot cell phones. Other day, I get in a cab. We're in crosstown traffic. The cabbie's got a cell phone in one hand, and he's fiddling with the radio dial with the other hand. He's yelling in the phone because he can't hear over the noise on the radio. Soon's we stop at a red light, I get out. Cabbie's screaming at me for his fare. I tell 'em, 'Shuddup, bub, or I'll have 'em pull your medallion.' They should all get brain cancer."

"Okay. I'm going, I'm going," Kate said, standing up. "Get off your soap box."

In the ladies' room, Kate tried Dolly's number at her apartment. No answer. She combed her hair, and freshened her lipstick. Tried again. Still no answer. She dialed Dolly's cell phone and got a message that the phone was turned off.

"Huh?" she said aloud.

"Something's wrong," Kate said, returning to the table. "She's not answering."

"Did you try her cell phone?" Jerry asked. He was on his second drink and drumming his fingers to the beat of the music.

"Of course."

Jerry pulled his eyes away from the stage long enough to say, "Did ya try the hospital?"

"No. I'll try now. Do I have to go back in the ladies' room again? I'll whisper."

Jerry turned back to Kate. "Sure. Call from here. Bobby's taking a break."

Kate finished her call to the hospital and reported, "No, she's not at the hospital. She never showed up. Now, I'm really getting worried. Something's wrong, I tell you. This isn't like Dolly. She would have called if something came up. And she never skips an evening at the hospital."

"Well, we can leave if you're really worried. It's a nice

night. We'll take a walk down Fifth Avenue and check on her at her apartment," Jerry suggested.

"But, Granddad, she's not answering the phone at her apartment."

Jerry gave her a thoughtful look. "Yeah, sweetheart, you said that."

JERRY TOOK KATE'S arm and started down Madison Avenue. He was much more concerned about Dolly than he wanted Kate to know. Kate was right, Dolly would have called if she couldn't make it. Dolly was considerate and would never leave them to wait and worry about her.

Unless she couldn't help it, he thought. He had visions of her lying on the floor, unconscious, after tripping over something. Or maybe she slipped and fell in the shower, he thought.

He talked, trying to distract Kate and himself. "You sure she didn't tell you she was going on one of her trips where she looks for pottery?"

"No, Granddad. When we had dinner on Tuesday night, she specifically reminded me that we were getting together at the Carlyle tonight."

Jerry didn't know what to say. "Well, it's a good thing Marty's off-duty, otherwise, we'd have him trailin' along behind us in that big limo."

"No. If Marty was here, he could drive us. Hurry up, Granddad. Can't you walk faster?"

"I'm walking as fast as I can. Here's a cab pullin' up. Let's grab it."

In the back of the cab, Jerry felt a cramping in his stomach. "Guess I got a little indigestion," he said. "Sorry I'm so grumpy." The truth is, he told himself, I got a pain in my gut from worry. What if something's happened to our Dolly? I got a bad feeling. Now I know what Ma meant when she said she could feel something in her bones. You do feel it in your bones when something bad's happened.

Kate patted his hand. "It's okay. I'm used to your grumpiness. It's part of your charm."

Jerry groaned. "Sure, my charm."

The cab bumped along to Seventy-second Street, then cut over to Fifth. The doorman on duty at Dolly's building ran to get the door for Kate. She didn't recognize him. "Where's Primo?" she asked. Primo was the building's regular night doorman.

The substitute wore a military-style uniform and seemed to take himself seriously. "He's off tonight. What can I do for you folks?"

Jerry stuck out his hand. "Jerry Callahan. Pleased to meet'cha. And this is my daughter, Kate. We're friends of Miss Devereaux."

Taken aback because few visitors shook hands with him, the doorman said, "I'm Carlo. And I know who you are, Miss. I'll buzz Miss Devereaux for you." He stepped inside the lobby to a panel with apartment extensions and a handset.

Jerry looked at Kate. "Let him try." They stepped inside the lobby after him.

"Sorry, folks, Miss Devereaux ain't home. She don't answer."

Kate said, "She was supposed to meet us two hours ago. We're worried. Can we go up and take a look?"

The doorman shook his head and gave them a disapproving look. "I'm sorry, ma'am. You know I can't let you do that."

"But she could be hurt. Or sick," Kate argued.

"Look, Miss Devereaux probably got the date mixed up, something like that. I can't let you go up there," he said officiously.

"Well, could *you* go up and make sure she's all righ
Kate asked.

"Miss Callahan, I'd sure like to help you out, but I c
leave my post. If I did, I'd have to lock the front door
the tenants don't like that. Tell you what, I'll try to f
one of the maintenance men and have him go up and ch
on Miss Devereaux."

"Kate, we can't do no more here," Jerry said.

"Okay. Thanks," Kate said to the doorman. "Here's
card. Call me at my home number. I'll be waiting."

Jerry handed him a ten. "We appreciate it, Carlo."

"That ain't necessary, Mr. Callahan."

"Go on, take it."

"Thanks. I'll keep a watch out for Miss Devere
and if she comes in tonight, I'll be sure to tell her yo
looking for her."

"Let's go, Kate," Jerry said, taking her arm.

"Johnny, the day man, would've let me in," Kate r
tered. "And so would Primo." She wheeled around to
doorman. "Carlo, what time did Miss Devereaux go
tonight?"

"I didn't see her go out, Miss. I came on duty at ei
She must'a left before then. Don't worry, Miss Calla
I'll have someone check the apartment for you."

Jerry steered Kate to the corner. Kate was dee
thought. Her thoughts chased around inside her hea
circles. "I wish I'd taken the key to Dolly's apartment
time when she wanted me to have one. I should have.

Jerry stopped. "Kate, this kind of second-guessing
gonna solve nothing. Dolly's all right. Something just c
up she had to attend to and she's gone off to take car
it. She'll call tomorrow and explain. There might eve
a message on our answering machine at home."

"I'll call home and see," Kate said brightly. "G

thinking, Granddad." But dialing her home phone for messages was a disappointment. "Nothing," she said. "No messages."

"Well, she'll call in the morning," Jerry said cheerfully. "Now come on, the rain's cleaned things up. Let's take a walk across Fifty-seventh Street, get some fresh air. I want to stop at Chantilly's and pick up a blackberry tart to take home. You remember how crazy your grandma was about their blackberry tarts."

"Granddad, how can you think about dessert at a time like this?"

I'm not thinking about dessert, Jerry wanted to say. I'm worried about Dolly, same as you. But if I let you see how scared I am, it'll be worse for you.

THE BLACKBERRY TART sat in the middle of the kitchen table, untouched. Kate couldn't swallow, neither could Jerry. "I'm too keyed up to go to bed," Kate complained.

Jerry picked up the pie and put it in the refrigerator. "Maybe tomorrow. Kate, everything's gonna be just fine."

The phone rang.

"Miss Callahan. This is Carlo. I got ahold of Richie and had him go up to check Miss Devereaux's apartment. He looked in all the rooms. Nobody home."

THE NEXT MORNING the day doorman tipped his hat. "'Morning, Miss Callahan, Mr. Callahan. You folks are out early this morning. Miss Devereaux expecting you?"

"No, Johnny," Kate said. "Would you buzz her apartment and see if she's there?"

"Sure thing. How ya doin, Mr. Callahan?"

Jerry didn't respond; he simply nodded. He'd had a bad night with chest pains that he hadn't wanted Kate to know about. Probably just indigestion, he told himself.

At about four A.M., he'd taken a healthy slug of antacid, finally falling into a restless sleep. When Kate woke him at seven, insisting that they had to go to Dolly's, he felt groggy and disoriented.

The crisp morning air had invigorated him though. Across Fifth Avenue, Central Park was green, shady, and inviting.

"She's not answering, Miss Callahan. But you say she wasn't expecting you? Funny, I didn't see her go out this morning," Johnny remarked.

"We're really worried about her, Johnny," Kate said. "She was supposed to meet us at ten last night and she never showed up. We stopped by here on our way home at about midnight, but she wasn't in. Carlo sent a maintenance man up to check on her but the apartment was empty."

Johnny pushed his hat up off his forehead. "I can see why you're worried, Miss Callahan. The last time I saw Miss Devereaux was sometime around four-thirty yesterday afternoon. She was going over to the hospital. Dressed in her clown suit, same as she does every day."

Kate squeezed her hands together. "Well, she never reached the hospital, Johnny. Will you take us up to her apartment, so we can look around?"

"Sure thing, Miss Callahan. Just let me get Richie up here to watch the door." Johnny reached for the house phone.

Ten minutes later, he was unlocking Dolly's apartment door for Kate and Jerry. "You folks take all the time you need. I know you and I trust you. Miss Devereaux wouldn't object at all to you being here. Use the intercom if you need me."

The apartment was unnaturally still. "Granddad, you check the kitchen, I'll check the bedroom and her closets."

"What am I supposed to be looking for?" Jerry asked. The chest pains were back and he broke out in a sweat. He turned his face away from Kate.

"I don't know. Anything unusual. Just look."

In the kitchen, Jerry sat down heavily and slumped over Dolly's kitchen table. I can see the entire room from here, he thought, so I'm checking the kitchen. Okay, heart, he told himself, calm down. Kate's got enough to worry about without you acting up.

In Dolly's bedroom Kate opened closet doors. She was looking for a gap in clothing on the rod, an open space to indicate that Dolly had removed outfits. But all the hangers ran close together, neat and orderly. Nothing had been pushed aside. In a hall closet, Kate found Dolly's luggage, and saw no empty spaces on the shelves where an individual piece might have once been stored, then removed.

In the bathroom, Dolly's medicine cabinet was well stocked, and again there were no gaps to indicate that medications or lotions had been taken. Nothing seemed to be missing from her lucite makeup box, and the paint box with her clown's grease paint was well-stocked and stored in the bathroom's linen closet.

Next, Kate went to Dolly's desk and lifted her appointment book. For each day of the week, a large "H" was penned in between the hours of five and eight. "H" for hospital, Kate told herself. For Friday, May 12, Dolly had noted, "Meet K & J at CC, 10." I never doubted that she was planning to come, Kate thought, but this proves it.

She walked through the other rooms. Everything looked the same as it always did. Nothing was disturbed. Dolly liked things neat. A place for everything and everything in its place, was her motto.

Kate had an idea and went back into Dolly's bedroom and straight back to her desk. She hit the REDIAL button on Dolly's telephone. After a series of rings, she heard her own voice asking that the caller leave a message. The last number Dolly had dialed had been to Kate's voice mail at the station. I got that message yesterday afternoon, Kate thought. Dolly had left a message saying, "Looking forward to a fun night out. See you."

Kate tried dialing *69. She got an automated recording informing her the last number that called Dolly's phone could not be identified. "So it was blocked," Kate said out loud. Still that meant nothing; every telemarketing outfit blocked its calls.

In the kitchen, she found Jerry peering into the refrigerator. Slamming the door, he said, "Well stocked with fresh produce. Doesn't look like she was going away. This place is sure neat."

"She wasn't going away," Kate said with certainty. "She was going to meet us last night. But something happened to her. And oh, Granddad, what are we going to do about it?"

THIRTY-SEVEN

DOLLY TRIED TO open her eyes but her lids were so heavy she could barely flutter her lashes. Her arms and legs felt like dead weights; they wouldn't move. What had wakened her? Oh, yes, the cold. She was terribly cold. Sometimes, if she was having a restless night, her satin comforter slipped off the bed. That must have happened. She had only to roll over and grab the edge of it and pull it back up onto the bed. That was easy to do. The comforter was as light as a feather. She didn't even have to open her eyes.

Why couldn't she roll over? she wondered. I'm so tired I can't move. Is that music I hear? Did I fall asleep with the stereo playing again? Before she could remember the answer to her questions, she sank back into a deep, dreamless sleep.

The next time she woke, she was aware again of numbing coldness and of a bright light shining in her face. The light hurt her eyes when she tried to open them. Her hand was resting on her knee. She lifted it to shield her eyes from the glare.

"Don't move," a man's voice commanded.

Dolly gasped and opened her eyes, squinting between her fingers. Who was in her room? No, this was not her room. This was a stark white room. A studio. Where was she? And who was this man? He was familiar, yet she couldn't place him.

She was so cold she shivered. Icy air flowed over her

bare skin, making the hair stand on end. Oh my God, she was naked!

Dolly struggled to get to her feet, but some unseen bond held her to the floor. "Let me go!" she screamed. "Untie me!"

"Sit still," the man barked. "You're ruining everything. And put your hand back on your knee."

"The light is blinding me," Dolly whimpered.

"Oh, all right, I'll dim it for a minute, but only if you'll sit still."

Dolly promised, thinking that if she could see the room better and get a good look at this man, she might know where she was and figure out why she was here.

The man moved a few feet to a wall switch and dimmed the lights. Without the light shining painfully in her eyes, Dolly lowered her left arm to her right knee.

The man crossed back to his position behind an easel. He's painting me, she thought. Not only has he removed my clown suit and makeup but he is making a painting of me nude. How did I get here? she asked herself.

And then it all came flooding back. The call from Randy the nurse telling her to hurry to the hospital because Kevin was worse. Rushing from the building. Seeing no available cabs. Hurrying over to Madison to look for one. Then the black van cutting her off, the man jumping out, grabbing her arm, thrusting her inside before she even knew what was happening. She looked at his face. Yes, he was the man who had grabbed her. She studied him. Her mind was so foggy, but he was someone she'd seen recently. Yes, now she had it. She placed him and knew exactly who he was.

She'd tried to open the van door but it was locked. She'd pounded on the window, hoping to attract someone's attention, but no one could see in through the tinted glass.

And with all the street noise, no one heard her fists beating the window. And then the man had lunged at her, and done something to her, for she had fallen asleep.

I've been kidnapped, she thought. He'll demand a ransom. He knows how rich I am. And he's some kind of amateur painter and he is amusing himself during the wait by painting my portrait.

She looked down. A long white silk scarf was draped over her left thigh and threaded between her legs. Under the silk she could feel the roughness of rope. Her bond. He did that, she thought. This man undressed me, touched me, bound my leg to the floor, then placed a cloth between my legs so that I would not be totally exposed.

"Don't move your head," he snapped. He stepped from behind the easel, a painter's palette in his left hand, a paint brush in his right, and started toward her.

Dolly lifted her chin. As long as he's painting me, he isn't touching me, she reasoned. Had he raped her? She felt no soreness. But her limbs did feel stiff and heavy. And she was cold. She'd been drugged, that was the reason for her light-headedness, her heavy limbs. Everything seemed unreal and distant. It was like she wasn't really here, like she was outside herself but observing what was happening to her. And it was so hard to think. She forced herself to concentrate on her surroundings.

She was half-sitting, half-lying on a pile of oriental rugs. To her right a blue and white Chinese *jardinière* contained a potted plant. Next to her left knee, there was a blue bowl filled with oranges. Beyond the bowl stood a marble-topped table. There was something familiar about the items that surrounded her. Where had she seen them before? If she could remember, she might know where she was. What this was all about.

She forced herself to sit still, although her legs and

arms cramped, and her cold flesh was covered with goose bumps. She didn't want to make him mad. She didn't want him to hurt her. Some worry was nagging at the corners of her brain. Her brain felt soft, like jelly, like mush. It took the most intense concentration to think through a single idea from beginning to end. Yes, she'd been drugged.

The worrisome idea was pushing its way forward. There was some flaw in her logic. What was it? Then the idea hit her brain like a shaft of white light. He could not ask for her ransom. There was no one he could ask. I have no family, she reminded herself. No one has access to my money but me, she realized.

He's going to kill me, she thought. She pulled against the rope that held her to the floor. Struggling to get up, she screamed, "Let me out of here! You've got to let me go!"

With exaggerated patience, the man set his palette and brush down on a table and picked up another object. As he approached her with it, Dolly saw that he held a hypodermic needle between his long, slender fingers.

"No," she cried. The needle's sting pricked her thigh.

THIRTY-EIGHT

In their Fifth Avenue apartment, located four blocks south of the Metropolitan Museum of Art, Jerry stretched out in his recliner. "This feels good," he told Kate. "I didn't sleep too good last night."

Kate was pacing. "I didn't sleep a wink." She paused to peer at Jerry. "You feeling all right? You look a little peaked."

"Nothing wrong with me that being fifty again won't cure," Jerry replied gruffly.

Kate resumed her pacing. "Granddad, if we go to the police, they'll just tell us that Dolly hasn't been missing for forty-eight hours so they can't do anything about it. What do you think of my calling Rick? He used to know Dolly. He knows she's not a scatterbrain."

"I think that's a fine idea. I'm worried myself," he admitted. *But much more worried than I'm gonna let you see,* he thought. "Do you mind if I just close my eyes for a bit while you call him?"

Kate came over and kissed him on the forehead. "No, Granddad, you go ahead and rest. Are you warm? Your forehead's clammy. I'll go make the call from my bedroom."

I forget that Granddad is getting old, she told herself as she dialed Rick's office number. *I think of him as immortal.*

Rick picked up on the second ring. "Detective Smith," he identified himself.

"Rick, it's Kate."

There was a brief pause before Rick said, "Hi, Kate, what can I do for you?"

All business, Kate thought. Well, that's what I proposed, isn't it? "Rick, I have a problem that I need your help with. Dolly's disappeared. You remember what Dolly's like. She's the most responsible person you'd ever want to meet, and she hasn't changed any in the years since you last saw her. If anything, she's more responsible and more considerate."

Over the speakerphone, Kate heard a creak as Rick's chair snapped into an upright position. "Tell me what you mean by disappeared, Kate. When was the last time you saw her?"

Kate could tell by the edge in his voice that Rick was taking her call seriously. He was, after all, heading an investigation of multiple murders that involved disappearing females, and where the outcome was the worst scenario imaginable.

Kate filled him in on Dolly's failure to meet her and Jerry last night, and of her efforts to locate Dolly.

"Okay, Kate, sit tight. I'll make some phone calls, then I'm coming right over. In the meantime, I want you to call Dolly's other friends and anyone you can think of."

"Thanks, Rick. I knew you'd help. Call me right away if you learn anything." Like, if Dolly was hit by a runaway cab and is now lying unconscious in a hospital, Kate thought, but dared not give voice to her fears.

Kate leafed through her address book and called the friends she and Dolly shared. The truth was they were few. Dolly, Jerry, and Kate were happy with the little family they'd formed. Dolly's time was occupied with her work at the hospital, Kate's with her career. The handful of people she called had not seen Dolly in weeks.

The hospital, Kate thought. Bet Dolly's closer to the nurses there than anyone else besides me and Granddad. She was dialing the Pediatric Oncology unit when her intercom buzzed.

"There's a Mr. Thompson here to see you, Miss Callahan," her doorman announced. "Should I send him up?"

Oh my God. It's Vaughn, Kate thought. She'd forgotten all about him and her date with him to drive to his country home in Greenwich. "Yes, send him up," she said. She'd just have to explain and apologize.

With Vaughn on his way up, she took a moment to check on Jerry. Asleep in his recliner again, she smiled. He'll complain about a crick in his neck all evening. But he looks so peaceful. She took an afghan from the sofa and covered him, then hurried to the door to wait for Vaughn so that the doorbell would not wake Jerry.

Stepping out of the elevator, Vaughn saw Kate waiting for him at her open door and was touched. She looked so pretty; her cheeks and lips were vividly pink, her hair tousled.

"Hi, Vaughn," Kate said softly. She'd never seen him in anything but a tailored suit. Today he was dressed for the country in a hunter green cashmere sweater and khaki slacks. He looked fresh and scrubbed. Kate smiled, for a moment forgetting her troubles. He probably has a convertible parked down in the street.

"Hi, gorgeous." He echoed her soft tone, mistaking her whisper for an intimate welcome. Impulsively he reached for her, drew her into his arms, covered her face with kisses.

Kate was too startled to react. And part of her didn't want to. She liked Vaughn, trusted him. He was her mentor and thanks to him she had her own show. She'd been so worried, so anxious. His arms offered shelter and strength.

Despite her firm resolve, she felt herself melting into the warm circle he offered. She was being held tightly and securely; her breasts were crushed against his chest. Then he was kissing her mouth, and for a fleeting moment her anxieties vanished and she gave herself up to the pleasure of being cherished by a powerful man. He'd protect her. He'd find Dolly. Her arms locked around his neck as she moved into a safe place where nothing bad could happen to her. The length of their legs touched, revealing the intensity of how badly he wanted her. She came to her senses.

She took a step back, breathing hard, and hugged herself awkwardly. Get ahold of yourself, she thought. Dolly comes first. "Granddad's asleep," she said, "that's why I'm whispering." Taking his hand she led him into her living room. "Oh, Vaughn, something terrible has happened to Dolly."

Vaughn sat with her on the sofa, put his arms around her and pulled her close. "Tell me what happened."

His fingertips stroked her hair and caressed her burning cheeks. Her lips stung from his kisses. She brushed them with her hand as if to obliterate her weakness.

"We can't find Dolly," she told him. She explained Dolly's disappearance. "I called Rick Smith. He's...he's an old friend. He's going to help."

Vaughn lifted her chin, peered deeply into her troubled eyes, kissed her lightly. "I know a first-rate private detective. I'll put him on the case right away. Naturally, we'll cancel our plans for this afternoon, but, Kate, I'm afraid we can't get out of the museum thing tonight."

"I know," she said numbly.

"Do you think you can get back into Dolly's apartment? I'll have the detective meet us there. He'll want to look around, see her appointment book, and her address book. And of course he'll need a recent photograph of her."

His arms tightened around her and his hand stroked her back. "Now don't worry about a thing. I'll take care of everything."

The doorbell rang and Kate excused herself to answer it. Vaughn took in the room. This was the first time he'd been inside Kate's apartment. At the television station they'd modeled a studio set to resemble her living room. Soft yellows and pinks covered walls, windows, and furniture. She decorated it herself, Vaughn thought. I'll give her free rein to do our homes any way she likes after we're married.

Kate returned with Rick Smith behind her. The two men shook hands. "I missed you the other night at the station, Detective Smith," Vaughn said warmly. "I've been wanting to meet you." Disarm your enemies, was his strategy. Vaughn Thompson had not built a television empire without knowing how to disarm his adversaries. He was well aware of exactly the role Rick Smith had once played in Kate's life. Well, he had his chance and he blew it. He's the loser, Vaughn thought. And I'm the winner.

Jerry, awakened from his nap by the doorbell, heard voices and wandered down the hall. He paused in the doorway, observing Kate with the two men. They're both in love with her, he thought. Well maybe this time, the green-eyed monster will give Joe Friday here a good kick in the keester. Whoever she chooses, I sure hope it works out. "Any news about Dolly?" he asked.

Rick shook hands with Jerry. "She's not in any of the hospitals, Mr. Callahan. And thank the Lord, she's not at the morgue. As a missing person's case, it's too soon to do anything. So—and I don't mean to alarm anyone, I'm just working the system—I'm including her disappearance in the strangler case. That way I can assign Detective Lori Martin to start tracing her."

"I'm Vaughn Thompson, Mr. Callahan," Vaughn said,

THIRTY-NINE

ROSALIE RUSSO DRESSED carefully for the Metropolitan Museum of Art gala. As Mr. Thompson's executive assistant, her presence was not optional. She had to be there, acting as his right hand. Thompson was hosting a cocktail party for all the bigwigs in the TV industry. Cocktail parties, they were always a problem. But Rosalie would say "No, thank you" to the cocktails and accept only soft drinks. She still went to AA meetings. "My name is Rosalie Russo and I'm an alcoholic," she stood up and said at each of them.

Yesterday she'd treated herself to a makeover at Elizabeth Arden's salon on Fifth Avenue. Her faded red hair, liberally sprinkled with gray now, was tinted a becoming soft light auburn. A cosmetician had demonstrated how to apply makeup, and Rosalie had purchased all the pretty cosmetics. She smiled at herself in the mirror. She had a lot to smile about. She'd never looked better. Her broad face looked rested and relaxed, the colors she'd applied looked, well, not glamorous, but pretty.

Her gaze strayed to the window overlooking the courtyard. There was that rabbit again. She took delight in watching him warily sneak from spot to spot, apparently thinking that if he remained resolutely still no one would see him. Then he hopped over to the lettuce leaves and ate his supper.

Rosalie would never move from this tiny house that was her home. It was so peaceful here; hard to believe that outside her little bit of heaven a noisy city loomed.

Those streets were mean. She knew that first hand, for once they'd been her home.

Rosalie Russo had once been addicted to alcohol. At thirty-five, she'd looked fifty, her current age, but worse, much worse. Every penny she earned—and she'd earned it the hard way—went for cheap wine which gave her a miserable hangover. So she'd start drinking again to escape the hangover.

Her favorite spot for panhandling was in front of the TNYC-TV Building on Eleventh Avenue, far enough north of the Javits Convention Center so as not to attract the cops. A remote area, where employees leaving the building hurried by in pairs or groups of three, but not before they dropped their change into Rosalie's lap. She was always there, she never caused trouble, and they felt sorry for her.

Late one night, when she was making up her bed on the grate, a really swell dude came out, his limo waiting for him at the curb. And when Rosalie asked for change, he made the mistake New Yorkers seldom make: he made eye contact with her. He stopped, frozen. "You look like an intelligent woman," he said, seeing past her grimy clothes and greasy hair. "Here." He pulled out a gold money clip and peeled off two one-hundred dollar bills. "Take this, and clean yourself up. If I can build this from nothing," and he indicated the TNYC-TV Center, "you can stop drinking." With that, he turned on his heel, ducked into the limo and was gone.

For the first time Rosalie saw herself through the eyes of a stranger, and the image made her sick. For the first time in how many? almost twenty years? she felt ashamed. She had two hundred dollars! That was her start.

She joined an Alcoholics Anonymous chapter that met at a modest Lutheran Church on the West Side. She slept on a cot among a row of cots in that church's basement.

She washed dishes and waited tables. She stopped drinking. Cleaned up and off the sauce, Rosalie was a pleasant-looking woman with a sincere smile and an eagerness to please. Her tips were good. She saved her money and the minister helped her to enroll in a secretarial school. Her first job was at a television station. She grew to love the industry, and moved from station to station, each move a step up, until finally she got a high-ranking top-paying job with Vaughn Thompson, her benefactor, the man who had given her a hand up out of the gutter.

Thompson never made the connection. And why should he? She certainly would never tell him that once she'd been the drunk who slept outside his building. He called her Mrs. Russo because she wasn't a kid anymore. And also because she wore a gold wedding band. It gave her respectability, she thought. Her story was that her husband had died in the Gulf War and she'd never found another that she wanted.

Rosalie called her boss Mr. Thompson, not Vaughn, as a show of respect. She owed him so much. The kind of loyalty he got from her couldn't be bought.

FORTY

KATE ARRIVED AT Vaughn's townhouse on Sixty-eighth Street between Fifth and Madison avenues promptly at seven. The reception at the Metropolitan Museum of Art was scheduled for eight. Kate was not in the mood for a party. This was the very last thing she wanted to do tonight, but it was a command performance for her. She was an important member of the New York media and she had to be there.

"It's work, Dolly," she'd said out loud to Dolly's photograph as she dressed for the party. "I can't get out of it. Otherwise I'd be out there scouring the streets with Detective Lori Martin, trying to find you."

Vaughn had sent his own car for her because Marty was off. "Wow, Miss Callahan! You look great!" Vaughn's driver, Tony Mastriani, said when he saw her. Kate wore a black strapless evening gown. Her hair was piled up on top of her head. The only jewelry she wore were a pair of teardrop pearl earrings.

On the sidewalk outside of Vaughn's house she was joined by Evan Wallace. "This is some ritzy place," he said. "Ever been here before?"

"No," Kate replied. "Have you?"

"Nope. Guess we're coming up in the world, Callahan. Look, he's even got his own garage. I hear he keeps a sporty Mercedes convertible worth ninety thou in there, and some sort of utility vehicle—a van of some kind." Evan grasped her elbow as he lowered his voice to a con-

fidential whisper. "And of course, he's got the limo and
Joe Palooka over there." Evan cast his eyes across the sidewalk to where Tony Mastriani waited behind the wheel
of the limo.

"Joe Palooka?" Kate asked, puzzled.

"You know, the comic strip character. The prize fighter.
Tony boxed on the inside."

"On what inside?" she asked. She felt slow and dull wit-
ted. What was Evan talking about?

"Yeah, inside. You know, the joint. Prison."

"Tony has a prison record?" she asked, incredulous.

"Sure thing. Take it from the investigative reporter: Tony's more than a driver. He's a bodyguard. And then some."

And then some? Kate asked herself. What is Evan hint-
ing at?

A maid held the street level door open for them as they
stepped into a well-lit formal entrance. Welcoming them,
she took their wraps, then directed them up a broad staircase to the main salon.

Part of Kate wanted to confide in Evan about Dolly's
disappearance. Another part did not want to talk about
it. Not that she wanted to keep it secret. She just couldn't
bear to recite the sad details one more time.

DETECTIVE LORI MARTIN had met her at Dolly's apartment
right after lunch. Rick came too. He presented his badge
to Johnny the doorman and they'd gotten immediate access to Dolly's apartment. Inside, Kate laid out the whole
story for Lori. She and Lori hit it off right away, and Kate
understood why Rick thought so highly of her. Lori took
Dolly's appointment book, address book, and a recent photograph with her when they left. "I'll start at New York
Hospital," she told Kate. "And then I'll come back here

around dinner time and talk to the tenants. Maybe some-body saw or heard something."

Rick had driven Kate home in his unmarked police car. He parked under a tree on the park side of Fifth Avenue, and they'd sat together in silence for a few minutes. Kate lowered her window. "Spring really is here," she said.

"Yeah," Rick said. He cleared his throat. "Kate, I know it's none of my business, but what's Thompson to you? Are you dating him?"

A little thrill shot through Kate's veins. Should she be brutally honest, she wondered, or mysterious? "He's a good friend, Rick, besides being my boss. We'd planned to drive to Greenwich for the afternoon so he could show me his country house. And when I told him about Dolly's disap-pearance, he was ready to bring in a private detective."

"Did he?" Rick asked.

"No, Rick. I asked him not to. Like you, I think Lori can do the job."

Rick placed both hands firmly on the steering wheel and stared straight ahead. Kate studied him out of the cor-ner of her eye. His profile was chiseled, his nose straight and handsome. There was a cleft in his chin, and when he smiled he had an adorable dimple in his right cheek. But he wasn't smiling now. How is it possible that he's become more desirable? Kate asked herself.

"A country house and a city house," Rick said. "I can't compete with that. All I've got is a one-bedroom apart-ment in Chelsea."

"I didn't know that you were in a competition, Rick," Kate said quietly.

Rick turned quickly toward her and the ache Kate saw in his eyes took her by surprise. She didn't know who moved first, but suddenly they were holding each other, sharing kisses so passionate it was as if the intervening six years had never happened.

"Ouch!" Kate said, as the stick shift jabbed into her thigh.

Rick laughed, and Kate reached out to press her fingertip into his dimple. Rick caught her hand. "You used to do that a lot," he murmured huskily.

Kate grinned at him. All of a sudden she felt light-hearted, as if for the past six years she'd been dragging around a huge bag of bricks and someone suddenly relieved her of them.

Rick's mouth found hers again. When they stopped kissing to catch their breath, Rick said in a burst, "Kate, I love you. I've never stopped loving you. I've missed you so much, it's like there's been a great big hole inside me."

"Oh, I know that hole well," Kate said tearfully. "Mine's felt like a crater."

Rick's cell phone chirped. After a few noncommittal responses, he disconnected, saying to Kate, "I've got to go. But, Kate, I want us to talk. I want us to spend the whole day together tomorrow. We'll talk everything out. I'll try to explain why I acted so stupidly."

"Shhh. We'll work it out," Kate said happily.

"Tomorrow? You free tomorrow?"

"Yes. Come at ten. We'll take Granddad out to brunch. Somehow I think he's going to be happier than either of us."

Rick took her hand and squeezed it to his chest. "That's impossible."

"THERE YOU ARE, KATE!" Vaughn Thompson called. He was standing at the top of the stairs, waiting for her. "Good evening, Wallace," he said as an afterthought. His gaze swept appreciatively over Kate's gown, lingered on the exposed swell of her breasts, settled on her upswept hair. "I like your hair that way. You look sensational." He kissed her cheek, then tucked her arm through his and led her into the room full of important people. "There's someone here I want you to meet."

Well, well, well, Evan said to himself. Old Thompson is in love. I think I'm looking at the next Mrs. CEO.

FORTY-ONE

EVAN WALLACE TRAILED along behind Thompson and Kate. Every once in a while, Thompson would remember him and good manners dictated that he include Wallace in his introductions. But always he pushed Kate forward to shake hands with the movers and the shakers of the television industry. Evan saw her face light up when Barbara Walters greeted her by name. He overheard Kate tell Miss Walters that she had learned how to conduct interviews by watching videos of Miss Walters' interviews again and again, and then imitated Walters' style.

Yet, overall, Kate was saying little this evening and was remarkably subdued, Evan thought. Wonder what's wrong with her.

"Imitation is the sincerest form of flattery, Kate," Walters said, looking pretty in a pale pink evening gown. "Let's have lunch together sometime soon. I'll have my secretary call yours to set it up."

Thompson looked like a cat with a bowl of cream, smug and knowing and lapping up the fat. Stick with me, Kate, his expression said, and I'll pave the way for you.

He must not feel too sure of himself, Evan was quick to deduce, otherwise he wouldn't be trying so hard to impress Kate. Well, that must be a first for Vaughn Thompson. From what Evan had heard, Thompson was quite the ladies' man. He specialized in twenty-year-old actresses who were trying to break into the industry. But now he's fallen for Kate, and the tables are turned. He's the one who's fawning. What goes around, comes around, he could hear his Scottish grandmother say.

"Come," Thompson said to Kate, his hand gripping her upper arm possessively, "there's something I want you to see."

You're not leaving me out in the cold, Evan said to himself, and stuck close to Kate. Seeing him, Thompson started to roll his eyes, but stopped himself. "Oh, and of course, you too, Wallace."

Thompson led Kate up a flight of stairs to the third floor. Through an open doorway, Evan noticed the master bedroom. Naw, he thought, that's too obvious.

But Thompson was leading them in the opposite direction, down a narrow carpeted hallway illuminated by art deco wall sconces. From his pocket he produced a key and inserted it into the lock in a door. Inside he turned on lights.

"Your own private gallery," Kate remarked politely.

Another collector, Evan thought. Seems like these rich dudes can't think of ways to spend their money except to acquire art collections. I think I'd spend mine on fast cars. And fast dames. He almost chuckled aloud.

He looked around. The room was cool and well lit. The pictures displayed on the walls were spotlighted individually. Gilt frames shone like the real thing.

I wouldn't know a Rembrandt from a Renoir, Evan told himself. Wonder if any of these paintings were stolen from their rightful owners by the Nazis? A private gallery like this, where people get in by invitation only, that's the perfect hiding place for stolen treasures. And that's how they managed to stay hidden for all these years.

Kate, usually vivacious, did not seem impressed, although she made polite remarks when Thompson asked her opinion. Something *is* bothering her, Evan thought.

Thompson was guiding her around the room from picture to picture. "This is an early Picasso I discovered in a small gallery in Madrid. Isn't it powerful?"

"Yes, of course," Kate mumbled. She turned to face Thompson. "I'm sorry, Vaughn, I'm not myself tonight. It's because of what we talked about this morning."

Evan thought she was being obscure for his sake.

"Of course, Kate, I'm being insensitive," Thompson was quick to say.

"I'd like to see your gallery another time. When things are...you know."

"Any time you wish."

Now what is that all about? Wallace wondered, his investigative reporter's curiosity telling him that whatever was bothering Kate was serious. He turned to the last wall. Now there's something I recognize, Evan thought, spotting an immense portrait. "That painting looks like one I've seen recently," he told Thompson. "It's a Sargent, isn't it?"

Thompson dragged his gaze away from Kate's face. He glanced at Evan and seemed distracted. Still, he cast his eyes where Evan indicated. "Yes, it's a Sargent," he said, turning back to Kate, but adding, "Probably you've seen his portraits at the Met."

Kate glanced at her watch. "Vaughn, we should be leaving now."

Thompson shot the starched cuff of his white shirt and checked his watch. "Yes, we'd better go." He strode rapidly to the door, his hand reaching for the light switch. "Coming, Wallace?" he called over his shoulder.

"Right with you," Evan said. The room went black, but in his mind he could still see the painting of a dark-haired girl in a long white dress.

Back out in the main corridor, he noticed another flight

of stairs leading to upper floors. "How many floors you got here?" he asked.

"Five," Thompson replied.

"So what's up there?" Evan asked. He was accustomed to asking people all manner of questions about any subject that struck his fancy. That was his job; ferreting out what people did not wish to reveal was what he did best.

"That's nobody's business," Thompson replied heatedly. "Certainly not yours."

Well, well, I've touched a sore spot, Evan thought. If Kate heard Thompson's rude retort, she ignored it. She was so preoccupied tonight. As Thompson and Kate started down to rejoin the party, Evan looked up the stairs to the dark landing thoughtfully.

On the floor below Rosalie Russo waited for her boss. "Mr. Thompson, we should get all these people into their cars and over to the museum now." It was Rosalie's job to keep her boss on schedule.

"We're just going, Mrs. Russo," Thompson said.

Rosalie smiled fondly at Kate. "How lovely you look tonight, dear."

Kate looked at Mrs. Russo's worn but attractively made-up face. She's been to a professional makeup artist, Kate thought, good for her. "You look awfully pretty yourself, Mrs. Russo," she said kindly.

FORTY-TWO

DOLLY WOKE FROM a sound sleep. It must be morning, she thought, because I feel so rested. And warm. She didn't remember going to bed, but she was resting on a comfortable mattress with clean sheets under a down comforter. For a moment, she thought she was at home, but then reality struck and she remembered she was being held captive. Yet, for the first time in what seemed like days, her mind was clear.

There were no windows. She had no idea if it was day or night. But it must be morning, she reasoned, I don't think I could sleep all day. My internal clock wouldn't permit me to. Then she remembered the drugs. Whatever he'd given her in the hypodermic needle was responsible for her deep sleep, for her constant drowsiness and disorientation.

But I'm not drowsy now, or disoriented, she told herself. I know I'm not at home. I want to go home. Last night I dreamed of Kate. We were children again, and Jerry and Babs had taken us ice skating at Rockefeller Center. It was the Christmas season; the enormous tree was ablaze with lights and decorations. How happy we all were then.

If I hadn't had Kate and her family every weekend while I was growing up, I'd have been so lonely, she thought. Kate shared her wonderful grandparents with me. We were like sisters. We still are. We don't have sleepovers every weekend now like we did when we were kids, but we do spend every Friday night together. It's our tradition. Most Saturdays we take in a museum or a concert.

Kate knows I'm gone. I was supposed to meet her and Jerry at Cafe Carlyle on Friday night. When I didn't show, when Kate goes to my apartment to check and finds me gone, she'll know something is terribly wrong. She'll go to the police. They'll start a search.

But they'll have no idea where to look. They'd never think to look for me here.

Suddenly the door opened. Her captor came in and she shrank against the headboard, pulling the blanket to her chin.

"I've brought you breakfast," he said pleasantly. He placed a tray on the bedside table. Lifting a lid with a flourish, he announced, "Cheddar cheese omelet. Bacon. Whole wheat toast. Fruit. And coffee." There was even a bud vase with a dainty pink rose. But no paper. No newspaper so she could see what day it was and read the headlines. Was her disappearance the subject of the headlines? she wondered.

"The bathroom's through there," he said, pointing to a door, "you may wander about at will in these two rooms. But I must keep the door to the hall locked. You understand."

Dolly only stared in terror.

"Eat up, my pretty," he said in a syrupy tone. "I am a rather good cook if I do say so myself. I had to learn how. I certainly couldn't rely on the women in my life to cook for me.

"Now, quickly, eat something. I'll give you thirty minutes, and then we'll get back to work. I've made a lot of progress but we have much to accomplish before tonight."

He closed the door behind him and left her alone. Tonight? What was the significance of tonight? Was he going to release her, after all? Maybe he'd blindfold her and drive her to a street corner and push her out. Would he? She could identify him. She'd seen his face. She knew who he was. He'd never let her go. Oh dear God, please save me.

The aroma of food made her realize she was hungry. She hadn't eaten since lunch on Friday. And this day was... what? Despite the terror in her heart, she managed to eat a little. She had to keep up her strength.

FORTY-THREE

"GRANDDAD, YOU LOOK a little green around the gills. Are you sure you want to go out to brunch?" Kate asked Jerry in the privacy of his bedroom as he knotted his tie. "Rick and Mrs. Greenbaum are waiting out in the living room, but they'll understand if you're coming down with some bug."

"Kate, stop your fretting. I'm feeling fine. Fine."

Kate shook her head. "Okay, your nibs, but I want you to call Dr. Stevenson tomorrow and make an appointment for a checkup."

Jerry threw up his hands. "My motto is 'stay away from doctors and stay alive!'"

At her insistent look, he sighed and said, "Okay, I'll do it."

OVER EGGS BENEDICT at the American Festival Cafe, Rick updated them on Detective Lori Martin's efforts to find Dolly. "Lori talked to many of the tenants in Dolly's building and to the doorman. The doorman saw Dolly leave the building at about four-twenty on Friday afternoon. She was dressed in her clown suit, had on her clown face and was wearing a wig. There weren't any cabs available, so Dolly hotfoot it around the corner of Sixty-second toward Madison. Mrs. Ella Hester, a tenant who knew Dolly, was walking her dog on Sixty-second at that time. She saw Dolly hurry past. When Mrs. Hester got to the corner of Madison, Dolly was gone. Mrs. Hester assumed she'd caught a cab."

"But she might not have?" Jerry asked.

"Mrs. Hester did not see Dolly get into a cab, and she did not see a cab pulling away from the curb. In fact, the curb was blocked by a black van with black-tinted windows. Dolly, she felt, should have reached that point."

Kate interjected, "Wait a minute. An insomniac across from Devon's Pub on Second Avenue saw a black van pull into the alley early on Monday morning when Regina Hoover was found in the Dumpster."

"But surely," Irma Greenbaum said, "there are hundreds of black vans in the city."

Kate was glad that the subject did not offend Mrs. Greenbaum's sensibilities. But then she'd been married to an emergency room physician and discussions about life and death had no doubt been a part of her daily routine. Irma was wearing one of her St. John's knit suits, this one in ivory with black braid, and she looked softly pretty but at the same time sophisticated.

I'm glad Granddad's found himself a companion, Kate thought, especially now that Rick wants back in my life. She wasn't sure how she felt about that. Rick had a lot of explaining to do. Over the years as a reporter, she'd gotten to know quite a few detectives. The stress of dealing with the seamy side of life, with murderers and rapists and serial killers, really took a toll on their personal lives. Their hours were long and unpredictable. They tried to shield their families from the brutality they saw every day. They seemed only truly comfortable when they were in each other's company. In some cases, the bond between detective and detective was stronger than the one between husband and wife. She and Rick needed to talk. Then, she promised herself, I'll just have to wait and see. But there was no

question that she still loved him. Just one quick sidel
glance at him and her heart turned cartwheels.

Rick was telling Irma, "Yes, Irma, there are hundr
of black vans in the city streets but I don't believe in
incidences."

"Neither do I," Irma said firmly.

The waiter refilled their coffee cups. Rick waited u
he'd moved to another table before saying, "Lori qu
tioned the staff at the hospital and learned that Dolly, n
definitely, did not arrive on Friday afternoon. They w
all surprised because Dolly never missed a day. She di
call and she didn't show up yesterday either. No one at
hospital has heard from her."

"It sounds like Mrs. Hester was the last person to
Dolly," Kate said, tears filling her eyes. She started to
up, to run to the ladies' room to have a good cry.

Rick grabbed her hand. "We're going to find her, Ka

"Yes, but how? Alive and well or dead and in a Du
ster?" Kate blurted.

Rick got up, put his arm around her shoulders. "Je
Irma, you finish your brunch. I think Kate needs a l
air. Come on, Katie." No one had called her that in ye
"Let's take a quick stroll around Rockefeller Center."

Over his shoulder he called to Jerry, "We'll meet
at the top of the stairs."

"I'M GLAD YOU decided to come with me," Rick said a
backed his unmarked car into a parking spot at the
on lower Fifth Avenue.

"Well, Granddad insisted that I get out of the hou
Kate said. "Do you think he wanted to be alone
Irma?"

"I think he wants what's best for you. He wants yo
keep busy and get your mind off Dolly. So do I. Yo

the one who suggested that Professor Haber might have known Courtney Dixon."

On the sidewalks of Greenwich Village, artists displayed their pictures on easels or by leaning them against fences. And the streets were teeming with sightseers. "I forgot about the sidewalk art show," Kate said, closing her car door. "Haber told me about it. His house is right around the corner. What if he's not at home?"

Rick joined Kate on the sidewalk. "Then we'll come back. It's best not to warn him that we have questions for him. Better to catch him off guard."

The afternoon was warm and sunny and many people had flocked to the annual event. From the fountain in the park, guitar music flowed, folk songs. They played those old Arlo Guthrie and Joan Baez tunes when I was a student here, Kate thought. Some things never change.

Professor Haber sat on a folding chair on Waverly Place, working the Sunday *Times* crossword puzzle with a pen. He seemed to be absently guarding a row of paintings that were propped up against the wrought iron fence in front of his house. Seeing Kate, his face broke into a wide smile. Then he noticed Rick and a certain wariness crept into his eyes.

Rick presented his shield and asked Haber if he'd known Courtney Dixon.

"I can't possibly know every student at the art institute," Haber insisted. "She wasn't in any of my classes."

"We know that," Rick said calmly. "But you might have met her just the same. At a lecture, perhaps."

"Well, if I did, I don't remember her," he said irritably. "These kids come to New York. They don't know how keen the competition is here. Just because they were first in their class back at Small Town High, they think the art world in New York is eagerly awaiting their arrival."

What a cynic he is, Kate thought. "Are these paintings yours, Professor Haber? You told me you painted." The paintings leaning against the fence were vibrant copies of Modigliani's, bursting with bold color.

Haber pointed. "The two on the end are mine. The others were painted by Rebecca Bernstein, one of my students."

The woman you were in love with, Kate thought, remembering how he'd confided in her. The woman who jilted you for someone else. Rebecca painted like a professional. By comparison, Haber's paintings were amateurish.

FORTY-FOUR

KATE'S DOORMAN HUSTLED across the sidewalk to meet her, his face screwed up in a grimace. He grabbed both her hands in his, surprising and scaring her. Something's wrong, she knew instantly.

"Miss Callahan, I'm sorry to have to tell you this but they took your grandfather to the hospital in an ambulance. The lady with him, Mrs. Greenbaum, said to tell you to come to Lenox Hill Hospital as soon as you got home. They think it's a heart attack. She'd said to tell you she's sorry she didn't call but she doesn't have your cell phone number."

Kate wheeled around to Rick and he grabbed her. Oh, Granddad, no, she thought. "We're on our way," Rick shouted.

With the blue light flashing on the dash, he drove furiously, darting in and out of traffic down Fifth Avenue and headed east on Seventy-second Street, then south on Second Avenue to the hospital on Sixty-third Street.

They found Irma in the ER waiting room. She was wringing her hands in her lap and that gesture told Kate just how bad it was. "Thank God you're here, Kate. They won't let me in. I'm not a relative."

Kate marched to the nurses' station. They weren't keeping *her* out. "I'll get us in," Rick said, flashing his badge and demanding that he be taken to Jerry Callahan.

Kate was allowed a brief visit. Jerry was on oxygen; a heated blanket covered his legs to his waist because he'd been trembling violently, the nurse said. "Hi, sweetheart," he whispered, and Kate ran to him and kissed his forehead. "Now don't you worry. I'm going to be all right."

His first thoughts are always for me. Never for himself, Kate thought.

"It's not a heart attack, Miss Callahan," Dr. Sharp told Kate. "We checked his blood for CPK, and happily there were no enzymes present to indicate heart muscle damage."

"I follow you, Doctor. My show did a series on heart attacks recently."

"Good," he said quickly. "We've had him on the monitor for an hour. I only wish my heart was as sound as his." He smiled and patted Jerry's shoulder. "We're running some tests, then we'll know more."

He steered Kate out into the hall. Rick and Irma hovered nearby. The doctor said, "Your grandfather says he doesn't have high blood pressure. Can you confirm that?"

Kate exhaled noisily. "It's always been normal when I can get him to have a check-up. Normal for his age, that is. Not like a nineteen-year-old."

Dr. Sharp crossed his arms. "Well, it was over the top when he came in. Has he been under any stress recently?"

Rick stepped forward. "I'm Detective Smith, a friend of the family. I'm investigating the disappearance of Miss Callahan's friend, a woman who's been like a granddaughter to Mr. Callahan."

"Granddad's been very worried about Dolly," Kate interjected. "Is that what this is about? Anxiety? Nerves?"

"I think so, Miss Callahan. I'll know more when the blood gases analyses come back from the lab, along with the results of his other blood work. We've taken chest X-rays and they're normal. Right now he's calm and his blood pressure is coming down. It's going to be a while so why don't you wait out in the lobby. I'll come find you when I know something."

"Thanks, Doctor," Kate said gratefully.

Kate encouraged Irma to take a break and get some coffee. "I'm so glad you were there with Granddad. It must have been frightening for both of you but I'm grateful to you for calling an ambulance."

"One minute he was clutching his chest. The next minute he was on the floor," Irma said. "What a scare that was. But I was a doctor's wife; I knew what to do. You're sure it's all right if I find the cafeteria and get some coffee. I could use the caffeine and maybe a Danish."

"It's fine, Irma. One of us should stay here in case the doctor comes looking for us."

"I'll bring you back some coffee," Irma said and headed for the elevators.

"Let's find a quiet corner away from all these people and that noisy television set," Rick suggested, and guided Kate down the hall and into a secluded alcove.

Kate slumped into a chair, her head in her hands. Tears streamed down her cheeks and her shoulders shook. Rick sat next to her, put his arms around her and pulled her close. "It's all right, babe, go ahead and cry. You've got too much going wrong these days, but for what it's worth, I'm here for you."

"It's worth a lot, Rick." Kate clung to him and cried until she was all cried out. He dabbed at her cheeks with his handkerchief and brushed her hair off her forehead. "I must look like a wreck," she said.

"A beautiful wreck," Rick teased.

Her eyes probed his. "Rick, how do you cope? You face life and death situations every day."

Rick steadied her shoulders with his hands as his eyes locked onto hers. "It's not easy, Kate. I've got Joe to talk to. He's a great guy. And he knows where I'm coming from. If it gets really rough, I go talk to one of the shrinks."

"Tell me what happened, Rick. To us," Kate whispered.

Rick whistled. "Whew. Yeah, I do owe you an explanation. I had planned for us to go somewhere quiet today and I was going to try to talk things through with you."

"Well, it's quiet here. For the moment."

He took her hands in his. They sat close, their legs touching, his hands holding hers in her lap. "Do you remember Izzy Anselmo?"

"Your first partner? When you were new on the force and we were engaged?" Kate pictured Izzy, a nice, warm-hearted Italian guy. "I remember him. And his sweet wife. We doubled dated once. What was her name?"

"Octavia," Rick said softly.

"She was from Italy," Kate recalled. "She'd only been here for a couple of years."

"Yeah, Izzy was crazy in love with her. Izzy was second generation Italian. He went back to Cortona for his grandfather's funeral. That's where he met Octavia. He brought her here to the States with him."

"Didn't they have a baby?" Kate asked.

"A boy. Isador, Jr." Rick smiled, but it was a sad smile.

"So what happened?" Kate asked.

"Well, Octavia was having a hard time adjusting to city life. She missed Italy, she missed her village and her family. We were working a bitch of a case, and putting in crazy hours. Izzy could have helped her adjust if he'd only had the time."

Rick's gaze held hers. "I knew something was wrong, that they were having troubles at home. Izzy started drinking on the job. One day he told me that Octavia had taken the baby and gone back to Cortona. He was so broken up. That was the night I broke our engagement. This job ruins marriages, Kate, ruins lives. I didn't want to do that to you."

"I'm sorry, Rick," Kate murmured. She was sorry for both of them. For all the years they'd wasted.

"Izzy's drinking got worse. I tried to cover for him, but the captain was no fool. He put Izzy on medical leave and referred him to rehab."

"What happened?" Kate asked. "Did he make it?"

"No. He skipped the appointments." Rick dropped his head. He couldn't face her. "He swallowed his gun, Kate. He was my partner, and he swallowed his gun."

"I didn't know," she said softly.

Rick nodded his head. "The Department hushed it up."

Kate cupped his face in her hands. She saw tears in his eyes and so much pain. "It wasn't your fault, Rick," she said, just as she used to tell him that it wasn't his fault that Mark had died and he had lived.

"Sure, I know that with my head, Kate. But not with my heart."

"Maybe because you're always trying to separate your heart from your head, and thinking you can protect everyone around you. Well, you can't." Kate got to her feet, too agitated to sit still another minute. "Just like I can't save him in there," and she pointed down the hall to the ER where Jerry lay helpless, "from old age and death. So what am I supposed to do, Rick? Say I'm sorry, Granddad, I'm not going to love you anymore because some day you're going to die and I don't want to go through the heartache."

She wanted to shake him. "Rick Smith, for a smart man, you sure can be stupid!"

He pulled her back down beside him. His eyes told her he wanted to hear more, even if she was being rough on him.

"Rick, you can't compare me to Octavia Anselmo. I'm

not a village girl from Italy suddenly thrown into the frenzied big city with a new baby. And you're much stronger than Izzy. We're both stronger."

"I know that now, Kate. Joe helped me to see it. He pointed out that with your job, you cover the same cases I investigate. You've got to be tough. But are you tough enough to put up with me and my job and what it does to me?"

She felt she had to ask, "Have you thought of doing something else? Teaching at the academy, for instance? Getting a law degree, perhaps?"

Rick frowned. "Yeah, I thought about those things. For all its drawbacks—the danger, the low pay—this is where I think I can make a difference."

Kate smiled. She knew what her answer would be if he asked her to consider another career. "Then go for it. I'm behind you."

"Are you sure, Kate? Can you put up with me and the crazy way I get when I'm going after someone like this strangler?"

Kate wound her arms around his neck. She saw love in his eyes, love spilling over, love for her. "As long as you don't shut me out, Rick, yes I can," she breathed.

"Miss Callahan," a voice called. Kate stood up and walked to meet Dr. Sharp. "We can't find anything wrong with him. I'm going to keep him overnight only because of his age. We've got him on a mild tranquilizer. As soon as he's settled in a room, one of the nurses will direct you there." He shook hands. "Good luck."

Kate held onto his hand. Her relief was acute, and her voice caught in her throat as she said, "Thank you, Doctor."

Rick put his arm around her shoulder. "I'm so glad everything's okay with Jerry, Kate. We'll stay with him for as long as he wants company."

LATER, RICK DROVE her home and rode up in the elevator with her. He'd suggested dinner but she'd said she wasn't hungry. "Well, I don't want you skipping meals and getting sick."

"I can't eat, Rick. I'd choke on the food," she protested. "I'm so worried. What happened to Dolly?"

"We'll find her," he said again.

She let them into her apartment. Its emptiness mocked her. "It's only been a few hours but already I can feel Granddad's absence."

Leading the way into the den, the room she thought of as Jerry's, she dumped her jacket and purse onto a chair. She went to the bar. "I need a drink. How about you?"

"Sure. Anything you've got will do." He moved up behind her and wrapped his arms around her waist, nuzzled her neck.

Kate set the brandy decanter down solidly.

"What can I do to make things easier for you?" Rick murmured in her ear.

She turned within the circle of his arms to look into his face. "Hold me, Rick. Just hold me. I feel like a scared little kid."

He gathered her closer. "Shhh," he whispered. "I'm here for you, Kate. And this time I'm not leaving."

He scooped her up in his arms and carried her out of the den. Then he stopped and laughed lightly. "New apartment. I don't know which way."

"Down the hall. My room's on the right."

In her bedroom, the scene seemed magical, for the sun's last rays were slanting through the windows, gilding tabletops and the bed, while shadows deepened in the corners.

Still holding her, he kissed her, reacquainting his tongue with the sweetness of her mouth. Then he lowered her onto the bed and knelt to slip off her shoes. She fell back against the pillows, her eyes never leaving his face. Quickly, he shrugged out of his jacket, tossed it onto a chair, pulled his suspenders off his shoulders. He stretched out alongside her. His arms reached for her, drew her close. "He's going to be all right, Kate. We're going to be all right." Sadly, he didn't mention Dolly.

Kate buried her face in his neck, smelled his aftershave, his soap, the musky scent of his skin. She let out a deep sigh, as if she'd been holding her breath for a long, long time.

He stroked her hair, kissed her eyes. She pressed in closer, heard and felt the moan that escaped from her throat, heard Rick's breath catch in a rasp.

"I love you, Kate. And I need you to love me back," he said huskily.

"All these years, I never stopped loving you," she whispered. Joy bubbled up inside her. The world and its cares disappeared, if only for a moment. She lifted her mouth and pressed her lips to his hungrily.

FORTY-FIVE

JERRY WALKED OUT of the hospital under his own steam. "I'm fine, I'm fine," he muttered grumpily to Kate, then bullied the attendant into letting him out of the wheelchair at the front door. Marty, who had Kate's limo ready and waiting in the driveway, tried to help Jerry across the sidewalk. Jerry shook him off.

But after he was seated inside the back with Kate, and Marty slid in behind the wheel, Jerry slumped back against the seat, exhausted. "Hospitals'll kill ya. I never shoulda let Irma call that ambulance."

"I won't listen to this nonsense," Kate declared. "You owe Irma a lot. I hate to think of what might have happened if you'd been alone in the apartment when you collapsed."

"I woulda come to and been fine," Jerry insisted. "There ain't no air in that hospital. You can't breathe." He waved an arm at the disappearing towers, as if waving goodbye and good riddance.

Jerry studied Kate out of the corner of his eye. "Well, you're looking a little better this morning. Did you get a good night's sleep?"

"Yes, Granddad," Kate said. "First good night's sleep I've had in a long time."

Jerry reached for her hand. "I'm happy for you, Kate."

He knows everything, she thought.

Then, "We'll find her, sweetheart," he said, again reading her mind.

Kate filled him in on the latest. "Detective Lori Martin

is getting nowhere. And now the media are spreading the story. All the networks are covering it. At least they haven't dragged us into it yet. And because Dolly is an heiress, the talking heads are speculating wildly, everything from kidnapping for ransom to Dolly fleeing the country so she won't have to pay income tax. Mike wouldn't permit such irresponsible journalism on *my show*!"

"No, 'course he wouldn't," Jerry mumbled. It had been his fear for Dolly that caused his collapse. And I ain't gonna let that happen again, he told himself sternly. Yet Jerry was afraid for Dolly. Because no one was mentioning the strangler. Rick said he'd included Dolly's disappearance in his investigation to expedite things, so he could assign Lori Martin to the case. The bureaucracy at Missing Persons would have held things up for days. And since there's been no demand for a ransom, the FBI ain't gonna be called in, Jerry reasoned. Law enforcement was so damned territorial.

I'm the only one who's thinking that maybe that nutcase got ahold of our sweet Dolly. For reasons known only to his depraved mind. A sharp chest pain reminded Jerry that he had to remain calm. It ain't my heart, he reassured himself, that's sound, thank you, Lord, it's just the anxiety. But anxiety is a killer too, Dr. Sharp had warned. And Jerry had witnessed the panic attacks Kate had whenever anything got wrapped around her neck. Even a silk scarf would make her think she was choking. A phobia. But with real physical symptoms. The mind is a funny thing, Jerry concluded.

AFTER A LIGHT LUNCH, and after Kate had tucked him under an afghan in his recliner with the telephone and the remote control at his fingertips, Kate left for the television station. She had a seven o'clock show to put on.

"Dolores, find Evan for me and tell him I'd like to talk

to him," she said as she passed through her assistant's office.

"And a good afternoon to you too," Dolores rejoined.

Kate stopped and set her briefcase down on Dolores's desk. "I'm sorry. I'm a mess today. Granddad spent the night in the hospital."

"I had no idea. You just said you'd be late when you called this morning. Is he okay?" Dolores said.

Mike Cramer was passing by. "Jerry sick?" he asked, concerned.

"Too much stress, Mike," Kate replied.

"He must be a wreck over Dolly. You too, Kate. You want Evan to go on for you tonight?" Mike offered.

"I'll think about it, Mike. The truth is I've got to keep busy or else I'll go crazy." Kate grabbed her briefcase and headed into her office.

"Staff meeting in thirty minutes, Kate," Mike reminded gently.

"I'll be there. I just want to talk to Evan for a few minutes."

In her office Kate unpacked her briefcase and returned phone calls to people she couldn't put off. There was a voice mail from Neil Lorneby. "Kate, I've located a breakfront for you. It's just what you wanted, one hundred and fifty years old and made in Ireland. Call me." Later, she thought.

"Kate, I left messages for you all day yesterday," Vaughn's voice said. "Did you get them? Call me. I'm worried about you." Again Kate thought: Later.

EVAN STUCK HIS head in Kate's door. "You wanted to see me."

Kate looked up. "Hi, Evan. Come on in and have a seat."

"Is this about Dolly?" Evan asked. "I heard the news. And I'm sorry. This must be really rough on you."

"Yeah, it is. Thanks, Evan."

"I was down at police headquarters early this morning and they've assigned a special team to work with Detective Lori Martin to search for Dolly. They've got two pictures of her they're showing all over the Upper East Side. One's of her in her clown suit with her face painted."

"Did anyone at headquarters have anything encouraging to say, Evan?"

Evan didn't have the heart to tell her that the mood at police headquarters had been gloomy. "They're determined to find her, Kate."

Kate inhaled and exhaled sharply. "Does anyone think she might have been abducted by the strangler?" She'd asked Rick that question repeatedly, but each time he'd told her not to worry, that with Dolly's money it was probably a kidnapping, and they'd get her back. But Rick was trying to spare her. She'd give anything to know what he was really thinking.

Evan said, "Well, her disappearance isn't part of the strangler case anymore. They're treating it as an independent disappearance."

So they were treating it like a kidnapping, Kate thought. Then, "Evan, do you remember those pictures you showed us of the dead girls."

Evan leaned back. "Yeah," he said cautiously.

"I'd like to look at them."

"Kate, are you sure? They're…"

"I know. Do you still have them?"

"In my office. Locked in my desk."

"Get them." Kate paused. "Please."

IT TOOK EVAN only a minute to return with the flat manila envelope. He placed it on Kate's desk. "Lock the door, please," she asked him.

Holding her breath, Kate slid the photos out of the envelope and spread them across her desk. "God, how could anyone do this?"

"What are you looking for?"

"I'm looking at the costumes. You thought they were significant," Kate said. "And the police think they're such a vital clue, they're withholding information about them from the public and the media. Let's see what we've got."

Kate studied the photos, focusing on the dresses, avoiding the girls' terrified expressions. "Ashley Fuller, the ballet dancer, is wearing a tutu and ballet slippers. Celeste Parker, the actress from Madison, Wisconsin, looks like she was dressed up in mismatched clothes that came out of a hundred-year-old rag bag. And Courtney Dixon, the Southern girl who was a student at NYU's art institute, has on a Gibson Girl-style suit. Then there's Regina Hoover, dressed in an old-fashioned long white dress."

"What are you thinking, Kate?" Evan asked. He respected Kate. She had a sharp, incisive mind.

"I'm thinking that Dolly was wearing a costume when she disappeared. A clown suit. So if the strangler's got her…" She doubled over in a sob. It hurt like hell to utter those words. She got herself under control and continued, "Maybe he was attracted to her by her clown outfit. That would mean he's been stalking her, maybe following her around at the hospital. This might not be about money at all. He might not even know she's an heiress."

AT SEVEN O'CLOCK a very subdued Kate went on the air. With a lump in her throat, she announced, "Dolly Devereaux, heiress to a copper mine fortune, is missing. Miss Devereaux was last seen at approximately four-twenty on Friday afternoon. Police are questioning the tenants in Miss Devereaux's apartment building, and the medical and security staff at New York Hospital where Miss Devereaux, in her role as Posey the clown, entertained children in the cancer unit. At this time the police have no leads as to Ms. Devereaux's whereabouts."

The screen split, Kate's face featured live in the left frame, a still-photo of her dark-haired friend's angular face in the right. Kate winced as she glimpsed their side-by-side countenances on her monitor. Just like in our picture at the Wollman Rink, she thought. It was hard to keep her voice steady and her attention on the teleprompter.

Kate tried to read the prepared text of Dolly's bio. Her voice faltered and she stared hopelessly into the camera. Then, slowly, tears slid down her cheeks. Inside, she was raging: Dolly, where are you? What happened to you? In the control room, Mike Cramer saw her distress and cut for a commercial break just in time. At her desk, Kate dropped her head into her hands and sobbed. Mike chastised himself: What was I thinking to let her deliver this story?

VAUGHN THOMPSON SLAMMED his fist down on Mike Cramer's conference room table. "Don't ever put Kate through that again!"

The news division staff had gathered for their usual postmortem after the show when Thompson burst into the room.

"I thought I could handle it," Kate said, attempting to defend Mike.

Thompson, still standing, glared at Kate over the heads of the others. She returned his gaze unflinchingly. Visibly, the fury drained from his face. "Kate, I'd like you to take a few days off. I think you need a break."

Kate got to her feet. "Are you suspending me, Vaughn?"

"Let's discuss this in private," Thompson said, starting for the door and expecting Kate to follow.

Kate stood her ground. "No. These are my colleagues. They depend on me. If I'm being suspended, they have a right to know."

Thompson pulled out a vacant chair and sat down with the others at the table. She has no idea what she means to me, he thought. She has no idea of the power she has over me. "No, Kate. No, Mike. No, Evan. Kate is not being suspended. But I do think, Kate, that it would be best for you, and best for the show, if you took a few days off. The strain is too much for you. A wise woman knows her limitations."

Mike Cramer folded his hands under his chin. "The boss is right, Kate. We all want what's best for you. And right now, you need a rest."

FORTY-SIX

HE HASN'T USED the hypodermic needle on me all day, D
told herself. Yet why do I feel so woozy? Why do I
in and out of consciousness? All day she'd posed for
reclining on the pile of carpets. He'd been kind to her,
ting her take breaks, but not too many. He'd even adju
the thermostat so she didn't feel so cold. He'd seemed
most friendly. And despite her embarrassment at be
nude, he never touched her in an intimate way. The
times he put his hands on her was to lead her from
room into the studio, then to arrange her pose to his sa
faction. And at those times he wore latex gloves and
wondered: How odd.

She'd tried to cooperate; she'd sat for hours on end w
out moving. Her arms ached; her neck ached. The so
he finished her portrait, the sooner he'd take her ho
she hoped.

He'd allowed her to eat lunch alone in her room. I
ner too. He was right when he'd said he was a good c
The food was tasty. But it must have been drugged
what else could explain her wooziness, her inabilit
keep track of time.

Dinner must have been hours ago. And now it i
be late. Midnight or later. She was so tired. She cou
hold this pose a moment longer. Tears flooded her e
brimmed over and spilled down her cheeks. Oh, K
please find me, please come get me and take me hon

"All done," he announced brightly, startling her. He set down his palette and brush with care on the worktable.

"Will you please take me home now," Dolly whimpered. "I promise, I swear to you, I will not tell anyone about this if you will only take me home."

"But don't you want to see your portrait first, my beautiful odalisque?" he asked, his tone offended. "This time I've really outdone myself."

"Yes, of course I want to see it," Dolly responded, thinking she would humor him.

Proudly he rotated the easel so that the painting faced her. Dolly gasped. The woman in the picture was grotesque, her features were distorted. Was this how he saw her? She tried to compose her face, to hide her distaste, but it was too late. He'd already noted her expression. His eyes narrowed into dangerous slits and his hands clenched and unclenched. She could see the blue vein in his temple pulsing rapidly.

"You don't recognize talent when you see it!" he yelled. Rage filled eyes bored into hers. His face grew bright red and to Dolly he looked insane.

"But I like it, I do," she pleaded.

He was out of control now, waving his arms and stamping his feet. "You're just like the others. You have no idea how talented I am. You think I'm a hack, don't you? Well, I'll show you. I'll show all of you."

Dolly shrank deeper into the carpets, lifting her arms defensively in front of her face. He advanced toward her, arms outstretched, fingers curling and uncurling. He grabbed the ends of the long white silk scarf with both hands and snapped it. He's a monster, she thought. He's going to kill me. "No!" she screamed. Kate. Kate doesn't know.

FORTY-SEVEN

KATE SLEPT FITFULLY, dreaming one nightmare after ano[...]
Each involved Dolly. Dolly was lost and Kate was st[...]
bling through a fog calling her name. Dolly was bound[...]
gagged by a monster, but Kate couldn't find her to free[...]
In the last dream, Dolly was whispering in her ear, w[...]
ing Kate that she must not trust... Kate could not hea[...]
name. She woke with a start. The intercom was buzz[...]

Dressed in only a nightgown, Kate's bare feet hi[...]
floor at a trot and she raced into the foyer. She presse[...]
button on the intercom before it buzzed again, hopi[...]
had not already awakened Jerry.

"Miss Callahan," her doorman said, "Detective S[...]
is on his way up."

Rick? What was he doing here so early? Back in[...]
bedroom she checked her bedside clock. Ten minute[...]
seven. She pulled on a robe, and still barefoot, ran to[...]
the door before Rick rang the bell. Then she starte[...]
shake.

When he got off the elevator and saw her stan[...]
there at the open door, Rick broke into a trot. Oh no,[...]
thought, it *is* bad news. All those dreams. Dolly!

Rick's arms went out to her, pulling her protecti[...]
against his chest. She leaned her head back to rea[...]
face. "It's Dolly, isn't it, Rick? Tell me the truth. Y[...]
found her, haven't you?"

Rick only pulled her closer, his arms tightening[...]
to shut out all harm. "Tell me, Rick. Don't torture m[...]

Rick spoke into her ear. "You're right, Kate. We found her. I'm so sorry, sweetheart."

"No-o-o-o!" Kate wailed, feeling her knees give way, her body slump forward.

Lifting her tenderly in his arms, Rick carried her into the apartment.

OVER COFFEE RICK told Kate and Jerry the details. Hearing Kate's cry, Jerry had wakened. The news almost knocked him off his feet too. But he hustled them into the kitchen and with trembling hands brewed coffee and set out coffee mugs, cream and sugar—all the while mumbling prayers for Dolly's soul.

Kate sat at the kitchen table, leaning on her elbows, her face buried in her hands. Rick had pulled his chair close to Kate's, his arms cradling her, trying to comfort her. But there is no comfort for this kind of news, Rick thought, remembering all the times he'd had to break the worst kind of news to worried families.

Kate took the coffee mug Jerry put in front of her. "Drink it," he said. Unsteadily she moved over to the big kitchen window that faced south on Fifth Avenue. Already the sun was warming the rooftops and streets below her. Out there it's just an ordinary Tuesday, she thought. Early morning joggers are already pounding around the reservoir. Later, it'll be pretty and the park will fill up with bikers and nannies and babies in strollers. Just another gorgeous spring day in Central Park.

But in here, I'm living my worst nightmare. "Where was she found?" she asked Rick.

Rick came to stand beside her, registering how she was staring unseeingly out of the window. He was watching for signs of shock. "Near a construction site over near the hospital. The foreman discovered her body at six when he came to work."

"In a Dumpster?" Kate faced him. "Tell me."

"Yes," he said softly. "As soon as I saw it was Dolly, I came straight here to be the one to tell you. Joe took over for me. I couldn't take a chance that a reporter might call you."

Kate placed her hand on his chest. "Thanks for that," she whispered. She turned back to the table, sank into a chair and grabbed Jerry's hand. "When did she die?"

Rick hovered over them, one hand on Kate's shoulder, the other on Jerry's. There was no way to spare them the details. And he knew that Kate would insist on knowing everything. He'd planned to feed her the information in bits and pieces, hoping to somehow soften the blow. But that was impossible.

"The coroner says she died late last night."

"Was she strangled?" Kate asked in a hush.

"Yes," Rick said gently.

Jerry had said little, now he made a harsh guttural sound in his throat. "Damn," he exploded.

"So she's the strangler's latest victim," Kate said.

"Maybe not," Rick replied.

Jerry's head shot up. "Whadda ya mean?"

"All of the strangler's victims have been dressed in costumes. We've been careful not to release that information to the press. Only a few trusted people knew about it. Dolly was undressed when she was found."

"You mean she was naked?" Jerry asked, outraged.

"She was unclothed," Rick said softly. "There was a white silk scarf…" He was about to say wrapped around her neck. He amended it to, "near her body."

"And that makes you think she was not killed by the

strangler, even though she was strangled, and her body was placed in a Dumpster like all the others?" Kate asked.

"That's what we're thinking. The method of execution, the dump sites, those details were known to everyone who's followed the strangler story. The stuff about the costumes, they don't know. We think this is a copycat murder. Maybe a kidnapping gone sour."

FORTY-EIGHT

"I WANT TO see her!" Kate insisted.

"Kate, I don't think that's a good idea," Rick said.

"Well, somebody's got to identify her, don't they?" Jerry growled. "A family member or a friend? Somebody other than the detective on the case?"

"I was going to call her attorney or her doctor, whichever I could locate first, someone who's not emotionally involved like you two," Rick said. The last thing he wanted to do was to escort Kate and Jerry to the morgue.

Jerry stood up. He seemed to gather strength from the crisis. "We're all the family Dolly has. There's no way we're gonna abandon her now. She needs us as much now as she's ever needed us. We ain't afraid of that poor girl's dead body, are we, Kate?"

Kate stood up too, supporting herself with her palms flat on the tabletop. Her hair was disheveled, her bathrobe soft from wear, yet to Rick she had never seemed more beautiful or lovable. He wanted to hold her tight and shield her from the hurtful things he knew the world had in store for her. He wanted to protect her so that nothing would ever hurt her again.

"I'll be ready in fifteen minutes," Kate said.

"I'm right behind ya," Jerry said.

Rick held out his open palms. "But I don't even know if they've taken the body to the morgue yet," he pleaded.

"Well, get on the horn and find out," Jerry snapped. "And for God's sake, stop calling her 'the body,' She's Dolly."

Jerry's right, Rick thought as he slumped in a chair to wait. Dolly was once my friend too, as well as Kate's. She was a good person. Too good for what happened to her.

IN FIFTEEN MINUTES Kate had showered, tied her hair back, and dressed in slacks and a sweater set. Jerry met them at the front door, his hair still damp from his shower, the lines in his face routed deeper today, but his gaze steadfast. He was going to look out for his little girl one more time; for what other purpose was the good Lord keeping him on this earth? He took Kate's elbow and they helped each other to the elevator.

Rick steered his unmarked police car east to Park Avenue and took Park south to Thirty-fourth Street, turned left, crossed Lex and Third, turned right onto Second Avenue, then doubled-back up First. Damn one-way streets, he thought. He was mad at everything and everybody today. He stopped in front of the New York City Coroner's Office next to Bellevue Hospital.

"They just brought her in," he said, as he escorted Kate and Jerry down long hallways and short flights of stairs. He didn't mention that there would have to be an autopsy and hoped they wouldn't ask, although he was sure they knew.

He left them in a small waiting room while he stepped inside a door marked "Restricted: Forensic Personnel Only." Jerry paced up and down past Kate who sat in a hard molded plastic chair, her hands clasped firmly in her lap because it was the only way she could control their shaking. Within minutes, Rick returned.

He sat down next to Kate and took her hand. "You won't have to go in there. I've arranged it so they'll use a video camera. You'll be able to see her on that monitor there. It'll just be a minute."

Kate looked at the flickering monitor. "No, Rick. This is not what I want. I want to see Dolly, to be able to reach out and touch her. I know you're just trying to make this easier for Granddad and me, but if I don't see her in person, I'll never be able to accept that she's gone." Kate sobbed, and Jerry put an arm around her shoulder. "I feel the same way," he said firmly.

"But it'll be easier on you with the monitor." Rick shrugged, defeated. "Okay, I'll do whatever you want."

He helped Kate through the door and into the restricted area. Sharp odors assailed Kate's nostrils, and Jerry blinked at the bright lights. Kate tried to avoid looking at her surroundings, focusing instead on the sheet-draped stainless steel gurney to which Rick led her.

Dolly's body appeared small under the sheet, although Dolly was not a small woman. Already death has diminished her, Kate thought hopelessly.

The coroner stood at the head of the table, his face impassive but not unkind. He does this every day, Kate thought. He's used to it. I've never had to identify a body before.

At a nod from Rick, the coroner folded the sheet back. Dolly's shiny black hair pillowed her head. Kate reached out a hand and touched the hair. It's so alive, she thought, yet Dolly is gone. I know this is Dolly's body, but Dolly herself is absent. "She's gone to a better place, Granddad," she said.

Jerry was overcome. He lowered his head and sobbed. "Look at her expression. The poor little thing was terrified."

Ugly raw bruises scarred Dolly's long, slender throat. Kate's hands flew to her own throat defensively. A great sob exploded from deep inside her. Rick reached for her, pulled her close. "That monster!" she cried. "Get him, Rick. Please, please, get him for me. Make him pay!"

Tears coursed silently into the grooves on Jerry's cheeks. Suddenly, and without warning, he kicked the wheel of the gurney savagely, sending it rolling smoothly over the tile floor.

FORTY-NINE

"I'VE GOT TO get back to headquarters," Rick said. "They
brought in a suspect and I have to be there."

"A suspect?" Kate asked. "Who is he?"

"Several of the nurses at New York Hospital repor
that one of the maintenance men seemed fixated on D
and followed her wherever she went at the hospital. .
parently he knew where she lived. We showed his pic
to her doorman and he said he'd seen the man hang
around the building."

"Is he suspected of killing the other girls too?" J
asked.

"We're going to check his whereabouts for the time
four of the women were murdered. We're not ruling
anything. And because of some similarities, the chi
keeping Joe and me on Dolly's case. I've got to go, b
Walk me out. Jerry, take care of yourself. Call me if
need anything."

"Will do," Jerry said from his chair at the kitchen ta
and gave Rick a smart salute.

In Granddad's eyes, Rick is forgiven, Kate thought
was grateful.

In the privacy of her foyer, Rick put his arms aro
her. "Promise me you'll take care of *yourself* too. Ta
few days off and get some rest."

"That's already been arranged," Kate replied. "Vau
insisted I take a medical leave. Evan's filling in for m
the show."

"Well at least Thompson and I agree about one thing." He stroked her hair with his hand. "I'm so sorry for all that you're going through, Kate. I wish I could make it all go away. Remember, I'm here for you. And this time, I won't let you down."

Kate kissed him lightly on the mouth. "I know you won't, Rick."

Rick had his hand on the doorknob. "I'll be in touch soon. I love you, babe."

"Me too," Kate whispered.

IN HER BEDROOM, the answering machine light was blinking. She played back her messages. Her friends from the station had called to extend their condolences and to ask how they might help her. An anxious Vaughn Thompson asked her to please call him right away, otherwise he was coming straight over.

Mrs. Russo put Kate through immediately, after she told Kate that her thoughts and prayers were with her and her grandfather. How nice of her, Kate thought, as she waited for Vaughn to pick up. She thanked him for his concern, and told him that all she wanted to do was sleep for the rest of the day.

After she hung up, she slipped out of her clothes, hung them up, got back into her nightgown, and turned back the comforter. The telephone chirped.

"Miss Callahan, it's Marty. I'm so sorry about your friend." Kate started to speak but stopped when she heard Marty sob. "This is a day we'll both never forget. My kid sister Debbie died during the night, peacefully in her sleep like I always wanted for her."

"Oh, Marty, my heart goes out to you and your mother. It's a blessing Deb didn't suffer," Kate said.

"There are things we've got to take care of, Miss Callahan, so I won't be able to drive you for a few days. If you want I can recommend somebody dependable for you," Marty offered.

"That's okay, Marty. I'm taking a few days off myself. You take as much time as you need."

"I knew you'd say that, Miss Callahan. There'll be a mass for Deb on Thursday at the Hungarian church on East Eighty-third Street. I know you didn't know her, but if you and your grandfather can come, it'd sure mean a lot to me."

"We'll be there, Marty." Kate replaced the receiver. Granddad and I will be attending two funeral masses this week, Kate thought.

SHE SLIPPED INTO bed and felt her whole body burrow deep under the covers. Cheerful sunlight peeped around the edges of her drawn draperies and warmed the room. Life goes on, she thought. Other people's lives. Mine has stopped for a while.

The apartment was silent. Granddad's napping too, she thought, probably in his recliner again. She smiled softly to herself.

Kate rearranged the pillows so that her head was propped up. And now Rick's back. And in a way it's like he's never been gone. I know he's the one. And I know that this time, he'll keep his promise.

"Dearest Dolly," she said aloud, picking up the framed photo of her best friend, "I miss you." Tears slid down her cheeks. What were you trying to tell me in my dream, Dolly? You warned me that I must not trust someone. Granddad always said that his mother, Granny Callahan, put a lot of stock in dreams. She believed loved ones could communicate across space and time through dreams. For what else does "communion of the saints" signify if not communication from those departed? Kate asked herself.

That's why it was so hard for me to accept it when Detective MacPeterson called from San Francisco to tell me he'd found my mother's grave. I always felt that I would *know* if Mom was dead. I still haven't told Granddad the bad news MacPeterson learned in San Francisco. Well, now it'll have to wait a long while. There's no way I'm going to hit him with Mom's death on top of Dolly's.

My grandmother, too, had faith in her dreams and her instincts. If you can't trust your feelings and instincts, she'd said wisely, what can you trust?

As Kate drifted off to sleep, one thought comforted her: Rick's got a suspect. The police wouldn't have taken him in if they didn't have good evidence. Now we can all rest easy and the killing will stop.

FIFTY

WHEN VAUGHN THOMPSON learned that Kate had returned to the news division, he took an elevator down to the news floor. "Kate, what am I going to do with you?" he asked, striding purposefully into her office.

Kate was on the telephone. "Call you later," she said and disconnected. She managed a smile. "Hi, Vaughn."

Vaughn strode to her side, grabbed a chair and pulled it up close. He cupped her face in his hands. "I thought we had an agreement. You'd stay at home and get some rest."

Kate pushed back. "Vaughn, I slept from yesterday afternoon until this afternoon. I'm all slept out." It wasn't the whole truth. Kate had cried off and on throughout the night. Her sleep had been fitful. At midnight, she got up to find Jerry in the kitchen making cocoa. He poured her a cup and she took it back to her room.

With a photograph album in her lap, she'd sat up in bed and looked at pictures of herself and Dolly that dated back to third grade. Sometimes she cried at the sight of them, but mostly she smiled. I've been lucky, she thought, I've had the best friend a woman could ever ask for. Some women never find a friend like Dolly. Now I've got to learn to cherish my memories of her and be grateful.

"Granddad says we've both got to go forward with our lives," she told Vaughn.

"He's a wise man. I thought it would be good for you to take some time off."

"No. That gives me too much time to think. I'd rather

keep busy. I'm not going to try to do the show, but I've got phone calls to return, mail to keep up with, and research for future shows." She smiled into his worried face. "I appreciate your concern."

"I told you about a piano bar I go to when I feel under the gun. It's a fun place, very low key, and a good place to unwind. Small and intimate. Let me take you there when you're through here. We'll have a few drinks and relax. Then I'll take you home."

"I don't know, Vaughn. I'm taking this day one hour at a time." She hated to disappoint him, he'd been so good to her, hated the disappointed look that crossed his face.

"Tell you what," he said. "I'll be there at about eight-thirty. If you change your mind, join me. It's called Broadway Melody on Sixth Avenue between Forty-eighth and Forty-ninth."

"I'll think about it, Vaughn," she promised.

Her phone rang. "I've got to take this."

"Okay, see you later then," he said, leaving.

"Kate, this is Thomas Shipley. I've got another seascape for you to look at. This is a real find. It's signed by a student of Winslow Homer. And the price is well within your budget. I'd like you to look at it right away because I've got another client who's chomping at the bit to own it."

Kate felt conflicted. She wasn't in the mood to look at pictures, yet she didn't want a really good painting to get away. "I'll try to stop by later," she said.

"Tell you what," he said, "we close at seven, but I've got some work to do in the gallery after hours. Ring the bell and I'll let you in if you come after seven."

No sooner had Kate said goodbye to Thomas Shipley, than the phone rang again. It was Neil Lorneby calling to extend his condolences and to remind her about the Irish breakfront. "It was put back when it didn't sell at auction.

The owner is willing to let it go for less than the reserve we established which was $2500. He'll let me sell it for $2200 if I can sell it fast. Come by after work and I'll show it to you. If we're closed, just ring the bell. There's a video camera at the door; I'll recognize you."

Kate had spent part of the morning calling their friends to tell them she was canceling Jerry's surprise birthday party. Still, she did want him to have a special gift. With her contacts at the gallery and auction house, she'd be able to give him both presents: the painting and the breakfront.

"I'll try to stop by, Mr. Lorneby. If not tonight, then tomorrow morning," Kate said. "And thank you for thinking of me."

"You've been a good customer, Kate, and you gave me an opportunity to present my side of this lawsuit fiasco on your show. Because of it, Shipley and his pals have dropped the suit. I owe you."

"Well, I'm glad it worked out."

Kate spent the next hour catching up and replying to email messages and opening her mail.

At six, she took the elevator to the station's cafeteria for a sandwich and a cup of coffee. Her colleagues hugged her and expressed their sympathy for what she was going through.

She joined Mike in the control room at seven to watch the show. "Evan did a good job," she said after the show was over.

"Tell *him* that," Mike said. "He was nervous about filling in for you."

"Evan? Nervous? I didn't think he had nerves." But she joined Evan on the set and after he offered condolences, she told him the show had been great. "No one would ever miss me if I was gone," she said.

"Don't kid yourself, Kate. There'd be a riot." Evan was

on a high. Kate knew well that feeling of exhilaration after a good show. Evan said, "I've got to attend Mike's post-mortem, but then I'm heading over to my favorite hide-away on Eighth Avenue, O'Brien's. It's a hole-in-the-wall bar, real sawdust on the floor, yuppies get the boot. Want to go? Drown your sorrows?"

"A hangover is the last thing I need, Evan, but thanks. And thanks for taking over for me."

"Hey, no problemo. I'll be at O'Brien's at about nine if you change your mind."

For the next hour, Kate surfed the Internet, searching the news bulletins for topics for future shows. At nine she called Jerry. "I'm on the Internet," she explained. "I think I'll work for another hour or so. I'll be home at my regular time."

"Well, I'm snoozing in my recliner. Those tranquilizers they gave me at the hospital must still be in my system, because it's hard to keep my eyes open. Make the security guard at the station find you a cab before you leave the building. Okay?"

"Okay, Granddad. See you later."

The phone rang just as she hung up. "Kate, it's Leon Haber. I'm glad I caught you before you left. I've just opened a bottle of Beaujolais to let it breathe. I make a red clam sauce to die for. Please come and have a late supper with me. I'll boil the fettuccini when you get here."

He doesn't know that Dolly was my best friend, Kate thought. Why would he? He doesn't know I'm in mourn-ing. "It's nice of you to think of me, Professor, but tonight's not a good time."

Haber laughed. "Please stop calling me professor, Kate. You're not one of my students. I'd really like to show you my house. Won't you reconsider? You've got to eat sometime."

Kate tried to sound gracious. "I had a sandwich earlier.

And my grandfather's not feeling well, so I want to get home to him. But thanks just the same."

"Well, I'm not going anywhere. I'll be here if you change your mind."

KATE STRETCHED HER arms over her head. Enough work for tonight, she thought. She turned off the computer, collected her things, and took the elevator to the lobby. Dolores had left hours ago, and she did not run into Mike in the hall. The news floor was unusually quiet. Well, Evan's over at his hole-in-the-wall bar, she thought, remembering the warmth and camaraderie such places offered. Bet he knows all the regulars and they swap "war" stories.

"Jesse, would you mind hailing a cab for me?" she asked the guard. "I'd rather not go out there alone."

"Sure thing, Miss Callahan. And you're smart not to stand out there by yourself. Not with that strangler on the loose!"

Within minutes Kate was thanking Jesse and climbing into a yellow cab. She was about to give the driver her home address when she had a sudden change of heart. Granddad's probably asleep in his chair, she thought, and I've got my second wind. Guess it's because I spent so much time in bed yesterday and today, but I don't feel tired anymore.

She leaned forward and gave the driver an address.

FIFTY-ONE

KATE TOURED THE small gallery while she waited for her host. She hadn't seen anyone when she arrived, but he'd explained that an associate had dropped by unexpectedly and they were just finishing up a business transition in another room. He respected her wish for privacy, he added. He'd get rid of the uninvited guest and join her in a matter of minutes. "In the meantime, make yourself comfortable. Enjoy my little collection."

The room was spartan, the walls painted white and spotlighted, the oak floor bare and austere. Kate approached the first painting, a Degas. This has to be a reproduction, she thought. A real Degas would be a museum piece. No one would display such a painting so casually otherwise. A placard mounted on the wall identified the painting as *The Dance Class* painted by Edgar Degas in 1873. The original hung in the Musee d'Orsay, Paris. So I was right, Kate congratulated herself. She peered at the legend. A sonnet composed by Degas was stenciled on the placard.

Kate moved on to the next painting, a large poster-size picture that depicted a can-can dancer. Immediately, she recognized the style of Toulouse-Lautrec. Even I know that Lautrec was a noted painter of Parisienne lowlife. The legend confirmed Kate's identification. "Jane Avril at the Jardin de Paris, 1893," she mumbled to herself. The poster was a reproduction, as well. The original was on display at the Museum of Albi. "Wherever that is," Kate said aloud.

She checked her watch. She'd give him two more

minutes, then she was leaving. I can do this tomorrow, she thought.

Jane Avril had bright orange hair. One long, black-stockinged leg was lifted straight up in the can-can kick. Her green, orange and mustard-colored skirts fluttered around her legs. She wore long black gloves and a floppy hat with a black plume. I guess I've seen another reproduction of this painting somewhere, Kate thought, because it's familiar.

The third picture was a sketch of a Gibson Girl-type figure. His taste in art is certainly eclectic, she thought. The lady wore a fashionable suit with a long fitted jacket over a pleated skirt. Her upswept blonde hair was crowned with a large, feathered hat. *Fluffy Ruffles* the legend read, created by Wallace Morgan, 1906. A feeling of dread spread up Kate's spine, constricting her throat. Something's wrong, she thought.

The hair on the back of her neck bristled. I know this picture too, she thought, although I swear I've never seen it before. She looked over her shoulder, feeling creepy.

The adjoining wall was empty, but a lighter outline indicated that a very large painting had hung there recently. The legend remained. Kate leaned forward and read, *Portrait of Emily Sargent,* by John Singer Sargent.

She gasped when she turned and saw the next picture. A nude. Straight black hair falling to bare shoulders, angular features, black eyebrows that almost touched. The similarity was incredible. "Dolly," she whispered, "it's you." A long white silk scarf was draped over the seated model's tan, folded leg. A long white silk scarf, just like the one found with Dolly's body.

What does this mean? she asked herself. She swallowed hard, feeling ill. I've got to get out of here. I've got to tell

Rick. But her legs gave way and she was forced to sit down for a minute to compose herself.

Her gaze swept over the pictures, back to the Degas. She got up and went to it. The first victim, little Ashley Fuller from Scarsdale, had been dressed in a ballerina's white tutu with a large blue bow around her waist, just like the girl in the Degas. The first victim had a red bow pinned in her hair, and wore wire-rim spectacles, just like the girl in the Degas. The first victim was wearing pink satin ballet slippers. Just like the girl in the Degas.

The first line of Degas' sonnet caught her eye. "She dances, dying...."

"No!" Kate cried. A blinding white light seemed to sear her eyes.

"I finally got rid of him," a voice said from behind her.

Kate whirled around to see him standing in the doorway. Too late, she thought, too late. She felt the terror on her face.

Intelligence sparkled in his eyes. "I see you've made the connection." He moved close to her until he was only inches away, threatening and intimidating, so that she stepped backward, afraid.

He seized her elbow and turned her. "I've saved the best for last. Have you seen her? She's magnificent. Look. Look at yourself, Kate," he commanded.

Kate's eyes were riveted to the portrait. She was mesmerized by it. She recognized the elaborate colors and rich gilt embellishments of a Gustav Klimt painting. The woman was stunning. Her pose haughty, proud, her expression slightly amused by the admiration she attracted from others. Her hand was on her hip, her chin lifted. Abundant ginger hair framed her pale oval face; hair exactly the same shade as Kate's. Her almond-shaped amber eyes looked out at the world as if from a distance, just as Kate's did.

"She's Emilie Floge, Klimt's lover," he said, his voice oily, seductive.

Now Kate knew what it all meant. She was going to die. He was a madman. He was going to kill her. Willingly and stupidly, she had walked right into the trap the strangler had set for her.

FIFTY-TWO

JERRY WOKE WITH a start, thinking he heard Kate calling him. Ow, he cried. Dammit, I've got that crick in my neck again. He got up and swallowed some Motrin in his bathroom. Then he went into the kitchen to brew coffee and start breakfast.

The apartment was quiet. He did not hear Kate moving around although it was nine o'clock. She musta got home late last night after I fell asleep. So she's tired. I'll just let her sleep. She needs the rest and she doesn't have to go in to the station unless she wants to.

He sat at the kitchen table, thinking of Dolly. It was like Babs and me had two granddaughters, he thought. We had Dolly every weekend. Her and Kate was like sisters. I'm glad Kate had her, that she didn't have to grow up alone, with just two old folks for company. Not that she ever complained. She knew how much we missed her mother and she tried to make it up to us.

Wonder when the police will release Dolly's body, he asked himself. We can't plan a funeral because we don't know when to plan it for. Hope it's not tomorrow. That's my birthday and I don't want Dolly's funeral as a memory on the few birthdays I've got left.

Jerry stacked the dishes in the dishwasher and carried a cup of coffee into his den. He switched on the TV, but kept the volume low. CNN didn't mention anything about Dolly or about the strangler. Thank the Lord. He couldn't bear hearing about it over and over. He watched some game shows and then showered and dressed.

Okay, it's almost noon. I think I'd better get Kate up. Maybe she'll feel like going out to lunch. He tapped on her door as was his custom and then slowly pushed it open. Jerry did a double take. Kate's bed was empty. It was made. It had not been slept in. He looked around for some sign of her, checked the bathroom. His legs gave out and he sank down on the bed. Kate, you didn't come home last night. Oh no, not you. He can't have you. Not my baby.

He reached out a trembling hand for the telephone. "Rick," he cried. "Rick. She's gone!"

KATE WOKE KNOWING that something was horribly wrong. She couldn't remember what it was but a terrible knowledge gnawed on the edges of her consciousness. She tried to open her eyes but her eyelids were so heavy it took the greatest effort just to flutter her lashes. Shaking off the dregs of a heavy sleep, she looked around her shadowy room. It must not be morning yet, she thought hazily, because there's no light penetrating the draperies.

Her limbs weighed a ton. Slowly, one leg at a time, she pulled herself up into a sitting position on the edge of her bed. Her legs were bare. She was naked. How odd. Why didn't I put on my nightgown before I went to bed last night? Kate asked herself. I never sleep in the nude.

And what's wrong with my room? she asked herself. When the room stopped spinning, it didn't feel the same. The walls were the same cheery yellow, the pink rose upholstery and draperies were the same too, but something was missing. Her brain was so sluggish. It was so hard to think. If only she could clear her head, she'd figure out what was wrong with her room.

The bed she sat on was her bed: mahogany four-poster,

crocheted tester, floral duvet. Her gaze swept the room. The furniture was similar but different. And where are my personal things? she wondered. Where are the photographs of my mother and of Dolly and me at the Wollman Rink that I always kept on my dressing table? And where is my silver brush and comb set? My perfume bottles? Only a small boudoir lamp glowed on the skirted table. "That's not my lamp!" Kate exclaimed aloud.

What is this? Where am I? This room is like a theatre set, a duplicate of my bedroom. It's like my set at the television station, a replica.

Kate's bare feet hit the floor. Dizzy, she reached out a hand to a bedpost to steady herself. Regaining some equilibrium, she tottered unsteadily to the windows. Reaching over the back of the chair, she pulled the cord to open the draperies. One view of Central Park and I'll know that I'm home, she thought.

Kate stared at a blank plaster wall. "No!" she cried, backing away. I'm going crazy. She stumbled to the door. "Granddad!" she screamed. Her hand twisted the doorknob. The door was locked.

She sank to her knees, too dizzy to stand. She beat the door with her fists. "Granddad, Granddad," she sobbed. "Where are you? Where am I?"

Suddenly her brain cleared and a memory so frightening it made her tremble struck with full force. Her heart thudded alarmingly. I remember now. I took a cab to…

The sound of a key grating in the lock on the other side of the door made her cringe. She scooted away. The door opened slowly.

He looked down at her, smiled pleasantly. "Good morning. Or should I say afternoon? It's almost twelve. I see you're up. I hope you like your room. I went to a lot of trouble to duplicate it for you because I want you to be

FIFTY-THREE

KATE STUMBLED TO her feet. The door behind him stood open. Unsteadily she took a step forward, then made a break for it. She darted past him, out into the hallway. She didn't know which way to go. She turned left, then realized she'd gone the wrong way because she came to a dead end and hit a blank wall. There was no way out. Shut doors lined the hallway. She tried each one, but they were all locked. I'm living my worst nightmare, she thought.

He didn't follow her. He stood near the door to her room, patient, watching her, knowing she had nowhere to go. I feel like a helpless fly caught in a spider's web, she thought. And the big evil spider's in the center, just sitting there, still and watchful. Certain that I'm going nowhere. Just keeping an eye on me until hunger strikes. Then it'll pounce. And the more I struggle, the more tangled I'll become. Until I can't move. Until I'm devoured.

Kate sank to her knees. Her head was swimming. She reached out her hands, tried to grab anything that would steady her. It was like experiencing the worst possible vertigo, like when you're drunk and hugging your mattress but it flies away with you. The hallway was spinning and she couldn't tell up from down. She curled up in a ball on the floor, naked, cold. Not even the floor felt stable.

Slowly, he walked toward her, knelt down for her, lifted her in his arms. Carried her back to her replica room.

KATE PUT ON the clothes he brought her. Although she longed to fight, she didn't have the strength. She didn't want to be hurt. *So far he hasn't hurt me.*

She drank the coffee he'd delivered on a tray, and forced herself to nibble on a croissant. "You didn't touch the cheese omelet," he complained, seeming genuinely offended.

"Sorry," she mumbled, "I'm not hungry." Then she asked herself angrily, *Why am I apologizing to a murderer?*

Shortly after brunch she became groggy and disoriented. The coffee hadn't revived her. *It's drugged,* she realized. *He's drugging me. I'll never figure out a way to escape if I can't think a coherent thought.*

She was as helpless as a small child. He helped her get into the gown he wanted her to wear. He zipped it up. His touch was impersonal, thank goodness. *But for how long?* she wondered. *How long before his fingers on my bare skin ignite his passion.* The thought of him attempting to make love to her was disgusting. *If it comes to that, I'll fight him off. I'll find the strength. I'll fight him off with any means available. He'll never have me that way.*

The dress she wore felt cool against her skin. It was made of the finest silk, a deep purple, covered with golden sequins. The sleeves ballooned around her wrists. He moved close and opened the neckline, gently parted the fabric, exposed the tops of her breasts. He said she looked just like Emilie Floge.

Then he led her into his studio. She saw the easel with the blank canvas, the portrait of Emilie Floge set on a second easel, the worktable covered with art supplies, his palette. He positioned her in front of a dark wall. Behind her head a colorful fan had been painted on the wall. The jewel-like colors framed her head like a halo. He fluffed up her hair, placed her left hand on her hip, turned her just so. Finally, when he had her posed just the way he wanted, he slipped a silk scarf around her neck.

"No," she cried. "Not that. I can't bear anything around my neck."

But he attached it to something on the wall behind her anyway. It felt so tight. She was choking. And she was anchored to the wall as securely as a butterfly pinned to a mat. She couldn't move.

This is what he did to my darling Dolly, she thought. This is what he did to all those other pitiful girls. He dressed them up, painted their portraits, then strangled them. Perhaps with this very scarf. And Dolly was naked when they found her because he had painted her naked. As fuzzy as my mind is, I can reach these conclusions now because it's all so simple. It's all clear now. And now it's too late.

Her knees grew weak. She gasped for breath. Her heart hammered. If I fall, I'll hang myself in this noose. "I can't stand this," she screamed. She felt herself falling. Brilliant spots exploded in front of her eyes. Nausea overwhelmed her. Then a velvety blackness carried her away to a peaceful place.

FIFTY-FOUR

ROSALIE RUSSO SAT in her office. She was very worried. Word had reached her that Kate Callahan was missing. Being in the chairman's office, there was not much that happened at the station that Rosalie was not privy to.

Oh, poor Kate, she thought. First Dolly Devereaux disappears, now Kate. Dolly turned up dead. A botched kidnapping, the police are saying. I wonder. Oh dear Lord, please don't let anything happen to sweet Kate, she prayed.

Her private line lit up before the telephone chirped. She lifted the handset and said her name. She recognized Mr. Thompson's voice at once. "Mrs. Russo, I'm not coming in today."

Rosalie was momentarily at a loss for words. This was extraordinary. Mr. Thompson never missed work. "Mr. Thompson, are you ill? Is there something I can do for you?"

"Nothing," he said, his voice dejected.

Of course, she thought, he's heard the news too. And it has made him sick with worry.

"Nothing," he repeated. "Just hold down the fort. And don't let anyone know where I am. No one. Do you understand?"

"I understand, Mr. Thompson. I'll tell no one."

He hung up without a thank you or a goodbye.

If there was anything Rosalie Russo knew how to do it was to protect her boss from unwanted intrusions. Naturally, it was possible that he was truly ill. If that was the case, she hoped he would have the good sense to call a doctor. If he calls me again, I'll advise him to do just that, she thought.

Now, how am I going to fill this day? she asked herself. Rosalie would never take advantage of her boss's absence to leave the office and go out shopping the way some of the secretaries did. She got paid a good salary to guard this place, and guard it she would. I'll keep in touch with the news desk and ask often if Kate's been found. I'll have the cafeteria send up a sandwich for lunch, she thought. And I've got the latest Mary Higgins Clark suspense novel. Clark is such good company for old gals like me. I'll just make myself comfy on Mr. Thompson's couch and read.

Rosalie buzzed the receptionist desk out at the elevators on the executive floor. "If you need to reach me, I'll be in Mr. Thompson's office. And if anyone asks for him, put them through to me as usual," she instructed.

"Yes, Mrs. Russo," the girl said. Up here, Mrs. Russo's word was law.

Rosalie took the book from her lower desk drawer and went into Vaughn Thompson's office, closing the door securely behind her. She tossed the book onto the couch but guilt prevented her from settling there. There must be something that needs to be done, she thought.

She went into Mr. Thompson's private washroom to verify that the janitor had cleaned it to her and Mr. Thompson's specifications. The room was spotless. Fresh towels hung on the rods, new bars of soap had been set out, and the room smelled of air freshener.

Back in his office, Rosalie walked to the window to look down. The day was gloomy, dark clouds were rolling in over the Hudson. Soon it will rain, she predicted. She imagined Kate out in that rain, unsheltered, maybe wandering the streets after an accident and suffering a loss of memory.

Turning, she noted that everything on Mr. Thompson's desk was in order. Checking the drawers, she verified that they were locked, as they always were when he was absent. She had her own set of keys to his office and his desk which she carried in her purse. But she'd never used them to open his desk drawers except the few times he'd called her from out of town and asked her to locate a file for him. He knew she'd never go into his desk uninvited, and she never would.

She opened the door to his closet. Well, the least I can do is take this suit to the cleaners, she thought. Maybe I will go out to lunch, after all, and I'll drop this off at that French dry cleaners on the next block.

She went out to her own office for a shopping bag, returned to his suite, and removed the worn-only-once suit from its hanger. She tossed the articles on the couch, then reached for the pants to fold them. Something pressed under her shoe, and to her dismay she realized she was standing on a paper that had fallen out of the suit pocket.

"Oh, dear me, what a klutz I am," she said out loud. "I hope I haven't ruined anything."

She reached down and picked up a small white paper, the back of a black and white photograph. She turned it over. "What!" she exclaimed out loud, immediately recognizing the person in the photograph and wondering about the informality of it. She felt puzzled and for an instant alarmed although she didn't know why. This is not a promotional piece, she told herself. You can see she doesn't know she's being photographed.

In the suit pocket Rosalie found a dozen black and white glossies of Kate Callahan. It was obvious that the pictures were taken without Kate's knowledge for she never once looked into the camera. Why is he taking pictures of her surreptitiously? she asked herself.

The photographs showed Kate shopping at a green grocers, entering and leaving a dry cleaning establishment, getting out of a cab and going into her apartment building. In the lower right side the date and time each picture had been snapped was printed in the corner. "What does this mean?" Rosalie asked the empty room. She was conscious of the fear she heard in her own voice.

Someone was following Kate Callahan around the city and taking photographs of her without her knowledge. It couldn't have been Mr. Thompson himself because Kate would surely have recognized him and looked up. Did he hire someone to do this for him? His chauffeur Tony came to mind. Rosalie had never liked the man. But he'd do anything for Mr. Thompson. Just like me, she thought. This can't be on the level. And now that poor girl is missing, just like all those other girls.

Rosalie Russo felt like the seams of her carefully constructed world were pulling apart. The man who had saved her life, the man she worked for and trusted, was involved in something underhanded. Her thoughts leapt along an uncharted course until she reached the ultimate, terrible conclusion. "No!" she cried aloud, and let the sheaf of photos fall from her hand.

FIFTY-FIVE

THE DOORBELL IN Jerry's apartment rang. Rick and Joe Mateer were there with Jerry, reassuring him that they were searching for Kate. She'd left the TV station in a cab on Wednesday night. The security guard had been the last person to see her. The police were checking with all the cab companies, going over the records, trying to locate the cab and its destination. Unless she'd taken a gypsy cab. Gypsy cabs were painted yellow too but they didn't have medallions. And gypsy cabdrivers didn't keep records.

"I can't remember if it was a gypsy cab," Jesse, the station's security guard, had said apologetically. "It was just a yellow cab. I didn't think anything about it. You're gonna find Miss Callahan, ain't you?"

Kate's face was broadcast on TV screens all over the city; every station was carrying news of her disappearance. Eight-hundred numbers had been set up for callers with information. Vaughn Thompson was offering one million dollars in reward money. That'd bring the rats out of their holes, Jerry thought.

The doorbell rang again. He pulled the door open abruptly. A woman was standing in the hall. Somehow she'd got past the doorman because she hadn't been announced. It had been many years but he knew her instantly. His hand flew to his heart. "Annie!" he cried.

"Hello, Dad," Rosalie Russo said. "I'm sorry to spring this on you now. I knew you and Kate had a good life and I didn't want to interfere. I know I'm bad news. But I've got information about Kate, and the police said that Detective Smith was here. May I come in?"

Tears flooded Jerry's eyes. The day he'd been praying for the past thirty years had arrived. "Come in? Of course you can come in." He opened his arms to her. "This is your home, Annie. Your home is wherever me and Kate are. No questions asked. No judgments made. Welcome home, sweetheart."

FIFTY-SIX

PHYLLIS STERN BURST out of the director's office in a rage. Her heart was pounding, and she knew her blood pressure was shooting sky high. That man's going to be the death of me, she thought. Museum attendance has never been higher, contributions are up, yet he's cutting the costume department's budget. Why do I have to put up with such idiots? she asked herself, thinking of the succession of directors she'd outlasted.

Maybe my critics are right, she considered. Maybe it is time for me to retire. I'm eighty-three, although they don't know that. I'm too old for this bottom-line accountant's mentality that is driving the museum these days. She remembered the old days when "art for art's sake" was the thing.

Too impatient to wait for an elevator, Stern took the stairs, her steel gray hair bobbing, her patent leather pumps flying like shiny black wings. She reached the mezzanine level and paused for breath.

All right now, old girl, she counseled herself, you've got the better of those bean counters in the past, you'll outsmart them again. What you need is a bit of time out. A stroll past favorite paintings to slow your heart rate and buoy your spirits.

Stern slowed her walk to a casual stroll and passed through the American Wing's Special Exhibitions in the M2 gallery. She headed for the M1 gallery and the late nineteenth and early twentieth century realists—her old friends. Hands clasped behind her back, she forced herself to a slow pace, took time to breathe deeply. Few visitors patronized the gallery so late in the day. She had it almost to herself.

She stopped to admire her old friend, *Lady at the Tea Table*, by Mary Cassatt. As a costume expert, Stern paid particular attention to the old woman's attire, her black capelet and white lace bonnet. The fact was, she knew these paintings the way a mother knows her children. She could have painted them herself from memory, had she any talent.

She moved on to her favorite. Each time she gazed at this fabulous portrait, she was struck with awe, no matter how many times that was. John Singer Sargent's rendering of *Madame X* was a larger-than-life seven by four foot canvas. The painting had been scandalous in its day. Madame X stood in a haughty pose, her head in profile, proudly showing off her large ski-slope nose. Stern had learned a lesson in style from that lady, specifically how not to try to hide the hawk's nose she'd been born with. Like Madame X, she displayed it proudly, with her sleek hair style, the black framed half-glasses that perched on its tip. And like Madame X, she was fond of the color black.

Stern admired the shimmery black satin gown with its deeply cut *décolletage*. If ever I were to paint, she thought, I would dress my subject in a daring gown such as this. Dress my subject… Oh my God, that's it! That's the key! She slapped herself on the forehead. What a dunce I've been.

Back in the stairwell, she raced down the steps to the first floor. Hurrying across the lobby, she ignored the greetings of volunteers. She swept into the gift shop, past the astonished clerks at the check-out counter. Everyone who worked in the museum recognized the legendary

Phyllis Stern on sight, but she'd never set foot in the gift shop before.

Stern pulled art books from the display shelves quickly, knowing exactly what she was looking for. It took her less than two minutes to find books on the French Impressionists, the Realists, and one book on Sargent. With her arms full, she rushed past the check-out counter, calling over her shoulder, "I'm taking these books to my office."

The young attendant raised no objection. Stern knew that everyone in the museum was afraid of her.

Hurrying to the lower level where the costume department was located, Stern closed herself in her office. She riffled the pages in the books, searching, seeking. "There!" she cried aloud, her long fingertip jabbing a page. "And there. And there. I've got it!"

Throwing a cashmere shawl over her shoulders and gathering up her purse, Stern swooped up the armload of books. Her heart beat too fast for comfort as she hurried down the hall and out the employees only door. On Fifth Avenue, a couple were just getting out of a cab. Stern jumped in. "One Police Plaza," she told the driver urgently. "Take the FDR Drive, it's the quickest. There's a fifty for you if you can get me there in fifteen minutes!"

FIFTY-SEVEN

AT FIVE O'CLOCK, Rick Smith's office was crowded, but things were coming together. Phyllis Stern had arrived with an armload of art books. She'd pointed out all of the pictures, indicating how the costumes in each resembled the clothing the dead women had been wearing. A detective was sent to retrieve all the costumes from the Evidence Room, and a comparison was made. "These costumes are identical to the clothing in the paintings," Stern said positively. "Don't you see? He's dressing them up like subjects in paintings."

"And then what?" Joe Mateer asked. "What's he doing?"

"Maybe he's using them as models for his own paintings. I don't know," Stern replied.

In an interrogation room, Detective Lori Martin was questioning Tony Mastriani, Vaughn Thompson's driver. And Mastriani was singing like a canary. Sure, he'd taken the photos of Miss Callahan but only because his boss told him to, there ain't no law against that. And yes, he'd followed her like Thompson had instructed, but that was just to make sure she was safe. Thompson was in love with her, worried about her. Tony didn't know why Thompson wanted the pictures. And after Tony had got Marty Sokolov the job driving Miss Callahan, Marty kept tabs on Miss Callahan.

But they didn't harm her. The last thing Mr. Thompson wanted was to have her harmed. He was flipped out over her. "I've told you everything I know," Tony said. "Now either let me go or book me."

"I'll do neither, Mr. Mastriani," Lori said. "But I can hold you for forty-eight hours, and that's what I'm going to do."

"Then I want a lawyer," Tony said heatedly.

"We'll get you one," Lori responded.

JERRY AND ANNIE had insisted on coming back to the station with Rick and Joe. Earlier at Jerry's apartment, Annie had shown the detectives the photographs she'd found in Vaughn Thompson's jacket pocket and suggested that they'd been taken by Tony Mastriani.

"Until you find Kate, I'm sticking to you guys like glue," Jerry had said when Rick protested his coming to police headquarters.

"You'll just be in the way," Joe Mateer had said.

The nerve of him, Jerry thought. He'd puffed up his chest and stuck his face in Mateer's. "Don't count me out just because I'm old," he growled. "If it wasn't for me, and guys like me, German would be your native tongue, sonny!"

Something inside me is breaking, he thought. My heart. Whatever. I'm not going to let it happen. I'm going to fight. I fought those Nazi devils and beat 'em, years and years ago. Now I'm going to fight again. My last battle. I'm going to get Kate back.

Mateer was impressed. Maybe he *can* help, he thought. Rick only smirked. He'd learned long ago when he'd been dating Kate that nobody won an argument with Jerry Callahan when Callahan's back was up.

At five fifteen Evan Wallace dropped by. "I'm on my way to the TV station and I thought I'd check to see if there were any developments." He looked at Jerry and

Thompson's secretary, Rosalie Russo, curiously. "Guess there are."

Rick brought him up to date. The hospital maintenance man had an airtight alibi for the night Dolly was killed. Then Rick told him that Rosalie was Kate's mother, Annie Callahan. "No shit!" Evan exclaimed. Then, "Pardon my language, ma'am. I just got carried away."

"I've heard worse," Annie said.

Phyllis Stern had left but the art books were spread on Rick's desk, their pages open to the relevant paintings. "There's that Sargent again," Evan said.

"What do you mean, again?" Rick asked pointedly.

"I saw that Sargent in Vaughn Thompson's house on Saturday night," Evan replied.

Rick stroked his chin as he weighed the evidence against Thompson. He had been stalking Kate. And one of the victims wrote to her sister that she was having an affair with a television giant. Now he's got the Sargent.

Rick reached for the phone. "Put Assistant District Attorney Jordan on the phone. This is Detective Rick Smith." Then, "Jim, I need a search warrant for Vaughn Thompson's house."

"Yes, that Vaughn Thompson."

"What am I looking for? A painting that is evidence in the strangler case. And any other evidence relating to the strangler case."

THOMPSON HAD BEEN DRINKING. His hair was rumpled and he was wearing a bathrobe. Granted the bathrobe was made of cashmere, still it was only six thirty in the evening. "Look if you want," he said. "I have nothing to hide."

"While they're searching, let's you and me have a little talk," Rick said. "In here." He indicated a small library. The bar was open, the cushions were crushed; this apparently was the room where Thompson had been doing his drinking.

"I'm distraught over Kate's disappearance," Vaughn attempted to explain, his voice tremulous, his eyes teary.

Now don't be pulling a crying jag on me, Rick thought. "That's why we're here," he said coolly. He felt no sympathy for this man who'd had Kate followed, photographed, and watched. All because he was obsessed with her.

"Mr. Thompson, did you know a woman named Celeste Parker? She was tall with bright orange hair, an actress who worked at a coffee shop on the East Side."

"No, I never heard of her."

"Are you sure?"

Thompson moved to the bar, refilled his glass. "What'll you have?" he asked.

Rick made a dismissive motion with his hand. "Nothing. Now, do you know Celeste Parker? Did you ever date her?" Rick repeated.

Thompson turned, weaving slightly. "I meet a lot of people, Detective. I don't remember all of them. But I do remember the women I date. And I've never dated Celeste Parker. Besides, I don't like tall women." His smile was lopsided, the goofy smirk of a drunk.

"Where were you on the night of Sunday, May 7th?" Rick asked, referring to the night Regina Hoover, wearing a dress straight out of a Sargent painting, had been killed.

Thompson struggled to concentrate. He flopped down in a chair. "That was the first weekend in May. I know, I remember. I was in Greenwich. I have a house there."

"Anybody see you?"

Vaughn frowned in an effort to think clearly. "Many people saw me on the golf course that afternoon. In the evening I gave a dinner party for twelve. I slept over and returned to the city on Monday morning. My driver drove me in."

"Yeah, we know all about your driver," Rick said with disgust. "Are you willing to give me a list of your dinner guests?"

"Naturally. I told you before I have nothing to hide."

Out in the hall, two detectives coming down the stairs struggled with a very large painting. "Where are they going with my Sargent?" Thompson asked, alarmed.

"It's evidence in a crime, Mr. Thompson. We're impounding it. You'll get it back. I'd like to know if you owned it on May 7th."

Vaughn blinked, attempting to focus. "On the weekend? No, I bought that painting several days later. On Tuesday."

"Who did you buy it from?" Rick asked.

"My dealer. Thomas Shipley," Vaughn replied.

"Okay, Thompson, you're off the hook for now. But don't leave town. Don't even go up to that fancy Greenwich estate of yours. I want you right here where I can find you."

Vaughn gave him a sly wink. "I'll have my lawyers call your lawyers." He raised his glass in a salute to Rick. Suddenly, he let out a loud grunt and threw the glass onto the carpet, its contents splattering in all directions. He lunged at Rick and grabbed him by the arm. "Find her, Smith. You gotta find her. I can't live without her."

Rick Smith pulled his arm away, turned his back and strode out of the room. "I got no use for slobbering drunks," he said out loud. "Rich or otherwise."

FIFTY-EIGHT

KATE WAS BACK in the replica room, lying on the bed. He sat next to her on the bed's edge, patting her wrists. "Kate, wake up. Wake up," he said.

Kate whispered, "I blacked out." He was acting very concerned for her. She decided to appeal to that side of him. "I have a phobia. I can't bear to have anything around my neck. I never wear necklaces or turtleneck sweaters. The feel of something around my neck causes me great anxiety, and I have a panic attack. Sometimes I pass out."

She grabbed his hands and pleaded, "Please don't wrap that scarf around my neck again. I'll pose for you. I won't move. I promise."

"Oh, Kate, of course I won't do it if it makes you uncomfortable. I want you to be happy here. That's why I fixed up this room just like your room at home. I copied every detail from the photo in *Architectural Digest*. I'm going to immortalize you and I want you to get as much pleasure from the experience as I do."

"Thank you," Kate murmured, falling back against the pillows. Tears filled her eyes and spilled from the outer corners.

"If you only knew how long I've been planning this. From the first time I saw you, saw your resemblance to Klimt's favorite model. You are both so beautiful. I have loved you for so long."

He's crazy, Kate thought, but allowed her tears to flow

unchecked. Feeling better because of them somehow. I've got to get away from him.

He was ranting. "It's important that you understand, Kate. I need to be understood by the women I love. But they never understand me!" His fist punched the mattress. Kate winced and slid away, trying to make herself smaller.

He softened his voice but still she detected the suppressed anger it in. "I have a mission, you see, a task that is my life's work. When I see a woman who resembles the subject of one of the great masters, I am compelled to paint her. Just as the artist himself did. Her hair and coloring must be the same, the costume she wears must be authentic, the setting must be an exact replica. I don't have any choice in this. This work has been entrusted to me. It is my destiny."

Kate didn't want to ask who had entrusted this macabre mission to him. She knew there was no one. She was locked up in these rooms with a madman, a psychopathic killer. Yet she had to learn about Dolly's last days. "Did you paint my friend, Dolly Devereaux? Did you immortalize her? I saw the Matisse. That's why she was nude, wasn't it? You were copying the Matisse."

He jumped up from the bed. "Copying? You've got it all wrong, Kate. The original paintings are merely sources of ideas. It's the girls themselves who provide the inspiration. Come, I'll show you."

He took her arm and helped her to her feet. From a key ring he produced a key that unlocked one of the doors in the hallway. At a flick of the switch, the room blazed with light. "My own very private gallery," he said with immense pride.

Quickly Kate surveyed the room. There were five paintings displayed on the walls. She recognized the costumes in each. From the Degas ballerina to the Lautrec can-can dancer to the Matisse nude draped with a white silk scarf. The fifth painting was immense and occupied a wall of its own. In it, a girl in a long white dress held a tennis racket. The paintings were similar in every way to the reproductions of the originals she'd seen last night. But with one terrible exception. The women portrayed in his paintings were grotesque.

Kate turned to the copy of the Matisse. This was supposed to be her dear friend Dolly. Dolly's kind, serene face had been depicted as hideous and evil. The first girl, sweet little Ashley Fuller, had been painted to look like a feral animal.

He doesn't see it, Kate realized. He thinks he's produced works of art, things of beauty.

He stood watching, waiting for her approval. Kate assumed a neutral expression; she would take her cue from him.

"Aren't they all lovely?" he finally asked. "Haven't I immortalized them, made them better than they were?"

Kate clasped her hands together as if overcome with admiration. "You're a genius. They are truly works of art. What did Dolly think of her picture when you showed it to her?"

His head snapped back as if she'd slapped him. "She knew nothing about art. She didn't have the sense to appreciate what I'd made of her."

Kate persisted. She had to know what had happened to her friend. "But I knew Dolly well. She had a fine appreciation of art. Are you saying she didn't like her portrait?"

He roared, "She hated it! They all hated their portraits. I couldn't bear the look of contempt in their eyes. I had to stop it!"

FIFTY-NINE

"LET'S TAKE a couple of uniforms and pay a little surprise visit on Thomas Shipley," Rick said.

"I'll call the A.D.A. from the car phone and have him get us another search warrant," Joe said. "I'll ask him to have it delivered to us at Shipley's, PDQ."

"And let's have Leon Haber brought to Shipley's," Rick suggested. "He's the art expert. I wouldn't know van Gogh from van Camps."

"What did you find at Thompson's?" Jerry asked from the backseat of the detective's car. He and Annie were holding hands and had waited impatiently while Rick and Joe went inside.

"Evidence that leads to Thomas Shipley," Rick replied, and filled him in.

The Shipley Gallery was about to close when the detectives arrived. Shipley opened the door himself. His assistant had left for the day, he told them. "What can I do for you detectives?"

"We've just had an interesting talk with Vaughn Thompson about a Sargent painting you sold him," Rick said.

Shipley looked from one detective to the other, nervously batting his eyes. "Is that illegal?" he asked hotly.

"You know the answer to that better than we do," Joe said.

Shipley closed the door behind them and began closing the shades. "What are you getting at?" He was trying to sound indifferent but his voice cracked.

Just like I suspected the other night, Rick thought, he's acting guilty about something.

"When did you sell the Sargent to Thompson?" Joe asked.

"I can't be expected to remember the details of every transaction I make. I'll have to look it up on the computer." Shipley went to a desk, sat down behind it, and tapped on the computer keyboard. He lifted his head. "I sold it on May 11th."

"Did you own it on May 7th?" Rick asked.

"May 7th?" Shipley repeated, and licked his lips. He consulted the computer again. "No, I acquired it on May 9th. What is this about? I insist on knowing why you're asking me these questions."

Rick ignored Shipley's indignant act. "Where were you on Sunday night, May 7th, Mr. Shipley?"

Shipley replied smugly, "On a night plane from London. Bringing the Klimt painting, *The Embrace*, back to Irma Greenbaum."

The doorbell rang. Rick went to the door, opened the shades. Two uniformed officers and Leon Haber stood outside. Rick let them in.

One of the officers handed Rick a document.

Haber looked from the detectives to Thomas Shipley. "Ship, what's going on?"

Shipley shrugged as if none of this had anything to do with him. "I wouldn't know. Ask them."

Rick handed the document to Shipley. "It's a search warrant, Mr. Shipley. We're looking for three paintings." He turned to Haber. "And you're here, Professor, because you're the art expert. We'd appreciate it if you would accompany these officers throughout the building and look for these paintings." He gave Haber the list of titles and painters Phyllis Stern had prepared: the Renoir, the Lautrec, and a drawing by Wallace Morgan. "We've already got the Sargent in custody."

Joe Mateer, the police officers, and Leon Haber began a search of the building, starting with the basement. Rick waited on the first floor with Thomas Shipley. Shipley got on his phone, tracking down his lawyer. Rick listened as Shipley left messages all over town for the attorney to come immediately to the Shipley Galleries.

Rick pulled up a chair and made himself comfortable. This was going to take a while. Jerry and Annie were waiting outside in his car. They'd have a long wait, but it couldn't be helped. They were as scared for Kate as he was. Where are you, Katie? he silently pleaded. Dear God, send me a clue.

To Shipley, he said, "We questioned your assistant and he confirmed that Regina Hoover had a job interview here the day before she disappeared. His story corresponds with yours except for one thing. He agrees that she was over-qualified for the job of a data entry clerk, but he says that after she left you picked up her résumé and took it into your office."

Shipley removed his glasses and used a handkerchief to mop the sweat from around his eyes. "So what?"

"So, you knew where she lived and what her telephone number was. The next day, she disappears."

"I did not kill her!" Shipley roared. "I did not kill anyone!"

"Whoever killed Regina Hoover had that Sargent painting in his possession on May 7th. You said you acquired it. Who did you buy it from?"

"From Leon Haber," Shipley said simply.

"Haber? Is he a dealer?"

"No. But he sometimes acts as a middleman. He's often asked to appraise works of art and that puts him in a position to know what's available. I had a client, Vaughn Thompson, who was in the market for a Sargent. I mentioned this to Haber. He said he knew of one for sale. He makes a tidy commission on the transaction."

Rick had to question Haber right away, but he needed him to help identify the three paintings. He wouldn't let Haber go home. After the search, he would take Haber into custody. Like Joe said, a cool head will solve this one. But will we be in time to save Kate? he worried.

Just then, Joe Mateer, the uniformed officers, and Leon Haber returned from the basement and began a systematic search through the various galleries on the first floor. Mateer paused near Rick. "The professor says none of the paintings we're looking for are down there."

Shortly after the group took the elevator to the third floor, Joe Mateer reappeared. "There're some locked doors up there, Mr. Shipley. You can give us the keys, or we can break the doors down."

The flush drained from Shipley's face, leaving it pale and tense. He reached into his pocket and produced a key ring. "Don't break anything," he whined.

Joe Mateer reentered the elevator. Ten minutes later, he was back, a furious Professor Haber bolting ahead of him. The uniformed officers each carried a gilt-framed oil painting. Rick jumped to his feet.

Haber, his face livid, marched up to Shipley and struck him across the face. "You are beneath contempt," he cried. Then grabbing the phone, he said, "The FBI will be interested in this."

Shipley slumped forward, his shoulders heaving.

Rick spread his hands. "Are these the paintings? What's going on?"

Joe Mateer smiled and waved a hand at the two paintings. "These are two stolen Klimts. Part of a threesome that included *The Embrace*. Shipley had all three of the stolen paintings all along. We'd better leave one of the uniforms here to guard him until the FBI arrives."

"What about the paintings on the list?" Rick asked.

"We went over every inch of the place. They're not here."

SIXTY

BACK AT ONE Police Plaza, Rick and Joe questioned Leon Haber. "We want to know all about the Sargent painting you got for Thomas Shipley. When did you get it and who did you get it from?"

"Am I a suspect?" Haber asked. "I've done nothing wrong."

"Where'd you get the painting?" Joe Mateer asked, leaning on the table and leveling his face with Haber's.

"I never wanted Shipley to find out because of the lawsuit he'd filed against Lorneby's, but I got the painting from Neil Lorneby. I've been dealing with Lorneby privately over the years. Occasionally, if I had a buyer for a painting, he'd hold it back and let it go on the side if the price was right."

"Is that legal?" Joe asked.

"It's not illegal," Haber said. "I don't involve myself in illegal transactions."

"When did you buy it from Lorneby?" Rick asked.

"On May 9th."

Rick and Joe turned to each other. "The day after Regina Hoover's body was found."

"Just for the record, Haber, do you have an alibi for Sunday night, May 7th?" Joe asked.

"I was with a friend," Haber replied reluctantly.

"All night?"

"Yes."

"A woman?"

"Yes."

"Will she confirm this?"

"Yes. But I don't want the University to learn of this. She's a student."

"Okay, wait in here while we check your alibi. Write down her name and number. If she confirms your story, you're free to go," Rick said.

Rick and Joe left the interrogation room, found Lori Martin, and assigned her the job of confirming Haber's alibi.

"I think we've got our man," Rick said. "Let's move."

One of the other detectives called, "Rick, call for you. She says it's urgent."

"Detective Smith, this is Elsie Hoover, Regina's mother. I just had a call from an employment agent wanting to know if she could set Regina up for an interview tomorrow. Guess she doesn't follow the news because she didn't know about Regina's death. She gave me some vital information."

"Yes. What is it?" Rick asked urgently. I've got to get to Kate! He switched the phone over to the speaker so Joe could listen too.

"Regina had a job interview with Neil Lorneby at Lorneby's Auction House on Friday afternoon. Regina did not call the agent after the interview as she was supposed to."

Lori Martin hurried into the detectives' office. "Haber's alibi checks out."

"Thanks, Lori, see that he gets released. Joe and I are on our way to Lorneby's. We think Neil Lorneby is our serial killer."

"Lorneby's?" Lori asked excitedly. "That's where they sell all those antiques. Gee whiz!" Lori whipped out her cell phone and ran out of the room.

Jerry and Annie returned to the office, paper coffee

cups in their hands. Evan Wallace was with them. "I came as soon as I could get away from the station," he said. "Something's breaking. I can tell by your expressions."

Lori Martin squeezed in, vibrating with tension. "I told them to let Haber go. *And* I just spoke to Ashley Fuller's mother. The Fullers' house is furnished with expensive antiques. Mrs. Fuller bought them at Lorneby's auctions. And Ashley often accompanied her to the exhibits there."

"There's Lorneby's connection with the Fuller girl!" Joe cried, as he and Lori hit a high-five.

Jerry said, "You mean you think Lorneby's got Kate. What are we waiting for? I'll kill that guy with my bare hands."

"Hold on a minute, Jerry," Rick said, scribbling something on a legal pad. Ripping off the page, he thrust it at Lori. "I want you to make some calls for me. We'll be on our way uptown. Call me with the answers on my cell phone. You got that?"

"Yes, Rick. Right away."

"Okay," Rick said, unable to conceal the anxiety in his voice any longer, "we don't have time to waste going through channels at the D.A.'s office. The commissioner has put a lot of pressure on us to solve this case, now it's payback time." Rick picked up the phone, dialed a number, and identified himself to the commissioner's wife. He was put right through.

"Commissioner, I'm calling about the strangler case. We need a warrant to search Lorneby's Auction House immediately and I don't have time to go through the D.A.'s office."

"What's at Lorneby's?" the commissioner asked abruptly.

"Kate Callahan and evidence that Lorneby is the strangler," Rick replied urgently.

"You're sure about this, Smith?"

"You can have my shield if I'm wrong, sir," Rick said.

"I won't be in any position to seize it, Smith. If you're wrong, I'll be out of a job. Now exactly what do you need?"

"We're on our way to Lorneby's now. I need someone to meet us there with a warrant. That place is as solid as an armory, so I need a lot of back-up to break through those doors. See if someone can locate Lorneby's security company and have them there too. They might be able to get us in faster. And because a hostage is involved, send a SWAT team."

"You got it, Smith!"

Leon Haber, passing the detectives' office, stuck his head in to say, "If you're going to question Lorneby, find out what happened to Rebecca Bernstein. She was his first wife, and after they divorced, he told everybody she moved to Paris. But I've never been able to find her!"

SIXTY-ONE

KATE HAD POSED for him all day. She hadn't moved in hours. The small of her back ached, her legs trembled with fatigue, and her neck was stiff. But as long as he's painting me, he isn't killing me, she reasoned. Please, dear God, let him be a slow painter.

"Neil, I have to take a break," she said. "I need to use the bathroom."

He set his palette down with exaggerated patience and wiped his hands on a turpentine-dampened towel, blowing out a frustrated sigh. "You use the bathroom more than any woman I know."

"I'm sorry," Kate replied meekly. "It's a problem I have. We've been working all day and I'm tired. How is it coming?" she dared to ask. She hoped he would show her the canvas. She hoped she would see a painting in the beginning stages. If it took days for him to complete, Rick might have time to find her. She knew in her heart that he was looking for her. And her grandfather would move heaven and earth to find her, if he had to call out the army, the navy, and the marines. She knew they were looking. She just had to hang on until they got here.

She was so relieved she'd been able to convince Neil not to tie the scarf around her neck. And he'd been leaving her alone in her room at mealtimes. She'd flushed lunch and dinner down the toilet. The only water she drank was what she could hold in her cupped hands under the tap.

She wasn't hungry. How could she swallow with a huge lump in her throat?

Without the drugs in her system, she'd been able to keep a level head and retain a semblance of calm. But to maintain the charade that she was eating his drugged food, when he walked her from her room to the studio, she behaved as if she was woozy. Many times she'd plead dizziness and ask to sit down. That helped in slowing his progress. He'll kill me when he's finished, she told herself, no matter how I praise the painting.

This is what my precious Dolly went through, Kate thought, shuddering. I'm going to get free, Dolly, she promised her dead friend. I'm going to get him for both of us.

She delayed in the bathroom until he pounded on the door. "You've been in there long enough," he yelled. "I'm opening the door."

He found her sitting on the floor. She gave him a meek, but confused, smile. "My legs are like jelly," she murmured.

He thinks I'm eating his drugged food, she reasoned. He'll know the symptoms I'm complaining about are the result of the drugs he's administering. Lifting her easily, he carried her back to the studio.

He'd placed a chair against the wall for her. "You can sit for a while. I'm working on your face and hair. I can do that while you rest."

"Thanks," she said in a compliant voice. "You're very kind, Neil."

At his worktable, he scraped the paint off the palette. "My paint dries out every time you ask for a break," he complained, irritated. He squeezed fresh paint from his many tubes onto the palette.

Kate followed his every move with her eyes.

"Neil, yesterday you started to tell me about your first wife," Kate said in a conversational tone, "the one you met through Leon Haber. Was she very talented?"

His reaction startled her. He flung down the palette onto the worktable. "She was a vicious bitch. And I don't want to talk about her."

"I'm sorry," Kate mumbled.

But he was on a tirade; nothing could stop him. "We used to set our easels up together, side by side, and paint the same subject. I always praised her work. But she had no respect for mine. She laughed at me. At times, I persuaded her to sit for me, but when she did, she ridiculed my efforts. I'm glad she's gone!"

He stormed around the room. Reaching a wall, he began to bang his forehead against it. Can I make a run for it now? Kate wondered. Just as she started to rise, he turned to face her, his anger spent. He picked up the palette, took a brush from a jar and resumed painting as if nothing had happened. Kate let out her breath.

After a moment, he said, "My other wives had no interest in my painting. All they cared about was the money. The furs. The jewels. The trips abroad. But for all their faults, they didn't belittle my efforts. Serena sat for me at times; she was so beautiful. When I showed her my paintings, she said she knew nothing about art. She said my work had energy and life. I liked her for saying that."

Lorneby's emotions are so volatile, Kate realized, I've got to be careful. She sat very still and waited for what she estimated was thirty minutes. "May I stretch?" she asked.

Lorneby smiled benevolently. He sure is a contradiction in emotions, she thought. "This is going well. Sure, take a break," he said pleasantly.

Kate stood up. She made a show of stretching her arms above her head. Slowly she moved around the room, rolling her shoulders, rubbing the small of her back. All the while she edged closer to the worktable.

Lorneby was dabbing paint, his attention focused on the canvas. Kate rounded the table behind him. Quickly she grabbed a palette knife off the table. As he turned his head to see what she was doing, she swung her arm back then down, plunging the knife between his shoulder blades.

Lorneby let out a howl. The palette and brush went flying. His hands reached behind him, groping for the knife. All the while he was screaming. Kate lifted her skirt, kicked off her shoes, and bolted from the room.

SIXTY-TWO

JOE WAS DRIVING. The light on the dash flashed blue. The siren screamed. Rick turned to Jerry, Annie, and Evan in the backseat. "Fasten your seat belts. Joe's gonna burn rubber, and I don't want you to get hurt."

"Don't worry about us," Jerry snapped. "We'll hang on. Just get us to Kate."

Joe got on the FDR Drive and floored it. Rick's cell phone chirped. "It's Lori, Rick. I made those calls for you. Phyllis Stern says 'yes,' the clothing could have come from an auction house. Especially, the Fortuny dress. And guess what? In May, Lorneby's auctioned off a Fortuny collection. Stern is positive about that."

"Any word from the guys working on the cab reports?" Rick asked.

"Yes. Their manifest shows that a woman was driven from the TNYC-TV center to Lorneby's Auction House at nine fifteen on Wednesday night."

"Good going, Lori! Anything else?"

"Yeah, I called Lorneby's fashion director at home. She told me that Courtney Dixon, the art student who worked as a model, was one of the models for Lorneby's when they auctioned off Hollywood costumes in early April."

"Good work. All the pieces are coming together."

"There's more, Rick. Neil Lorneby frequented Flo's coffee shop. He always asked to be seated in Celeste Parker's section."

"Thanks, Lori." Rick said to Joe, "Lorneby's connected

to them all." Hang on, Kate, we're coming. His foot ground into the floorboard, urging the car forward. "Can't you go any faster?"

Seeing a break in the traffic ahead, Joe said, "Can do," and the detectives' car shot through the opening.

KATE DID NOT make the same mistake twice. She turned right and ran down the corridor in the opposite direction from the route she'd taken when she'd darted past Lorneby that first day, the blind route that had led to a dead end. Ahead were the elevators. Behind her, she could hear Neil stomping and cursing in his studio. She didn't think the palette knife had inflicted a fatal wound. She thought the tip was lodged in muscle. Soon, he'd yank it out. But she had gained herself some valuable time. Now she had to find a good place to hide. In this immense seven story building with all its storage rooms and furniture, she'd find that place.

She punched the elevator button and the doors glided open. She had no idea of the time, or of the day either. She thought it was Friday. Oh my gosh, Granddad's birthday, she thought. Counting the meals he'd served her that day— breakfast, lunch, dinner—she had to assume it was now about ten or eleven at night. The auction house would be closed to the public. All the employees would have gone home. Neil would have seen to that. And there were no security guards after hours, she remembered him saying. The building was a fortress.

If she could find a place to hide through the night, tomorrow the building would fill up with people and she'd run to them for help. She had to remain level-headed, not to give in to the fear that threatened to destroy her ability to reason.

Her mind raced. She hit the CLOSE DOOR button. She

tried to anticipate what Neil would do, to put herself in his shoes. He would go to his command center to watch the monitors. He'd be able to see every inch of the entire building. She forced herself to recall everything he'd told her about his security system when she'd toured this building with him last Thursday.

There were cameras everywhere, he'd said, plus heat sensors and motion detectors and silent alarms. When the alarms go off, he'll be watching me on the monitors. Then he'll come for me. But he'll have to leave the command center to return to the elevator. And that's when I'll switch places.

Where could she go? She remembered the carpets and tapestries room. I'll go there. I want him to see me stepping between the rows of carpets.

The overhead panel indicated she was on the seventh floor, his penthouse. Now, if only I can remember the layout of this place. Where was that rug room? Ah yes, on the sixth floor, down the hall from his office. And that gave her an idea.

She pushed SIX. The elevator descended smoothly and slowly. Hurry! she urged. The doors opened and a bell dinged dully. As she stepped off, Kate hit the button for the first floor. The doors closed behind her and the elevator started its descent. Maybe he'll think I'm trying to escape from the lobby. In any case, this will buy me more time.

Kate appraised her surroundings. Think fast, Callahan, you don't have time to waste. The hallway was dimly lit and shadowy. Along the walls there were Chinese urns and narrow tables. She vaguely remembered those objects from her tour. At the distant end of the hall was a door she believed led to the rug room. She ran down the middle of the hallway where there was the most light, hoping that Lorneby was watching her on a monitor. The sign that identified the rare carpets and tapestries room was large and legible. This is it.

Kate opened the door, praying that a silent alarm was going off, and that a flashing light on a panel in his security command center was alerting him that the rug room door was being tampered with. Inside, a solitary lightbulb dimly illuminated the gloomy space. Kate forced herself not to look up for the cameras. She made a great show of choosing which row of carpets to hide in, then stepped between the heavy hangings. Dust billowed up and she sneezed. She forced herself to count to ten.

He'll be running to the elevator now, she thought. But it will have to come all the way up from the first floor. And his wound will slow him down. I've got a minute, maybe two. He's probably bleeding a lot. He won't take the stairs. He'll want to make this as easy on himself as possible. He's feeling sure of himself. He thinks he knows where to find me. He plans to kill me quickly, then get medical help for himself.

On the count of ten, Kate sneaked out of the room and melted into the shadows. Out in the hall, she pressed her back against the wall and inched along in pools of darkness. The elevator was humming. Her plan was working. As she passed the elevator she saw on its overhead numerical panel that it was ascending from the first floor. Good, her plan was working. He was waiting for the elevator. He was not watching her on his monitors.

The door to Lorneby's office stood wide open. He's got such a tight grip on the staff, he knows no one would dare come in here, she thought. Light from office buildings on Park Avenue filtered through the windows. Quickly she moved to the sarcophagus in the corner. It was tall enough to conceal her; she'd squeeze behind it.

The stone sarcophagus was wedged tightly into the

corner. She couldn't get it to budge. Impossible! she thought. Through the open door she could hear the faint hum of the elevator. He's coming!

Her fingertips groped along the sarcophagus's rim. There should be a latch, she told herself. Her fingers fumbled, clumsy and stiff, then encountered something that felt like a bent pin. She depressed it and the lid released smoothly. Out in the hall, the elevator bell dinged dully. Neil's here! She thought her heart would burst through her chest, it was beating so hard.

Kate yanked the lid open with both hands. A sour, musty smell assailed her nostrils. This thing hasn't been opened in decades, she thought. She squeezed into the tiny, dark coffin and pulled the lid after her. Inserting her fingertips into the crack, she held the lid open about an inch. The coffin was airtight; she didn't intend to be trapped inside to suffocate.

There wasn't much room inside the sarcophagus. It had been designed to hold one body. And there was already a body in it. Kate felt dry bones and tattered cloth, and something like parchment that she thought was human skin. She stifled a cry as she heard Lorneby stumble off the elevator and lurch down the hall in the opposite direction. Will this be the first place he looks when he doesn't find me in the rug room? Please, dear Lord, help me. Rick, I need you. Hurry!

WAS THAT THE elevator humming again? Where is he going? Kate wondered. And then she thought she heard her grandfather calling her name. I must be having a breakdown, she thought. The air inside the sarcophagus was foul. Kate pressed her nose to the one inch opening between the lid and the frame. I'll go mad if I have to stay in here with this mummy much longer, she thought. Yet, I can't risk getting out. Neil might be lurking out there in the hall, waiting for me to show myself. Or, maybe when he couldn't find me, he returned to his command center and he's watching the monitors. I have to stay hidden until morning.

"Kate!"

There, I heard it again. That wasn't my imagination. Is Neil Lorneby imitating my grandfather, calling me, so I'll show myself?

"Kate! Where are you?"

That *was* Granddad! The elevator had brought him to the sixth floor.

"Kate! We're here. You're safe. You can come out."

Rick? That was Rick's voice.

Kate pushed the lid open with both hands and stepped out. "Here! I'm here," she called. She felt dizzy and reached out a hand to the wall to steady herself. Pounding footfalls ran toward her.

Rick reached her first. Arms opened wide, he pulled her close, crushing her against him. "Thank God, we got here in time. I thought I was going to lose you for the second time. I never want to be without you."

"And you never will." She trembled. "Oh, Rick, this has been so awful."

Jerry broke through the throng of uniformed police officers. "I'm here for you, sweetheart." He reached for Kate, and Rick passed her into Jerry's arms.

"Granddad. How did you find me?" Kate asked. Then, "You're panting. Slow down. Take a deep breath. I don't want anything happening to you now."

"It's a long story. Rick did a bang-up job." He lowered his voice to confide, "I never seen a man so scared, honey. That man loves you. And we had lots of help. Phyllis Stern, the museum curator. Elsie Hoover, Leon Haber, Detective

Martin, everyone chipped in some piece of information, and it all led here to Lorneby."

Kate leaned into him and felt safe for the first time in days. "I hid in the sarcophagus," she said over her grandfather's shoulder to an anxious-looking Rick. "But there's a mummy in it. It was terrible."

"Mummy?" Rick said thoughtfully. The sarcophagus lid hung open and he peered into its dark interior. He remembered Professor Haber asking him to find out what happened to Lorneby's wife. Rick beamed his flashlight into the interior. "That's no mummy," he said. "We ran an extensive background check on Lorneby. That's gotta be Rebecca Bernstein. She never moved to Paris like Lorneby told everyone all these years. What a ghoul. He's had her in his office all along."

SIXTY-THREE

WITH HIS MASTER KEY, Neil Lorneby secured the elevator on the seventh floor. There were other passenger elevators in the auction house, and freight elevators as well, but none traveled to the seventh floor except the one he was shutting down. The steel fire stair doors to the seventh floor were locked. It would take the police some time to break through. And by that time he would have resolved everything.

The terrace beckoned and he moved through the darkened apartment and stepped out through French doors. The night air cooled his fevered skin. Lights from Park Avenue towers shone down on him like starlight. As happened each time he went out onto the terrace, he thought of his mother, pictured her watering the potted plants. She'd never been the same after they'd left their native England.

His father hadn't seemed to mind the uprooting. He'd always immersed himself deeply in the family business. The Lorneby International Auction House was everything to him, and he wanted Neil to share his dedication. When, as a young man, Neil had expressed his desire to become a portrait painter, his father had voiced his disapproval in no uncertain terms. Painters die paupers, Neil, he'd said. You know enough about the art world to know that. Selling dead painters' pictures, now that's where you'll make your mark. I never want to hear this absurd notion mentioned again.

Neil had made lots of money, but what good had it

done him? His ex-wives got most of it. Except Rebecca, he thought with grim satisfaction. She got what she deserved. There was no justification for her cruelty. I had no choice but to silence her jeering and ridicule forever.

He leaned his elbows on the wall that enclosed the terrace. The wound in his back throbbed. He was losing a lot of blood. I loved all those women I painted, he thought. If only they'd liked my paintings. If only they'd praised my work. But they all reacted the way Rebecca had, with loathing stamped all over their faces.

I thought Kate Callahan was different. I thought she understood. But she's been my downfall. Never underestimate a pretty face: that had been his father's advice.

He wasn't surprised to see rifles trained on him from adjoining rooftops. He knew they wouldn't shoot him. He looked down into broad Park Avenue. Law enforcement vehicles lined the avenue in front of his building but he wasn't interested in them. He wanted one last look at the flower beds. Under the high-powered streetlights, the red azaleas in the median took on a purplish hue. Like dried blood, he thought.

Neil climbed up onto the wall. I've had a good run of it, he thought. I've done everything I wanted to. Despite Father's injunction, I became an accomplished portrait painter. And I was a master auctioneer. There's nothing left for me to do.

Quickly, he slipped off the wall.

SIXTY-FOUR

"I NEVER TRULY believed you were dead," Kate told Annie. "Even when the private detective I hired said he had proof, I found it hard to accept." Kate sat close to the woman known to her for years as Rosalie Russo.

They were in Kate's living room. It was about midnight, but they were too keyed up to think about sleep. Kate swirled brandy in a snifter. Jerry handed Rick a brandy. "As many times as I been to Kate's station, I never ran into you, Annie," Jerry said. "If I had, I'd have known you right off."

Annie's nervous hands clutched a glass of club soda. "I owe you an apology, Kate, Dad. I know you've worried about me, but I didn't think I'd do you any good by coming back into your lives again."

"You were wrong, Annie," Jerry said gruffly in an attempt to disguise the catch in his throat. "Me and Kate needed you."

"I was an alcoholic, Dad. It took me years to get myself straightened out. And by then, I thought it was too late."

Rick leaned forward in his chair. "How did you become Rosalie Russo?"

Annie swallowed a sip of club soda. "Rosalie Russo was my best friend in San Francisco. We had so much in common. We were both from New York; she'd grown up in foster homes in Queens. My addiction was alcohol. Rosalie's was hard drugs.

"We'd both had babies. Rosalie was determined to keep

hers. Because she'd been an orphan, she refused to give her baby up. But the streets are no place to raise a child and her little boy died."

"Oh," Kate cried. Annie had led such a hard life.

Annie caught and held Jerry's eye. "That's when I knew I had to bring Kate to you, Dad. So she'd survive. And you and Mom did a wonderful job with her. I owe you so much."

Tears flowed down Annie's cheeks, and Jerry's too. Rick cleared his throat. He needs to hear this, Kate thought, he's part of the family now.

"Rosalie and I were staying in an apartment that belonged to the friend of a friend of a friend. You know how loose things were back then. No, maybe you don't.

"After her baby died, Rosalie took more risks with drugs than before. On the day she died, she got cocaine from somewhere. I could see she was on a bad trip. She went into convulsions. I tried to help her, but I didn't know what to do. When she was scarcely breathing, I called 911. I knew she wasn't going to make it, so before I left, I exchanged identification with her: a clinic card, a soup kitchen card. Everyone would think that Annie Callahan was dead. And that suited me just fine. Then.

"When I returned to New York, I didn't have the courage to claim my own name. So I remained Rosalie Russo."

"Well, you ain't her no more. You're Annie," Jerry said, agitated and pacing around the room. "I want you to get your stuff and move in here with us. That's the best birthday present anyone could ever give me. Right, Kate?"

"We'd love to have you, Annie." Kate could not yet bring herself to call this woman mother. Her grandmother had been the only mother she'd ever known. "I just want to get to know you."

"Dad, I don't think that's a good idea," Annie said

softly, almost apologetically. "And I really like the little house I live in. But I'll spend lots of time with you and Kate. Nothing could keep me away now."

"I just wish your mother and I had been able to help you, Annie. We tried, but nothing we did was right. I'd sure like to shake the hands of the people who done right by you. You've become a fine woman. Your mother would be proud of you."

Annie dropped her head. Her memories caused her shame. "You can start by shaking hands with Vaughn Thompson, Dad. He gave me two hundred bucks and told me to clean up my act. Of course, he has no idea that the wino he was kind to and the woman who is his assistant are one and the same."

"Vaughn is a good man," Kate said. "He really cared for me."

"But he wasn't the right one for you," Jerry said. He looked from Kate to Rick. "So, when's the wedding?"

Rick moved across the room to put his arm around Kate. "Any day Kate names."

Kate grinned. "I believe there's a three-day waiting period, Granddad. Next weekend soon enough for you?"

Oh, Dolly, if only you were here to share this with me, Kate thought. But Dolly was a part of her; Dolly would remain in her heart forever. She could almost hear Dolly's lusty laugh: Way to go, girlfriend!

* * * * *